LEGACY
OF THE
KEYS

LEGACY OF THE KEYS

Book One: Guardian Of The Holy Keys

Bill Floyd

Copyright © 2012 by Bill Floyd.

Library of Congress Control Number:		2012905726
ISBN:	Hardcover	978-1-4691-9185-0
	Softcover	978-1-4691-9184-3
	Ebook	978-1-4691-9186-7

All rights reserved. No part of this book may be reproduced or transmitted in any form or by any means, electronic or mechanical, including photocopying, recording, or by any information storage and retrieval system, without permission in writing from the copyright owner.

This is a work of fiction. Names, characters, places and incidents either are the product of the author's imagination or are used fictitiously, and any resemblance to any actual persons, living or dead, events, or locales is entirely coincidental.

This book was printed in the United States of America.

To order additional copies of this book, contact:
Xlibris Corporation
1-888-795-4274
www.Xlibris.com
Orders@Xlibris.com

I dedicate this book in honor of my wife Carey, who has put up with me for the past 47 years. She is a great wife and wonderful mother of our four children. This is for you, my angel.

Foreword

Pope Alexandro was just finishing his evening meal. Sitting around the table with him were his wife Helena, his son Gepedtro, and his daughter Angelina. It had gotten dark earlier than usual. An ominous dark cloud had rolled over Rome. Rain pelted the windows, echoing through the chamber like small drums. Lightning flashed, giving the room an eerie light, and thunder seemed to boom louder and louder. Alexandro had been pope for just over five years. He had used his power mercilessly, crushing all who challenged his authority. Many who had come against him had disappeared without a trace. Stories swirled around Rome like a coiled deadly snake about to strike and of dark shadows coming from the palace and terrorizing his enemies. Alexandro spent money seemingly without an end. He had liaisons with many women from the best and worst families in Rome and many children whom he supported and did not bother to deny. He was a member of the Sufraz family, the eldest son of the Duke of Milan. His family had threatened, cajoled, and paid off enough of the cardinals in the college to garner enough votes for him to be elected pope. Since becoming pope, he had elevated many of his friends to the rank of cardinal, assuring their cooperation. Many of the most powerful families in Italy were not happy with this pope and were meeting in secret, plotting his death. Among them were the Medici from Florence and the Lords of Perugia—the Borgias and the Baglioni.

In another part of Rome that night, sat another man of the cloth. Within the church men of courage, honesty, and loyalty could still be found. Among them was a priest of one of the small churches on the outskirts of Rome. St. Johns was still a place where the values of the church were upheld. Father Andre Loren was the confessor for most of the college of cardinals. They chose him because of his honesty and virtues. He was a man that could be trusted to hold their secrets between him and God. This had been proven over and over as he heard the confessions of their sins, which were many and varied. People flocked to his church for every Mass, eager to hear him speak of God's love and mercy. Wherever there seemed to be a need, Father Andre was there. The people of Rome loved him. His mother was the daughter of Alberto Baglioni, the younger brother of the current Lord of Perugia. His father came from an old-landed family from Perugia who owned a vineyard, whose wine was sought after. They wanted him to go to school in Milan and study law, but he always wanted to be a priest. After seminary, he continued his studies in church history and ancient languages. He taught in a school in Rome before taking the assignment at St. Johns.

Father Andre sat in the kitchen of the rectory finishing his evening meal. He was enjoying another glass of his father's wine, watching the flames flickering in the hearth.

The rain made a rhythmic sound on the thatched roof, echoed by another sound as it hit the ground almost having a tune. The sight of the lighting flashes illuminated the stained-glass windows, making brief rainbows float across the room. His attention was jarred every now and then as thunder boomed, shaking the dishes stacked on the table behind him.

The nuns who cared for him had left for their rooms next door. He enjoyed the time alone where he could contemplate life, love, and the human condition. He loved his charges and took great joy in his calling. He had no doubt that he was God's man.

Back in the pope's apartment Alexandro called to his wife "Helena, see to the care of the children. It is time for them to retire to their rooms, then have another bottle of wine sent to my study."

"Yes, my Lord." Helena gathered the children and left with the nuns in charge of their care.

Alexandro got up from the table and made his way to his study. It was not long before a monk arrived with the bottle of wine. As per his duty, the monk opened the bottle and poured himself a small glass and drank it in front of the pope. Alexandro pulled out a ledger from the desk and began to look through it. The monk continued to stand near the pope. After the prescribed time, the pope said, "Leave me." The monk poured a glass for Alexandro and then backed out of the room. He made his way out of the papal apartment complex and into the street that led toward the house where he and the other monks lived. He began to stagger, his breathing became labored, his eyes began to blur, and there was an awful burning sensation in his stomach. He leaned against the wall to steady himself.

Deep in the shadows, he was being watched. Two men dressed as monks in dark robes watched as he slipped to the ground. Red foam was coming from his mouth and nose. Death came quickly. The two men picked up his body and took it to a waiting cart. He would never be seen again.

Three families met that night—the Medici, the Baglioni, and the Borgias. "Are you sure that was a slow-acting poison?"

"Yes," answered Thomas Borgias. "We have been perfecting this poison for a while. Having someone taste your wine will no longer make sure you are safe drinking it. You see, most people ask their tasters to wait only ten to fifteen minutes. This poison takes forty-five to work."

There was a knock on the door, and one of the men dressed as a monk came in. "It is done, my Lord. He lasted until he was outside and nearly home. His body has been disposed of as you instructed."

"Well done. Let us drink to the end of this pope and to his successor of our choosing."

Around ten thirty, the bells of St. Peters began to ring, signaling a problem at the pope's residence. The sound was repeated around Rome as each church picked up the chiming. Father Andre awoke when one of the nuns began to pound on his door.

"Father, Father, we have just gotten word the pope is dead. Shall I have our bell rung?"

"Yes, Sister, I will be up in just a minute."

Helena had gone to the study to join Alexandro just before ten and found him slumped over his desk, blood foaming from his mouth and nose. His eyes were open, and he had a surprised, pained look frozen on his face. In front of him was an ornate chest with a key lying in front of it. She stood in the doorway and began to scream. The screams echoed through the halls, giving those who heard a chill. The nuns and monks in charge of the household came running. Seeing what had happened, one of the brothers raced to the apartment of Cardinal Belerousi, head of the curia.

Death puts different processes into motion—the decay of a body, the beginning of grief for some, and a celebration for others. In this case, it put the well-oiled wheels, greased with money and the thought of power running on the well-worn path of election of a new pope, in motion—victory for some and defeat for others.

The funeral will go smoothly; the interworking of the curia and the college of cardinals had seen this many times before. A camerlengo was selected to oversee the church until a new pope was elected. Papal families, mistresses, and children had to be evicted, and the papal apartments had to be sealed. The new camerlengo, Cardinal Donotello, was well versed in the process, having assisted in this duty before. He knew that certain things must be retrieved and safeguarded. His friend, Cardinal Belerousi, was the first to be called. He immediately took the key that was lying on the desk along with the chest. He also removed the key from around Pope Alexandro's neck. He stored these things in his apartment and placed his personal guards on duty to keep them safe.

It took two weeks for the cardinals to gather in Rome for the funeral Mass for Pope Alexandro. They had a hard time finding anyone wanting to say Mass for this pope. The chapel was readied for the conclave to begin. St. Johns and its priest, Father Andre, were busier than usual the two days before the funeral Mass and several days before the conclave. Many cardinals sought out their confessor to rid themselves of their many sins. There were more involved in this pope's murder than Father Andre had thought. There were many days during this time that Andre's heart was so heavy, hearing sins of those in charge of the church, that he thought it would break. He could not eat or sleep. He was looking forward to the days of convocation when the cardinals would be locked behind closed doors and he would be free to let his spirit rest.

The last of the cardinals walked into the conclave and took their place. The door was shut, locked, and a guard was posted. Over the past several days, money had been passed around, threats made, and promises for loyalty was rampant among the powerful families and the cardinals. Several favorite sons were in contention, none of whom were in the college of cardinals but that had never made a difference. Some were bishops and archbishops from the families. Those on the inside knew that the process could not be done on the first ballot. Some still had not made up their minds or been paid enough. Which of the evils would be the lesser one? Whoever lost the election, their family could cause many repercussions to echo through the church.

On the first ballot, the votes were nearly equally divided among the families, but each family's candidates name was out there. The cardinals representing these candidates began to circulate around the room vying for support. This went on for the first day and again on the second day without much movement of the votes. That night, the brothers brought in tables and the nuns set out the evening meal. Several of the brothers began to pour wine into the cups set before the cardinals. They began to eat and drink, discussing in close groups the votes of the last two days.

Without warning, two of the cardinals tried to stand, clutching their throat, and fell across the tables before toppling to the floor. The rest looked on in stunned horror, dropping their wine goblets. This had never happened before. No one had ever broached the sanctity of the sacred college. This was never supposed to happen. Was there no honor among the thieves and rogues running? Probably not, because the stakes for money and power had never been higher, and these two cardinals represented the same family. Suddenly, the room was in a panic. The cardinals began to run for the door. It was locked, so they began to pound on it, screaming to be let out. Several were on their knees and had begun to cry. It took a while, but the Camerlengo Cardinal Donotello finally restored order.

Each remaining cardinal took his seat. Before them were the tables and the two dead cardinals lying on the floor. Donotello pulled the bell cord in the sequence that only he knew and then stood at the door. When it was opened, he directed the brothers and nuns to remove the tables, food and the two dead cardinals. Word quickly spread through the palace and Rome as to what had happened.

Day three was approaching. It had been an uneasy night. The politicking had ceased, and all was silent within the chapel. Each cardinal's heart jumped at the sound of the chapel door being opened the next morning. There was no rush to approach the food that was being laid before them. They watched in silence as the brothers and nuns left and locked the door. Seeing that no one was going to eat, Cardinal Donotello asked, "What shall we do?"

"Vote" came the reply.

As the ballots were read, a new name was called again and again. There were no dissenting votes.

"We have elected a pope," Donotello announced. A sigh of relief swelled throughout the chapel. Donotello went over and pulled the bell cord.

"Ring the bell. We have a new pope," he said when the door was opened.

Soon the bells on all the churches in and around Rome were rung. Cardinal Donotello and Cardinal Belerousi made their way through the streets of Rome to the small church they knew so well. They walked up to the door of the rectory and knocked. When it was opened, they knelt before Father Andre, "Holy Father, will you serve, and what name will you take?"

Andre stood looking down at their upturned faces. Somewhere far off, he heard himself say, "Yes, I will serve, and I will be Leo—a lion for God."

The new pope was escorted back to St. Peters and dressed in the papal white robes. He was led into the chapel and seated on the throne of Peter. Each cardinal came to him and knelt and kissed his ring, swearing their loyalty to him as head of the church. After blessing them, he was escorted to the papal apartments. Later that night, Cardinal Donotello knocked on his door. When Leo opened it, the cardinal presented him with an ornate chest and a beautiful golden key on a chain.

"This key, Holy Father, had come down to each pope since the reign of Peter. Within the chest is an ancient manuscript that holds the secret of the power that has been bestowed on each pope. This power has not always been used wisely as you have seen. God has chosen you to be worthy of this power."

Leo took the key and hung it around his neck, tucking it into his alb. He took the chest from Donotello. "I will do by best to be worthy of this honor."

Donotello bowed and turned and walked back down toward the exit. Leo closed the door and walked over to his desk and put the chest on it. He opened the chest to find the manuscript and another key that was in two parts. It looked very much like the one that he had just placed around his neck. He took that one off and compared it to the one in the chest. Many of the symbols were same on both keys; some he recognized and others he could not. He lit another candle and sat down. He pulled the manuscript out. It was bound with leather straps tipped with gold balls and around it was a leather sheath. The sheath was well worn and the papyrus sticking out was yellowed with age. When he removed the manuscript and began to unroll it, two more keys fell out. They looked very similar to the one he was wearing, but the symbols were different. He could tell that the manuscript had been added to over the years by several of the popes from the condition of the papyrus. The Latin and Greek were old verbiage, but Leo had no problem reading it. Most of the new additions were warning to the new popes of the danger written within the pages. How the power could become addictive, making the user evil.

The older pages were written in Hebrew and Egyptian symbols. At the sides of these were Latin translations and some in Greek but these were few. Leo was fascinated, shocked, elated, and unbelieving as he waded through parts of the manuscript that he could read. He seemed to be drawn into the pages themselves, loosing sense of time and space. The sun rising and shining through the window brought him back to reality. He had been reading all night. He rolled up the manuscript, placed two of the keys inside it, and put it back into the sheath and then placed the other two key parts on top of it. He took the key he was to wear and inserted it into the lock. He locked the chest and placed it under his desk.

Over the next several months, with the help of several scholars, he finished reading the manuscript. Now he knew why he was chosen to be pope. He must keep the keys that were inside the chest secretly and separately from the manuscript. One could not work without the other. The human race was not ready for the three key secrets within the manuscript or the keys themselves. He could not allow anyone person until the time was right to hold such power again.

Leo took the manuscript apart, dividing it into three parts. To each part of the manuscript, he wrote in Hebrew, clues to the hiding place of the other parts. These were written is such a way only a man worthy would be able to figure it out. The first half of the key was hidden in a book within the archives that were being collected and housed in the basement. He had a niche built into the wall and the chest placed into it, holding the first part of the manuscript, which was then sealed, and a bookcase placed in front of the wall. The other half of the key was hidden in a secret compartment in one of the bookcases. The other two parts of the manuscript and the keys were placed in golden chests and taken out of Rome to undisclosed locations in Europe. Only he and the two monks knew where they were hidden.

Was the time that the first Leo envisioned at hand? Was the new pope going to once again reign with full power?

Chapter 1

Jesus said to him in reply, "Blessed are you, Simon son of Jonah. For flesh and blood has not revealed this to you, but my father in heaven. And so I say to you, you are Peter, and upon this rock I will build my church, and the gates of hell shall not prevail against it. I will give you the keys to the kingdom of heaven. Whatever you bind on earth shall be bound in heaven; and what ever you loose on earth shall be loosed in heaven." (Matt. 16:17-19)
I will place the key of the house of David on his shoulder; what he opens, no one shall shut, when he shuts, no one shall open. (Isa. 22:22)

Pope Leo walked down the hallway leading to the archives. It was late afternoon, and he was sure the office of Archbishop Valanti would be empty. If anyone were there, it would be a member of the Swiss Guard outside Valanti's door. Leo kept looking over his shoulder, making sure no one was following him. Being pope made it almost impossible to be alone. Several times, he felt like something or someone was watching him. He could feel the hair on the back of his neck bristle under the cassock. Rounding the corner, he saw Valanti's office at the middle of the hall and sure enough there was the Swiss Guard in place.

"Good evening, Holy Father," he was greeted as he neared the guard.

"Bless you, my child," he said as he passed him and opened Valanti's door. As he thought, the office was empty; the archbishop had gone for the night. Leo walked across the office to the door that led into the papal archives. He inserted his key into the top lock and turned it; then doing the same to the bottom lock, he turned the handle and went inside. The smell of musty paper and old books assailed his nose. Feeling for the light switch, he turned on the lights. The archive is a big open room filled from floor to ceiling with bookcases and tables covered with ancient papers. This room was off limits to anyone, except the reigning pope or the keeper of the archives with the pope's permission. Since Leo had been pope, this room had only been opened three times. To his knowledge, he was the only one to have been here. This first time was to make sure the key was still in place. He remembered well where to look. He had been left a letter from the dying Pope Gregory with instruction to memorize how to find the hiding place of the key. He had read the letter then burned it as instructed and flushed the ashes down the commode in his private apartment.

Leo had been having nightmares for the past several weeks and been visited by what you would call, and what he could only think of as an evil spirit. There would be a feeling of panic, and the hair on his arms and neck would stand up. The worse part was that the oppressive presence seemed to crush his soul with accusations of past sins, some that only he and God knew about and the blackness that came with it. Then summoning all of his strength, he would mentally fight off the presence, ordering it to be gone, in the name of Jesus. After this he would be worn out. He could feel his strength fading away quickly. Now he must see if the key was safe and write a letter to his successor and leave it with his secretary Monsignor O'Rourke, telling the new Pope what had been told to him. God had warned him that time was short.

Leo made his way around the tables in the middle of the room and walked over to one of the bookshelves at the back, where he counted over sixteen books from the right hand side of the shelf and seventeen down from the top and pulled out an old, dusty book; the binding was so fragile some of it came apart at his touch. He gently opened the book to the twenty-second chapter, and his face became ashen as the place where the key should have been was empty. Only the cutout image of a key looked back at him. Hopefully, whoever had opened the book had only half of the key. Closing the book, he carefully placed it back where it belonged. Quickly, he walked over the other side of the room where he got down on his hand and knees. Feeling for the latch under the bookcase, he pulled and a section of the ornate case opened. Leo felt inside, hoping to find the top half of the key still there. It too was gone. His heart sank, knowing that the thief had both pieces. This meant that the manuscript had also been found, and it must also be gone. This explained the evil he had felt, and he knew where it had come from. He had to get in touch with Archbishop Valanti immediately.

He closed the secret compartment. He did not want whoever stole the key to know that he was onto them. Glancing around to make sure everything was back in order, Leo walked toward the door. The magnitude of knowing that the key was missing weighed heavily upon him. As he reached for the light switch, the hairs on the back of his neck stood up, and he could hear the taunting voice coming from a distance toward him. Quickly he closed and locked the doors and rushed back across Valanti's office.

Leo startled the guard as he yanked open the door and ran into the hallway as if being chased.

"Holy Father, what's going on?" yelled the guard after him.

Seconds after the pope passed, the guard was knocked to the ground by a dark force he had not seen. Glancing over his shoulder, Leo saw the guard fall, and a dark shape following him, but he kept on running. Night was falling over the Vatican, and Pope Leo had to get to his apartment. As he entered his room, he could see the day's last light filtering through the window that led to his balcony. It would soon be dark, and according to Leo, this is when the nightmares began. There would be the feel of death, and the dark smoky presence that had chased him from the archive would try to surround him again, and he would hear screaming, and he would realized that the screams were coming from him, and he would begin to fight back the thoughts that kept entering his mind. Each of these episodes took a toll on his aging body. He was getting tired and knew he could not hold out much longer. He finally realized the darkness which surrounded him could not harm him physically, but the memory of old sins it brought caused him much pain, and each time he had to go through this trial, he would become weaker. Leo walked over to the window and gazed out onto the city he loved and the plaza below. There were visiting nuns walking around near the fountain, and looking up, they saw Leo looking out of the window. They began to call him, "Papa, Papa," and hearing this, Leo waved at them and smiled. Turning back into the room, he walked over to his desk, which was across the room in the corner. He was weary from the long day; he began his prayers before sunup. As he sat down, Leo pulled out the drawer to his desk and took out three pieces of paper. He was going to write a letter to each of his most trusted friends and one to the man who would succeed him as pope. The first one was to his secretary Monsignor Patrick O'Rourke; he had important instructions for him to be carried out if something happened to him. The second was to his old and dear friend Archbishop Valanti. Valanti was the keeper of the papal archives. Only he and the pope had a key to these important rooms in the Vatican. The last one and the most difficult would be to the cardinal who will take charge of the church after Leo's death—the next pope. He will leave the letters in the meantime with his secretary Monsignor Patrick O'Rourke. Leo looked around his study, which consisted of a desk, a chair, and a large selection of books and artwork. Much of the furnishings and books had been here since the first Leo. Leo finished writing his letters and walked into his bedroom, which opened off of his study and placed the letters in his old, worn Bible that was lying on the nightstand beside his bed. Reaching around his neck, he took off the key he had worn for the past ten years that he has been pope, reopened his Bible, and dropped the key into the envelope addressed to Patrick. Feeling his energy failing, he lay down on the bed. The sun had now set, and the only light in the room came from the light on the plaza below. A cool breeze was coming in through the open window, but Leo did not have the energy to get up and close the drapes. It seemed to him that darkness was settling down upon him like a blanket. Leo closed his eyes, letting his body sink down into the soft mattress. Soon there was the foreboding feeling of death that began to seep through the open window, and Leo felt the presence that he had felt before. With all the strength he could muster, he rose up, and with his hands raised and with all his will power, he spoke to the dark presence. "I command you in the name of Jesus, be gone. I command you to be gone," he screamed again. Leo falls down beside the bed in exhaustion.

Lying there, he wondered how much longer he can hold out. His mind drifted back to that faithful day three months ago when he had been working at his desk. He had dropped his pen on the floor, and it had rolled under the desk. He bent down and tried to reach it without getting out of his chair but could not. He pulled his chair out into the room and got down on his hands and knees and got under the desk. The pen had rolled near the right rear leg of the desk. As he reached to get it, the sun rays coming through the window reflected on a round shinny medallion attached to the inside of the leg catching his eye. He retrieved his pen and decided to get a flashlight so that he could get a better look. Shining the light on the plate, he saw that it was engraved with a key emblem on it. He reached down and felt the impression, the pressure of his touch caused a small draw to pop out. Inside was a letter from the first owner of the desk—the first Pope Leo. He got out from under the desk and sat down and read the letter.

LEGACY OF THE KEYS

Dear Holy Father,

You have been led to find this secret drawer I had built into the desk during my reign as pope. When you became pope, you were handed a letter telling you about a key that was hidden in the papal archives. This key is one of the three keys Jesus gave to our first Pope Peter. It is the key to Hell. It is also known in legend as the Key of Solomon. Solomon was reputed to use the demons from this realm to keep his people in line and to build his temple and palace. For them to do your bidding, the key must be put together and the ancient Hebrew commands used. One part of the key is in a book sixteenth from the top and seventeenth over in the old bookcase at the back of the archives in a book titled **The Rule of Solomon.** *The second half is located in a secret compartment in an ornate bookcase across the room under the carved piece; running across the bottom, you will find a latch which opens a small door the other half of the key is inside. There is a chest with a lock and the key that you wear will unlock. In this chest is a manuscript older than I am. This manuscript holds the secret of how to use the key and the location of the other two. The chest is sealed away in a niche behind the bookcase where the first half of the key is located. These three keys hold great power for good and evil. There was so much corruption within the church when I became pope and the power of these keys were so savagely used that I decided such power should not be given to one man until one come along that is worthy. I have hidden the other two keys in distant locations. The clues to those are encoded in the manuscript. If you are that man who is worthy, God will assist you in your quest; if not, may God have mercy on your soul.*

Leo I.

After reading that letter, Leo put it back in the leg of the desk. Over the next few days, he pondered on what he should do. He decided to go down to the archives late one night to see if the key was really there, and he found both parts. The bookcase was too heavy to move, so he called one of the brothers that had helped him in the past with translations of old manuscripts to come to the archives late one night. Together, they had moved the bookcase, and behind it was a niche with a key symbol on it and a keyhole. Leo took the key from around his neck and fitted it into the keyhole and it fit. He turned it and a drawer slid out. Standing on a chair, he looked inside. There was the chest, which was written about in the letter he found. He and Brother Sebastian took it down and lay it on a table, and Leo opened it and inside they found a manuscript. Under it was a single page with pentagrams and names along the edges. In the center were the words in old Hebrew "Come and serve me." Pope Leo took out the manuscript, left the page closed the chest, and placed it back in the drawer. He and Sebastian replaced the bookshelf. All looked as it was before they came. Leo gave the manuscript to Sebastian with instruction to translate it for him so that he could find out where the other two keys were and what they could be used for.

Chapter 2

Monsignor Patrick O'Rourke is one of five brothers raised in an Irish Catholic family. He always wanted to become a priest. He met Pope Leo when the pope visited Ireland six years ago. He was serving as the secretary to the bishop of Dublin. The pope was so impressed with Patrick that he asked him to come to Rome and work in the curia. He was so successful in his job that the pope asked Patrick to be his personal secretary and raised him to the rank of monsignor. Patrick was Irish through and through with his rugged good looks, reddish-blond hair, and bright blue eyes. Patrick was always a good athlete in school and kept up his workouts. The women visiting the pope were in awe of Patrick's movie-star good looks, and many unashamedly flirted with him. Patrick was also very smart, graduating in the top ten in his class from Trinity College in Dublin, and from there, he went to a Catholic seminary in London. Patrick loved the church and was fiercely loyal to the pope who thought of him as a son.

It had been a long day, and the pope had an unusually large number of people that wanted an audience with him. After the pope had gone for the evening, Patrick had a lot of paperwork to catch up on before he left. He also had to amend the schedule for the following day. Pressing the save icon on his Mac and closing the lid, he was finally ready to leave. Patrick had a room in the Vatican on the hallway that the pope's apartment was located on, so that he would be close by if the pope needed anything. Leaving his office and closing the door, Patrick had a satisfied expression on his face; it had been a successful day on many fronts. One good thing was he didn't have to deal with Cardinal Joseph Pulaski, the head of the curia, the governing body of the Catholic Church. Patrick did not have any good feeling about this cardinal. Going down the hallway to his room, Patrick passed the door to the papal apartments, and just as he passed, he heard the pope scream out. He could not understand what was said; it was just a scream. Being concerned, Patrick knocked on the door. "Holy Father," he called. "Holy Father, are you all right?" There was no answer, so Patrick knocked again this time harder. "Holy Father," he called out again. The door slowly swung open due to the power of his knock. Looking inside, there was only darkness with just a wee bit of a light coming through the open window. As his eyes adjusted to the darkness, Patrick saw a white shape lying on the floor beside the bed. Patrick rushed over and knelt beside the pope and gently called his name, "Holy Father, can you hear me?" Patrick placed his hand on the pope's neck and felt a heartbeat, and feeling the touch, Leo began to stir.

"Patrick," the pope whispered, "Help me sit up next to the bed." Putting his arm under the pope, Patrick gently lifted him up and laid him next to the bed. "Patrick, you must go and find my dear friend Archbishop Giorgio Valanti. I must see him immediately. It is of upmost importance. Go quickly," said the pope as he tried to sit up. Patrick got up from his kneeling position and turned to leave. "Wait a moment," said the pope. Patrick turned back to Leo, who was sitting now on the side of the bed. Patrick watched as Leo picked up his old worn Bible from the nightstand and leaned forward giving it to Patrick. "Guard this with your life," said Leo. "Now run as fast as you can and bring me Archbishop Valanti." Patrick turned to leave, looking over his shoulder one last time at the pope, who had slumped back down onto his bed. Patrick lifted up his cassock so that he could run at full speed to where Archbishop Valanti lived, which was just outside the Vatican walls.

As he was running, Patrick passed Jason Sitzler, the captain of the Swiss Guard, who was responsible for the safety of the pope. Patrick knew Jason well; this was his second year here at the Vatican, and he and Jason had become friends, playing squash or having a beer after work.

"Hey, Patrick, what's the matter?" Jason called. He was on duty tonight, and seeing Patrick running from the direction of the pope's apartment, he knew there must be something wrong.

Looking over his shoulder, Patrick yelled to Jason, "Get over to the pope's apartment ASAP, and guard him well! The pope wants to see the Archbishop Valanti immediately, and I was sent to get him." Now it was Jason's turn to run. Nearing the pope's apartment, he was out of breath, but he noticed a strange smell, and the closer he got to the apartment, the worse it became. The pope's door was closed, and he dare not enter without permission. Jason posted himself outside the door with his Glock pistol drawn. The odor was very strong here, and Jason was not sure what to do. This was not a smell that should be coming from the pope's apartment. Jason decided to knock on the door, and as he did so, it swung open. It had not been closed all the way. Inside, the room was dark, and he could make out the window, which was open with just a little light coming in from below. Lying beside the bed Jason could just make out in the dim light the shape of what looked like a man curled up on the floor. There was no sound coming from the room; it was eerily quiet, but Jason could hear the pounding of his heart drumming in his ears from running or was it fright? As he began to step through the door, the odor, which he would later describe as the smell of death, filled his nostrils, and he was enveloped in a terrifying darkness. He felt a crushing weight on him, and he was both nauseous and dizzy at the same time. It was as though every organ in his body was being invaded at once. His mind was suddenly filled with a sense of dread, and memories of all the sinful things he had done were being played in his head like he was viewing them on the big screen. He felt his legs begin to give way and then there was only darkness.

Chapter 3

The lights were quite dim, and the café was filled with people milling around at the bar, just the kind of place that Cardinal Joseph Pulaski and Cardinal Martin Louis liked. Without their clerical dress, they blended in quite well. This was a little café at the edge of Rome, just far away enough that they would not run into anyone that they might know.

Cardinal Joseph Pulaski was the head of the Roman Curia. He was one of the most powerful men in the church. He was a heavy-set man with small black eyes, which made him look like a weasel. He was in his midfifties and grossly overweight. He was a very ambitious man. He wanted to be the next pope, and he did not care what he had to do to make this happen. He felt like it was his destiny.

Cardinal Martin Louis was the lone American in the curia. He and Pulaski were friends and allies; they both shared the same evil ambition. They had attended college in Rome together. They also shared a selfish, ruthless nature. Both had climbed the ladder to become bishops on the backs of those who served them. They would do anything to gain more wealth and power.

This was not their first meeting. They had been plotting against Leo almost since the day he had become pope. They had agreed that whoever became pope would have the immense power that belonged only to the pope. Each pope had a secret source of power and wealth, and it had been used for both good and evil through the years. Many had used it to preserve the church during the dark ages; others had exploited it in indulgences and agreeing to pay a hefty sum of money to free a relative from hell. Pulaski had become the head of the curia and used his position to find out many things. Among them was that the pope wore a key under his cassock, and it was rumored that he never even took it off, even for bath. Once when he was sick, the doctor wanted to do an MRI on him, and he refused because of the key. This had pricked Pulaski's interest. He began to do research, and in a letter written two hundred years ago, it was revealed that the pope received a key when he ascended to the throne of Peter. Going back much further, he found another mention of the pope having keys, so there must be more than one. In the book of Matthew, it is written that Jesus gave Peter, the first pope, the keys to the kingdom. One of the keys, the one mentioned in Isaiah 22 and that the Apostle John wrote about says that Christ held the key of David which can open a door that can never be shut, and he who controls this key controls who has access to the kingdom. He also wrote in the book of Revelation that the key opens a door into the very presence of God. He had found references that one of the keys unlocks the door to hell. This one was also known as the key of Solomon. Solomon was known to practice some kind of magic, which he used to control the people and build the temple. It was legend that Solomon could call spirits to do his bidding. The third key was to a place containing vast wealth or knowledge. Pulaski reasoned that if Leo only wore one key around his neck, the others must be hidden somewhere, maybe even here in the Vatican. He spent a great deal of his time seeking the hiding place for the keys and had enlisted Martin to help him. They met every week outside the walls of the Vatican to share information. They sat in the rear of the café, sipping a glass of red wine. Something in Joseph's demeanor was not quite right, and Martin could not put his finger on it.

"Joseph," Martin said, "You are not your usual self. Is there something bothering you?"

"No," replied Joseph. "I am just a little tired. I have been doing a lot of research lately, and it is tedious work looking through all of the old letters and notes from the archives."

"Have you been able to get access to the pope's secret archives?" Martin asked. "You know I would have to drug Archbishop Valanti to get in there. He is very loyal to Leo," replied Joseph.

Martin had the feeling that Joseph was hiding something from him. He wondered if he had indeed found a clue in some of those old letters and diaries he had access to by being head of the curia.

Joseph rose to go. "I have some business I need to take care of. See you tomorrow, my friend."

Watching his friend leave, he still had the feeling of distrust. Something was going on, and he intended to find out what. One thing

Martin had learned was the saying, "There is no honor among thieves" holds true with friends who are both seeking power and influence. *Joseph Pulaski was not a man to be trusted,* thought Martin finishing his glass of wine.

Chapter 4

Patrick was running down the hall as fast as he could. He was holding up his cassock to give him all the running room he needed. Rounding the corner, he saw the door for the staircase leading down to the first floor and the exit he needed. Busting through the door, he began to take two steps at a time, being careful not to trip and fall. Reaching the first floor, he opened the door to the outside and felt the cool night breeze hitting him in the face. Looking around, he needed to make a decision whether to head for Valanti's apartment or to the place he usually ate supper. It was still early, so he decided to go to Valanti's apartment. Valanti lived in the new section of Rome that had just been built where they had torn down some old apartment building that had begun to rot. This meant that Patrick would have to cut through the papal gardens, which would be full of tourists at this time of year.

    Reaching down and once again pulling up his cassock, he began to run toward the gardens. As he got closer, he saw a couple of the tourists that had met with the pope today along with several of his colleagues. Seeing the monsignor running through the gardens like bandits were chasing him could cause quite a stir. Hoping to minimize the impact, Patrick tries to smile and wave as he passes through the crowd. At the end of the garden, Patrick paused to get his bearings. He felt the sweat running down his back and his face. Even though the sun was down, it was still quite hot. May in Rome with the heat rising from the pavement is not the place to be running. Turning north, he once again picks up the pace and runs the four blocks to where Valanti lives.

At Valanti's house, Patrick rang the bell for his apartment 210 on the second floor. At first, there was no answer, and Patrick heart sank. He has made the wrong choice. Patrick decided to try one more time before he went to the café. This time a gruff-sounding Valanti answered, "Who is it?"

"Patrick O'Rourke" Patrick replied in a winded voice.

"Who did you say?" came the voice of Valanti.

"Archbishop, it's Patrick, the pope's secretary, and I must speak to you right away"

"Okay, my son, please come up," said the archbishop, and Patrick heard the door buzz so that he can open it. Climbing the steps, two at a time, Patrick quickly found apartment 210 and knocked on the door. Archbishop Valanti opened the door. He was dressed in casual attire, having taken off his alb and had a napkin tucked into his shirt. "Patrick, my friend, please come in. Can I get you something to drink? You look like you have been in a race. I am just finishing some dinner. Would you care to join me? As usual, I have bought more than I can eat," Valanti said.

"Thank you, but I have no appetite at the moment, but a little water would be good. The pope has sent me go get you. It is very important that you come with me to see him immediately," said Patrick.

"Let me change clothes, and I will be right with you."

"No! No! There is no time. We must go now. The pope will not care what you are wearing," Patrick pleaded.

"Very well. Let me just put this unfinished meal away," Valanti said as he quickly cleared away the table. He reached down and picked up his keys and followed Patrick out the door.

Patrick walked at a fast pace causing him to get further ahead of the older man. Patrick knew that Valanti could not run or even trot, but he hoped that he could walk a little faster. They had not even reached the entrance to the gardens yet, and to Patrick, it seemed they had been walking for hours. Patrick could hear Valanti panting, trying to catch a breath. Looking behind him, Patrick could see the sweat pouring from Valanti's face, so he began to slow a little, giving Valanti a chance to catch up, and he did not want him to have a heat stroke. At the entrance to the gardens, Valanti sat down on a bench. He was trembling and looked very white. Looking around, Patrick saw a Taxi coming their way, and he flagged it down. He helped Valanti into the backseat and told the driver to get them to the Vatican plaza as quick as he could. Leaning back in the seat, Valanti began to revive.

"What is going on, Patrick? Why this rush?" Putting his finger to his mouth, Patrick let Valanti know he could not talk about it in front of the taxi driver. Up ahead, Patrick could see the gate that led to the Vatican. It would not be long now.

Pulling up to the curb, Patrick paid the driver and helped Valanti out, and they climbed the steps to the building, leading to the papal apartments. Patrick knew that Valanti would not be able to climb the stairs, so he led him toward the elevator. Patrick punched the button and the door opened, and he and Valanti entered. Patrick pushed the button for the second floor. When they exited, they hurried down the hallway that led to the pope's apartment. He was always a couple of paces ahead of Valanti and had to wait on him to catch up.

Patrick could sense something was wrong as soon as they turned the corner. He did not see Jason stationed outside the door, and the door stood open. Seeing this, he grabbed Archbishop Valanti by the arm and began to pull him down the hallway. "Hurry, hurry," Patrick began to shout at Valanti, "something is terribly wrong. Jason is not at the door, and it is open."

Chapter 5

Jason began to stir. The suffocating blackness was no longer present. He felt weak, almost like he had just finished a five-mile run in heavy gear in the desert. His head ached, his stomach churned, and he felt dizzy. He closed his eyes, hoping he would not vomit. At first, he did not know where he was. It was dark where he lay on what appeared to be the floor of a room, and he could see lights coming through the door from the hallway. Jason's eyes were beginning to focus and adjusting to the dim light. He was lying on his back in the doorway with his head inside a room and his legs in the hallway. Rolling over to his stomach, he could see the inside of the room. Lying in the floor was what looked like a white sheet balled up, but Jason knew it must be the pope. The fog that filled his mind was beginning to lift, and it was all coming back to him. Patrick had sent him to guard the pope and then something happened. A horrible helpless feeling, the mind filled with every sin he had ever committed, a crushing weight trying to enter his body, and then only blackness. Getting up on his hands and knees, Jason crawled over toward the pope. As he neared him, he could hear the labored breathing. Jason tried to get up but found that he was not ready to stand yet and sat back down next to the pope. Jason reached up onto the bed and got the pope's pillow and placed it under his head. Feeling the nausea returning, he leaned back on the bed, trying not to be sick. Using his cell phone, he placed a call to the command post.

"Sergeant Major Nordstrom here, sir" came the reply.

"Have someone contact Sister Judith Bridget immediately and bring her here to the pope's apartment. Someone or something has attacked the pope. I was also attacked and knocked to the ground."

"Yes, sir," comes the reply.

Jason, feeling a little stronger was able to stand now. He walked over to the window and breathed in the cool night air. Turning back into the room, he switched on the lamp on the pope's desk. The pope looked old and fragile lying on the floor, and Jason felt like he needed to get him off the floor and onto the bed. Sliding his arms under the pope's shoulders, he grabbed him under the arms and raised him to a sitting position. Sliding his arms under his legs and holding him around the center of the back, he tried to lift Leo, but he couldn't. Even though Leo was small and light, Jason was still too weak to lift him. So he gently laid him back down on the floor and covered him with a blanket against the cool night air and sat down beside him.

Sister Judith Bridget had a room one floor down from the pope at the bottom of the staircase. Once someone alerted her, it would not take long for her to be here. Jason placed his hand on Leo's neck to feel for a pulse. He found one, but it was weak and not stable. The pope was his responsibility, and he could not believe that he had let this happen on his watch.

Jason heard footsteps and voices coming toward them. He was hoping that it would be the pope's nurse and the help he had called for. The voices were getting louder and both were men's voices. One of them sounded like his friend Patrick. It was Patrick; he must be coming back with Archbishop Valanti. The footsteps came quicker, and the voices grew louder as they neared the apartment.

Patrick rounded the corner first and burst into the room. What he saw stopped him cold in his tracks, letting Archbishop Valanti nearly run over him. There was the pope, lying on the floor, with Jason sitting next to him and leaning up against the bed. Jason looked awful. His normally healthy looking complexion was a pasty white; all the color was gone from his face and hands. He had put a pillow under the pope's head and covered him with a blanket from the bed. The pope was not moving. His eyes were shut, and Patrick had a hard time making out if his chest was moving. Patrick and Archbishop Valanti walked over slowly to where the pope lay. Kneeling down, Patrick touched the pope's forehead, and it felt sticky yet surprisingly cool. Patrick put his hand on his friend's arm, trying to assure him that it was going to be all right. Jason's eyes were filled with the pain of failure. He had not only let the pope down, but he felt like he had also let Patrick down.

Before Patrick could ask what had happened, there was the sound of what seemed like an army running down the hall, coming their way. Looking toward the sound, Patrick could see Sister Judith Bridget leading the pack as she came through the door with her black bag in her hand.

Sister Judith Bridget has just been assigned to the Vatican. She had spent much time in the mission field as a nurse and midwife sometimes assisting doctors in surgery. She had received her degree in nursing from Emory University in Atlanta, Georgia. Her order had asked her to come to Rome and help care for the aging pope.

All the men following her were armed, with their weapons drawn. From what they had been told, there had been an attack on the pope and their captain. The sergeant major stationed his men, one at each of the doorway and the others at the staircase entrances. There would be no way for anyone to get by them without being seen. Once this was done, he walked over to his captain to make sure he was all right and if there was anything else that needed to be done. Squatting down, he leaned close to his captain so as not to be heard and asked, "Sir, who did this? What did they look like?"

"I am not sure. All I can remember is knocking on the pope's door. I was overcome by a feeling of dread, and I felt like I was being crushed, in blackness. That is all I can remember," Jason answered.

Nordstrom extended his hand to help Jason stand. Jason was still a little wobbly on his feet, so leaning on Nordstrom's shoulder, they made their way out of the room and into the hallway.

Chapter 6

Sister Judith wasted no time upon entering the room. She gently pushed Patrick aside along with the archbishop so that she could kneel beside Pope Leo. The first thing she did was to find a pulse by placing her finger on Leo's neck. Sister Judith felt a weak and erratic pulse. His breathing was also shallow. She motioned for one of the guards to come over to her, and she asked him go back to her room and bring up the portable oxygen tank. This being done, she dug down in her black bag and found the blood pressure cuff. Gently, she pulled down the blanket and reached for Leo's left arm. Sister Judith pulled up the sleeve of the pope's alb to expose his arm. Sister Judith was surprised at just how thin his arm was. He could have been one of her patients in any one of the African countries in which she served. The arm had no color; it was pasty white. This was not a good sign. The pope could be going into shock. She remembered that Leo was somewhere in his mid eighties. No wonder he was so fragile. She wrapped the cuff around this arm and began to pump up the cuff while placing the stethoscope into her ears and the other end onto the crook of his arm. The readings were not good; eighty over fifty-five and a pulse rate of only forty. Then she opened the pope's alb and placed the stethoscope on his chest to listen to his heartbeat first and then to make sure his lungs were clear. The heart, although slow, sounded strong, and the lungs sounded clear.

Sister Judith motioned to Patrick to kneel beside her, and she asked if he would help her lift Leo onto the bed. While Sister Judith placed her arms under Leo's shoulders, Patrick slipped his arms beneath Leo's legs. Sister Judith said to Patrick, "On the count of three, we will lift him together. One, two, three," she counted, and both of them lifted the pope onto his bed. After placing Leo on the bed, she reached down and retrieved the pillow and placed it under his head. Patrick picked up the blanket and handed it to Judith, and she placed it over Leo.

Hearing some commotion in the hallway, Patrick and Sister Judith both turned toward the door only to find that it was the soldier returning with the oxygen tank. Since he didn't know whether to come or not, he stopped in the doorway. Sister Judith motioned him to come over, and he entered the room with reverence, pulling the tank behind him. Sister Judith thanked him, and he backed out into the hallway, remembering that no one ever turned his back on the pope.

Sister Judith gently lifted the pope's head and placed the oxygen mask's strap behind it and placed the mask over the pope's nose and mouth. She turned on the oxygen, and once again took the pope's pulse. It was still slow, but his heartbeat was much stronger and less erratic. "Holy Father," Sister Judith whispered, "can you hear me?" Sadly, there was no response.

Archbishop Valanti walked over to where the pope was lying and asked Sister Judith, "May I sit beside my friend for a moment?" Sister Judith nodded and moved aside. Archbishop Valanti sat down on the bed beside the pope and took his hand in his he closed his eyes and said a prayer for his dear friend. Valanti continued to sit with Leo, holding his hand.

Sister Judith walked over to Patrick and asked, "What's going on?"

"I saw the pope this morning, and he was not in this shape. Something has caused him a lot of trauma, and this happened in the last couple of hours," she continued.

Patrick looked down at her and slowly shook his head. "I don't know."

"I stopped by earlier and heard the pope call out, and when I entered his room, he was on the floor."

Sister Judith looked at him quizzically. "Why didn't you call me?" she asked.

"The pope told me to run as fast as I could to get Archbishop Valanti. It was of utmost importance, and I did as he asked," Patrick replied sheepishly.

"That's no excuse!" Glared an angry Sister Judith.

"Sister, Sister," called Valanti, "I can see the pope's eyes fluttering, trying to open."

"Gustav," he whispered. "It is Antonio," Archbishop Valanti said, calling Pope Leo by his given name. The name, he knew him by when they were young and in school together. "Can you hear me, my dear friend?"

Leo opened his eyes and tried to smile at his friend. Valanti felt the pope squeeze his hand. With his head, he motioned for his friend to lean in closer. Through the oxygen mask and in a weak voice, Leo managed to say to his friend, "I need to speak to you and Patrick alone," and then he closed his eyes. Valanti stood and allowed Sister Judith to sit beside the pope. Once again, she placed the blood pressure cuff on his arm, and this time, the pressure was up a little, and his breathing was less shallow. Leo opened his eyes and winked at his nurse above the oxygen mask. She reached down and took his hand, and Leo gave her a reassuring squeeze.

Archbishop Valanti walked over to Patrick and told him what the pope had said and asked him to clear the room. Patrick walked over to the two guards and told them to wait outside, then he walked over to Sister Judith and said, "Sister, the pope asked everyone to leave the room. He has to speak privately to Archbishop Valanti and me." Grudgingly, she stood up and glared at both of them and walked to the door. Turning, she said, "I'll be right outside. I expect to be called back in immediately if there is any change in his condition." She walked out and closed the door behind her.

Chapter 7

Standing outside the café, Cardinal Pulaski's cell phone began to ring. Since he was the head of the curia, if anything went on within and sometimes outside the Vatican, he would be one of the first to know. He pulled his cell out of his pocket and looked to see who was calling. It was one of his office staff—Father Anton, a Jesuit priest, who had spent much time in Rome and knew the ins and outs of politics there. Father Anton was his most loyal ally. He knew how to keep his mouth shut, and what Pulaski liked the most about him was that he knew his place. "Yes," said Pulaski.

"I thought you would like to know there is something going on within the Vatican, and it has to do with the pope," answered Father Anton.

"Why would you say this?" inquired Pulaski.

"I was going through the papal gardens about an hour or so ago, and I saw Monsignor O'Rourke running through there like he was being chased by the mafia," Anton replied.

"Well, what does that have to do with the pope? I've got my own suspicions about the monsignor."

"Well," continued Anton, "I decided to follow him just out of curiosity, and he went to the home of Archbishop Valanti. I decided to hang around for a while, and I am glad I did. Not long after he went in, they came out, and the archbishop was not in his cassock and was literally being dragged along by the monsignor back toward the Vatican. I went as far as the entrance to the gardens, and there lost them, because they caught a cab."

"Good work, Anton. Get back to the office, and I will meet you there," Pulaski said. Looking around to see if anyone was close enough to hear what had been said, he walked out to the curb and hailed a taxi. He wanted to get back to the Vatican as soon as possible. Things were happening faster than he had thought, and he wanted to make sure that nothing could be tied back to him. He also needed to make sure that his recently acquired helper was properly returned to where it came from. If he were caught, the triple crown of Peter would be lost to him forever.

As he was opening the taxi's door, he heard his name called. Cardinal Louis came bursting out of the café door like someone who had not paid his tab, and the waiter was running after him. "Wait up, Joseph!" he called. "I have news that might interest you." Cardinal Pulaski stepped into the taxi and held the door open for Martin. "I just got a call from security," he reported. "Seems like someone broke into the pope's apartment. All hell has broken out over there. The captain of the guard has been injured, and Sister Judith has been called in to care for the pope."

Cardinal Pulaski's cell began to ring again. This time, it was the duty officer from security. Looking at Cardinal Louis, he said, "It's the security. Excuse me a moment. I need to take this call."

"Hello," he answered. "Yes, I see. Is the pope all right? Is anyone else hurt? I am on my way back to the office. Have a report ready when I get there" and he hung up. Turning back to Cardinal Louis, he tried to hide it, but there was a faint smile playing across his face and the look of satisfaction instead of concern. "Martin, you were right," he said. "The duty officer just confirmed all that you had said. We will know more once we get back to the office. Driver, get us back to the Vatican as quickly as possible."

They sat in silence for the rest of the ride back to the Vatican. Cardinal Pulaski's mind was churning, trying to figure out his next move. He had to be careful even more so than usual. There was much at stake here. He kept going over in his mind everything that had led up to this moment. Every step he had made had to be kept secret. Who knew or could know any of it. Martin knew something was going on, but he had taken care of his only real accomplice—poor Brother Sebastian. In every struggle for power, there has to be a few casualties. This is the one place that he could be in trouble. He was not able to take care of the problem himself, and he contracted out the job to one of his mafia contacts. So there was still someone out there who could tie him to Brother Sebastian's death. Almost everyone agreed that it was a horrible accident. It seemed like our dear departed brother had the yen for female company or at least that's the way it looked. He had been seen in the company of a local prostitute and had spent several days with her, or at least, that was the way the don had made it look. They had rented a boat and were out in the Bay of Naples on it drunk when both of them fell overboard, and a poor innocent boater ran over them and the prop of the boat hardly left anything to bury or to even do a blood test on. Hopefully, the sharks that had been seen that day had a good meal.

Cardinal Louis calling his name, and the cab coming to a stop, pulled Pulaski out of his thoughts. "Joseph, we are here" Cardinal Louis said as he opened the door and gathered his packages and stepped out of the cab. Joseph leaned back and stretched out his leg so he could retrieve his billfold from the pocket of his pants and paid the cab driver. The bill was eighteen euros, so being the big tipper that he was, he gave the driver a twenty and told him to keep the change. Sliding across the seat, he got out, and closed the door, and he and Martin stood, looking up at the Basilica. It is an awe-inspiring sight to see St. Peters—the seat of power for the Roman Catholic world—lit up at night.

"Well, good night again," Joseph said. "I must get back to my office right away. I will give you a call if I find out anymore than what we know." Turning, he walked up the stairs toward the main entrance of the church, leaving Martin, at the bottom of the steps, staring after him with a lot of question running through his mind.

Chapter 8

Watching Sister Judith close the door, Patrick and Valanti walked over to the pope's bed and knelt down beside him. "Holy Father, it is okay to speak," Patrick whispered. "We are alone." Pope Leo turned toward Patrick and Valanti, and struggling, raised his hand toward his face, trying to remove the oxygen mask. Seeing this, Patrick gently lifted Leo's head and slipped the band from behind it and removed the mask. Leo smiled at Patrick and patted his arm.

"Since we have been working together, you have learned to anticipate what I need," Leo said in a struggling voice. "The things I need to tell you are of utmost importance," Leo continued. "Where is the Bible I gave to you, Patrick?" he asked.

"It is right here in my cassock, Holy Father."

"Good," said Leo. "I have written three letters, and there are detailed instructions in them for both you and my dear friend Antonio. Also you will find one for the next pope. Do not share this information with anyone until there is a new pope elected and maybe not even then. That all depends on who is elected."

"We will do as you wish, Holy Father," they replied. Patrick placed his hand in the pocket of the cassock and felt the old, worn-out Bible and felt some comfort in touching it. Both noticed that the pope was beginning to look more pallid, and his breathing has become more labored. Patrick reached over and took the oxygen mask and once again placed it onto the pope's face. Leo moves his head to the side, tossing off the mask.

"I can't talk with the mask on, and I must continue what I need to tell you that you must know," Leo gasped. "Antonio, lean closer," Leo said. "I think someone has gotten into my secret archives."

"Gustav, that's impossible," Antonio whispered. "We are the only people who have the keys, and I have mine here around my neck." He said, reaching up and pulling out a gold key and showing it to the pope.

"I have worn mine also until today," said the pope, but I have taken mine off and placed in into the envelope that I have sealed and given to Patrick. Turning to Patrick, Leo looked up into his blue eyes and saw surprise. "I have given my key to you, Patrick, to hold onto and at your discretion to pass onto the next pope. But be very careful and make this discussion based on the feeling of your heart. Trust no one in this matter, only the leading of your heart."

"Antonio, your family has been working for the church for centuries, and I am sure you have heard many stories. Not all of them are true. But you will be surprised at the ones that are true," said Leo, smiling at his old friend. "One of the oldest legends is true. Our Lord Jesus gave to Peter, the first pope, the keys to the kingdom, and I fear that one of them has been stolen. This key was kept in the archives, and I thought only I knew where it was. It is the most dangerous of the keys." Leo wheezed. Archbishop Valanti and Patrick looked at each other in shock, not knowing if this could be true or it was just the fantasy of a dying man. Because looking at Pope Leo and listening to his breathing it did not take an expert to see that he was slipping away. Leo took a shallow breath and continued, "I have been told that there is another entrance into the archives through the crypt, and I am sure I am not the only one to have this information," Leo gasped and closed his eyes.

Looking at Archbishop Valanti, Patrick asked, "Should I get Sister Judith?" Feeling the pope's fingers tighten on his arm, Patrick looked down to see his eyes open again. The pope used all the strength he could muster and shook his head.

"The letters I have written and the manuscript that I gave Brother Sebastian will give you clues to where the other two keys are. I have never had them. They were hidden over a century ago by one of my predecessors. Each pope has lived in fear that they will fall into the wrong hands once again. Sebastian's death was no accident. You must find the manuscript and get Sister Judith's father to finish what Sebastian started. I have written down in each letter only a part of the clues as they were passed onto me. It will take both of you working together to read them. Share with no one what I have written and then burn the letters and wash the ashes down the sink when the time comes. The clues in the manuscript are written in ancient languages, so you must have help to translate them. You must find them, and it will be up to you, Patrick, to guard them and pass them to the right pope.

"Now I must warn you that both of you are in great danger. Never share this information with anyone you can't absolutely trust. Only share the information when the stolen key is found. You will be safe then," he said, still gripping Patrick's arm. Leo reached over to Antonio and took his hand, and taking another breath, looked both in the eyes and said, "Swear to me you will do as I said."

Both men looked down at Leo and said, "We swear, Holy Father, to obey you."

Leo took a deep breath and lets it out slowly and whispered, "Only your faith and a pure heart can save you from this evil." Patrick and Antonio felt his grip loosen on them and knew that he is gone.

Patrick's eyes began to water as great waves of grief swept over him. Leo had treated him like a son. Looking over at the Archbishop, Patrick saw tears running down his cheeks. Both had just lost a good friend, and the church had lost a loyal servant. Slowly, Patrick ran his hand down over the pope's face, closing his eyes for the last time. Using the side of the bed to help him, Archbishop Valanti got up with great difficulty and stood looking down at his friend. Patrick rose and turned toward the door. He was not looking forward to telling Sister Judith or anyone that the pope was dead. Protocol now took precedence over what happened next. There were things that needed to be done.

Patrick opened the door and walked into the hall. Looking around, he saw Sister Judith talking to Jason, making sure that he was all right. Patrick walked over to them to tell them the news, but the look on his face and the tears in his eyes said it all.

Sister Judith didn't say a word, but ran into the pope's room. Standing there with Jason, Patrick told his friend that the pope's room had to sealed off and that only certain people should be allowed in. A camerlengo would be in charge of the church until the election of the next pope. He would be the one who will certify that the pope is dead.

Jason's shoulders slumped. He was not only saddened by the news, but he felt responsible because he did not protect his pope. Patrick, sensing his grief, placed his arm around his friend to comfort him, and reassured him that he did all that he could do. He wished he could tell his friend that there was nothing he could have done, but he was not really sure what this thing or evil as, the pope called it, was.

Patrick released Jason and turned to leave, saying, "Post guards, for only Archbishop Valanti, Sister Judith, myself, or the camerlengo are the only ones allowed inside unless the archbishop needs someone, until I return. I need to make some calls. If you need me, I will be in my office."

Chapter 9

Sister Judith quietly opened the door to the pope's apartment and slipped in as quietly as she could. Archbishop Valanti stood beside the bed, leaning over the pope, giving him the last rites of the church. Hearing the door open, he turned to see Sister Judith coming into the room. She walked over to where he was standing and looked down at the pope. She took the pope's hand in hers and leaned over and kissed his ring. "He was such a good man. I can't believe that he is gone. His hand is still warm to the touch." She laid his hand down beside him.

"Sister, I will have one of the guards go over to the Jesuit house and bring Father John and Father Ralph over to sit with the pope while we wait for Monsieur Loren the undertaker from Rome to come and do his work. I will go and call him."

"I will be all right, Father. I do not mind being alone with the Holy Father until he arrives."

"I know, my child, but there are protocols to follow." The archbishop turned to leave, and glancing back over his shoulder he said to Sister Judith, "I will also call the mother superior to send over Sister Mary Margaret to help you get the clothes ready to dress the pope after Monsieur Loren is finished." But nothing can be done until the camerlengo arrives.

Reaching the door, the archbishop stepped into the hall and gave the instructions to one of the guards about what he and Sister Judith had discussed. Looking back through the door, he watched as Sister Judith took the oxygen mask off the bed and began folding up the tubing and packing her black bag. Valanti walked back into the room and pulled the pope's chair across the room, next to the bed, and sits down. All of a sudden, he felt very old and very tired. He was not used to running up and down the streets of Rome or the emotional pain of loosing a dear friend especially under these circumstances.

Seeing the fatigue on his face, Sister Judith asked, "Father, is there anything I can get for you?"

"Thank you, but no, my child. With God's help, I will be able to continue the work that has been laid out for me."

Sister Judith walked over to the cupboard where the pope's clothes are kept and began to select the garments that he would wear. Both Sister Judith and Valanti were quiet, being lost in their own thoughts of what lay ahead for both of them.

A knock on the door brought both of them back to reality. "I will see who it is," she said, moving toward the door. Opening the door, she lets Father John and Father Ralph in. John was carrying a processional cross and stand, and Ralph was holding a candlestick with a tall white candle on it. They proceeded over to the bed that the pope was laying on and bowed their heads in prayer, then John placed the cross at the pope's head, and Ralph placed the candlestick at his feet.

"Now that you two are here, I am going down to Monsieur O'Rourke office," Valanti said, and rising from the chair, he continued, "and call Monsieur Loren and make arrangements for him to come over tonight." Turning to Sister Judith, he said, "While I am gone, why don't you finish packing up the medical supplies and go back to your room for a while. It is going to be a long night. One more thing, ask mother superior to send over a couple of the sisters to clean up the pope's apartment. It would not be good for the cardinals to see it looking like this."

"Yes, Father, I will do as your say and have mother send over the help you requested." Judith replied as she continued to pack her black bag.

Turning back to the two priests, he said, "John, you and Ralph should not leave this room until I return, and do not let any one take anything out of this room with my knowledge. The only people who has any business in here tonight is the camerlengo, and it will most likely be Cardinal Emilio Recto Alveraz, Monsieur Loren, and the nuns that mother superior sends over, and you should know all of them." Satisfied that he was leaving things in capable hands, he turned to leave.

By this time, Sister Judith had finished packing her things and pulled the oxygen tank she walked toward the door behind Valanti. Reaching the door first, he held it open for Judith to pass through. Stepping into the hallway, he told the guards stationed there who has permission to enter and who does not. Both of the Swiss Guards nod in unison. They still had their weapons drawn and were ready for any emergency.

Walking down this familiar hallway, he began thinking of all that had happened and the information the pope had given them, and it made Valanti feel very uneasy. He was anxious to read the letter the pope had written to him. It was still in his Bible that Patrick had in his pocket. He decided to cut through the pope's audience room, thinking it would be empty this time of the night, but he found that he was wrong. Standing just beyond the door stood two members of the curia. Trying to skirt them did not work.

"Archbishop Valanti, wait a moment please," one of the cardinals called out. "We would like a word with you. Archbishop, what is going on? There have been rumors that the Holy Father has been attacked in his own apartment. The Swiss Guards are on full alert at the palace with their guns drawn. Is Leo all right?"

"I cannot speak of the rumors about the attack at this moment. We are still trying to find out what happened." Looking at the three, Valanti continued, "It is my sad duty to tell you that about forty-five minutes ago, the Holy Father died. I am on my way now to his secretary's office to call Cardinal Pulaski and inform him what has happened. I cannot tell you more than this, but I will keep you informed. As you know, I must call Loren the mortician from Rome to embalm the pope." Having said this, Valanti turned and left, leaving the three cardinals speechless.

Valanti continued through the audience room and into the hallway that led to Patrick's office. Behind him, he could hear the three cardinals coming out of their shock, and all three were talking at once. He had walked this hallway many times, and the office he was headed to used to be his a long time ago. He had once been the secretary to a pope. He stopped outside the door for a moment, trying to recall all that the pope had said. One thing that continued to ring in his ears were these words, "Never share this information with anyone you do not trust, and only your faith can save you." Now, he wondered who other than Patrick could he trust and was his faith strong enough or was Patrick's?

Valanti knocked softly on the door, and he heard Patrick say in a muffled voice, "Come in." He entered to find Patrick behind his desk talking on the telephone, and from what he was saying, he was talking to Cardinal Pulaski, the head of the curia. He has wanted to talk to Patrick first before this call was made. Patrick looked up and gave him a pained look, and as quickly as he could, he ended the conversation.

"Was that who I think it was?" asked Valanti.

"Yes, that was one call I wanted to get over with."

"Have you called the camerlengo?"

"No, that was to be my next call. I needed to make sure it was going to be Cardinal Alveraz."

"You need to make it right now. Nothing can happen until the pope is officially declared dead."

Patrick picked up the phone and placed a call to the residence of the camerlengo. "Hello, this is Monsignor O'Rourke. May I speak to Cardinal Alveraz?"

"This is Sister Joan Marie" came the answer. "Is it important? The cardinal is having dinner?"

"Yes! It is of utmost importance."

"I will go and get him for you, Father."

In a few minutes, Cardinal Alveraz came on the line. "Hello, Patrick, is everything all right?"

"No, Cardinal, it isn't. I have grave news. I am sorry to inform you that Pope Leo has died, and I need you to come to his apartment in the Vatican and confirm this."

"I will leave immediately. Does any one else know?"

"Yes, Father. Archbishop Valanti, Sister Judith, the captain of the Swiss Guard Jason, Father John, and Father Ralph from the Jesuit house and myself," said Patrick, "and there is one other I just got off the phone with, Cardinal Pulaski."

"I see. Well, seal off the pope's apartments until I get there."

"Yes, Father."

Chapter 10

Cardinal Pulaski hung up the telephone. There was something Monsignor O'Rourke was not telling him, or there was someone else in the room. He thought he had heard a knock on the door while they were talking. So Leo was dead. This left the door open for him to become the next pope, but he had to play his cards just right. He had to be the most humble of all the cardinals and one of the most clever. He also had to make sure that all of his tracks had been covered.

He had only one loose end, and he was not sure how to deal with it. You did not mess with a mafia boss very easily, nor could you get rid of one without causing a lot of attention. This was going to be a very delectate matter. But handling delectate matters was what he had always done best. He was a master of putting the blame on someone else even for one of his own blunders.

Father Anton had become a very useful ally in his plans, and he was very loyal. He also shared with the cardinal a propensity for evil. Then there was Cardinal Louis; he too would be useful. He was putting together a good team that should bring him to victory in the race for the papacy.

He had some other very potent help, but he had to be very careful how this particular help was used. It had worked very well so far, but he did not know all that had happened tonight, and the monsignor was playing it close to the vest as it were.

There had been some wild rumors floating around the palace tonight. That sounded like a wild tale and that is exactly what he wanted everyone to think. The presence of evil coming out of nowhere and someone, or as he had heard, something had attacked the pope and the captain of the guard. Jason was not saying much of anything. He and Patrick were good friends, and Pulaski was sure Jason had been told to keep his mouth shut by either Patrick or the archbishop. And why did Patrick leave the pope and run and bring the old man to the palace anyway. Leo and the archbishop went back a long way, and they were good friends. The archbishop was the only person other than the pope who had access to the secret archives or so, they thought.

The cardinal smiled to himself. *I wonder if they will ever figure out that there is another way in? It does not matter. Once I am the pope, I will have the keys, and I can come and go in front of anyone. At that time, I will have the other way sealed off, and it will be my little secret.*

What a stroke of luck that Brother Sebastian who had worked for him in Poland had been transferred to Rome to help sort out some old documents and papers of a tenth-century pope who was also a Leo. One cannot say enough about loyalty from one's protégé. He had been nice to Brother Sebastian, helping him through school to become a librarian and giving him a place to live. He did not know at the time how important this brother would be to him. Now, dear Sebastian, God rest his soul was about to give him the crown and power of Peter. *I must say a Mass for Sebastian, or better still, I could release him from hell myself,* smiled Pulaski.

Leaning back in his chair, he closed his eyes, letting his mind drift back to the time Brother Sebastian came to him again for advice.

Chapter 11

Camerlengo Cardinal Emilio Rico Alveraz looked like a blaze of red and white as he entered the Basilica of St. Peters. He had his driver let him off at the main entrance so that it would be just a short walk to the building and the elevator that ran up to the floor where the papal apartments were.

The place was quiet; it was dinnertime for the Vatican. The only people he passed were the guards at the door. He entered and noticed that they were on high alert and their guns were drawn. This seemed a little strange to him, but he had other things on his mind. He looked down the hall toward the way he had just come and saw another contingent of guards passing through; they were also armed. Pushing the up button, he watched as the numbers changed, and he could hear the elevator descending. As the door opened, another couple of guards stepped out and held the door open for him to enter. Then they joined him in the car, pushing the third-floor button for him.

"Why is everyone armed tonight?" asked the cardinal

"Father, we are on high alert. Our commander and the holy father were attacked in the pope's apartment earlier tonight."

"Is everyone all right?"

"We don't know, Father. We have just come on duty and were sent to meet and guard you."

"Do you think that I am in danger?"

"We do not know. All that we know is that our orders are to guard you and lead you to the pope's apartment."

The car arrived at the third floor and the door opens. Both of the Swiss Guards step out and hold the door open for the cardinal and then accompany him down to the pope's apartment. Entering the hall to the papal apartment, Cardinal Alveraz saw two more guards standing at the entrance to the apartment and two more down the hall in front of the pope's bedroom and still two more outside the pope's audience room. The pope's apartment consisted of several rooms all opening onto this central hallway.

Cardinal Alveraz stopped in front of the door leading into the pope's bedroom and study. He reached for the handle and tried to turn it. It did not budge. The door had been locked from the inside. He knocked. He could hear movement inside the room and then the door opened. Facing the cardinal was Brother John. He stepped aside and allowed the cardinal in. Passing through the study he entered the pope's bedroom. Seated beside what looked like a sleeping Pope Leo is Brother Ralph. Ralph rose on seeing the cardinal and stepped away from the bed.

Cardinal Alveraz walked over to the bed and gazed at the peaceful face of Pope Leo, then he reached into the pocket of his cassock and pulled out a small, silver hammer.

"Gustav Augustus Felinni, are you dead?" asked the Camerlengo Cardinal Alveraz, calling Pope Leo by his Christian name, while tapping him on the forehead with the silver hammer. Getting no response, once again, the cardinal intoned while tapping the pope on the forehead. "Gustav Augustus Felinni, are you dead?" Still getting no response, he asked a third time while taping the pope on the head. "Gustav Augustus Felinni, are you dead?" Having gotten no response, he turned to the two witnesses and said, "I declare that the pope is dead. The pontificate is officially ended." The camerlengo leaned forward and removed the Fisherman's ring from his finger.

To the two Jesuits, he said, "You may return to your house. Your work here is done. I will call you back when it is time to prepare the pope for the viewing." Both of the fathers bowed their heads and left the room. Hearing footsteps, he turned to see Sister Judith and Sister Mary Margaret coming through the doorway leading from the study.

"Mother superior sent us over to do whatever you think needs to be done," Sister Judith told the bishop.

"After the undertaker leaves, the fathers will return to dress the pope, and he will be moved to St. Peters for the public to pay their respects, and for nine days, Masses are to be said for his soul. Once the pope is moved, his clothes and personal belongings need to be moved out and the apartment cleaned. Then it will be sealed until the next pope is elected."

"We will go back to our rooms until you call us."

The weight of his responsibility until the next pope is elected began to settle in on Alveraz. He walked over to the chair that was beside the pope's bed and sat down. It was going to be a long night, and he had not had time to finish dinner. He could hear the guards milling around just outside, which was a comfort to him, considering the circumstances surrounding Leo death. He wondered if there had really been an intruder and who would attack this pope in his own bedchamber? How could they have gotten past the guards? Then it dawned on him. Just how safe was he if the intruder had not been caught?

He had many things to attend to over the next nine days that the pope would be lying in state. He had to call all of the bishops to Rome for the convocation to elect the next pope. But for now, he had to take care of the funeral arrangements. He also needed to talk to Monsignor O'Rourke and Archbishop Valanti. They had been the last ones to see and talk to the pope before he died. According to tradition, Patrick should have been given a letter for the next pope. He needed to find out if Patrick had such a letter, and if he did, being temporary head of the church, he should have the letter. He would have a talk with the monsignor first thing in the morning. He also had to let all of the pope's staff know that they have nine days to clear out their quarters and make them ready for the new pope's staff.

There was a knocking on the door that brought the camerlengo back to the present. "Come in," he said.

"Your grace, the undertaker is here from Rome. Should I let him in?"

"Yes, I have been expecting him."

Chapter 12

There was an awkward silence for a moment when Patrick hung up the phone. He and the archbishop just looked at each other in silence. Finally, Patrick said, "What do you think is going on? The pope was old, but for him to die so suddenly and in such a strange way, just doesn't make any sense."

"I know, Patrick. I feel the same way. He and I are the same age. Leo told us that he had left us each a letter and that he had given them to you in his Bible. Where is that Bible now?"

"I have it here in my cassock pocket" he said, then reached in and pulled the Bible out. Sticking out of it are the three letters. Patrick removed them and handed the archbishop the letter addressed to him and he lays his own on the desk in front of him along with the one addressed to the next pope.

The archbishop recognizes the fine handwriting of his friend Leo on the front of the envelope. It is addressed to Archbishop Antonio Valanti. Valanti opened the letter and unfolded it, and to his surprise, he is unable to read it. It appears to be written in a shorthand or a foreign language. None of which he is familiar. "Patrick," he said. "Open your letter"

Patrick opened his letter and as he did, a golden key on a chain fall to the desk. And as he unfolded his letter, he too was looking at words he was unable to read. "You are the pope's secretary. Can't you read his letter?"

"No, I can't. It is written in a language that I do not know. How about you?"

"It is the same for me How are we going to be able do as Leo asked, if we can't even read his instructions?" the archbishop asked.

"While you were in seminary, did either of you take ancient text or a course in shorthand?" Patrick asked.

"Not that I can remember. For the pope to have written to us in this manner must mean he thought we could figure out what it means."

"I agree."

The last thing he told us was "It will take both of you working together. He also said that we should memorize what he wrote then destroy the letters."

"I agree. But first we need to be able to understand what is written here."

Patrick picked up the key and began to examine it. It was a gold key with an ornate design and it had several symbols engraved into it. Patrick recognized one of the symbols; it was the one used for the pope and crown and orb, but he did not know what the other symbols were. There was something strange looking about the design running around the key. "Archbishop, you also have a key. Can I look at it?" The archbishop reached into his cassock and pulled out a golden key, and it was very similar to the one Patrick was holding. It was on a chain around the archbishop's neck. Valanti pulled the chain up and around his head and handed the chain and key to Patrick.

"I have not had the key off my neck since the pope gave it to me. I even stoop down to unlock the archives door so that I do not have to remove it."

Patrick took the key and looked at it; he noticed that it had the same ornate design, and it also had the same symbols engraved on it. To his eye, the key looked exactly the same. "Archbishop, I know the pope's symbol, but I do not know the other ones, do you?" Valanti reached over the desk and took his key back from Patrick and began to examine it.

"I too recognize the pope's symbol and one of the other symbols is for the keeper of the archives. The last three I do not know. Who in Rome could help us with this? It may be important in helping us find out what is going on."

"We have a church history scholar from the States who the pope invited to help us catalog some ancient papal letters and documents that Brother Sebastian was working on before his tragic accident last week. His name is Mat Mason, and he just arrived today so he has not come to see me yet. Maybe he can be of some help," observed the archbishop.

"He also has degrees in ancient languages and other religions. He teaches antiquities at Emory University in Atlanta Georgia."

"How did we come to know about him?" asked Patrick.

"The pope's nurse Sister Judith told the pope about him. It turns out that he is her father. He was more than willing to come and help. He has not seen Sister Judith in several years and wanted the opportunity to spend some time with her."

There conversation was interrupted by a knock on the door. Hearing the sound, both men quickly grabbed their letters and hid them. Patrick picked up the key the pope had given him and quickly placed it around his neck being careful to tuck it out of sight. "Come in." Beckoned Patrick. Sister Judith and Sister Mary Margaret entered.

"We have just left the Camerlengo Cardinal Alveraz," said Sister Judith. "He has pronounced that the pope is dead and has taken his ring and seal. Once the pope is prepared for viewing and moved to St. Peters, the apartment will be sealed after it is cleaned. We are going to our rooms until we are called, but I thought I would stop by here to see if it would be all right to leave the Vatican and visit my father who just arrived today?"

"Yes, that will be fine, Sister," replied Valanti. "Just keep your cell phone on, and be ready to return at a moment's notice."

"I will, Father"

"By the way, Sister, have your father call me in the morning. We still need him to do the work the pope called him to do. I also have something I need to ask him."

"Yes, Father, I will," she replied as she and Sister Mary Margaret turned to leave.

Chapter 13

Brother Sebastian sat shivering in the damp and cold conditions of the catacombs. He had been down here in the darkness for the past week. He dared not venture out during the day, and he had only gone out at night to get a blanket, some food, and a few candles. Hearing the scratching of the rats, made his skin crawl and at night a few of them had nipped on his shoes. There were puddles of water standing where it dripped from the roof of some of the tunnels. Rome and the Vatican were built over a series of catacombs, and these were used by the early Christians to hide from the Roman oppressors. After the church was built, these catacombs were used as a burial ground. The graves of many of the popes and martyrs were down here. Aside from the darkness and the rats, it was the constant dampness and the cold that was beginning to get to Brother Sebastian.

He had a lot of time to think this past week. He had made his regular report on the work he was doing on the papers of the first Leo. He had already given Cardinal Pulaski the map of the secret passage from the pope's palace to the secret archives. Leo had built this so that he could come and go without anyone knowing what he was doing. The last thing he had given Pulaski was the hiding place of a key that according to the ancient manuscript was a very important key that had been passed down since the time of Peter, the first pope. Pulaski seemed especially excited with this news and made Sebastian promise not to tell any one about this passage way or the key. He had made him promise on the Holy Bible, so there was no danger of Sebastian telling anyone. He took his oath very seriously.

He did not think much about what he had told the cardinal, he thought the pope already knew all about the passage way and the key. He was heading back to his room when a big dark car pulled alongside of him, and a man sitting in the backseat rolled down the window to ask him directions. He felt a sharp pain in his neck and then everything went black. He woke up several hours later in a room, lying with his hands bound behind his back on the floor. The room was dark, and the only window had a black plastic bag taped across it. The building must have been old because the wooden floor was smooth, having been worn down by much use. As his eyes adjusted to the darkness, he could make out by the light coming in from under the door. The room was filled with packing and shipping crates. The only furniture was a folding metal chair, lying up against the wall. He must be in some kind of warehouse. Why would anyone want to kidnap a monk? What did they hope to gain?

He could make out the sound of voices in the next room. Several men were talking, and he also heard a woman arguing with one of the men. He could not make out what they were saying; he could only hear the voices. Every now and then, he thought he smelled the ocean or heard water lapping against a dock. He also heard the sound of a foghorn in the distance, so he knew he must be somewhere near the bay.

Sebastian tried to free himself but the tape was too tight. He could scream, but he did not want the men or the woman coming into the room yet. There were several crates nearby on the floor, and if he could sit up, he might be able to rub the tape on the edges of the crates and begin to tear the tape. He rolled over onto his side and drawing up his knees, he began to push himself, inching like a worm toward the crates. He tried to be as quiet as possible. Nearing one of the crates, he rolled onto his back, and using the leverage of his feet, began pushing himself up against the crate until he was in a sitting position. From this position, he could move his hand up and down on the rough corner of the crate and hopeful begin to tear or weaken the tape.

Sebastian had not been doing this too long when he heard the woman scream and then there was a silence. The men began talking again, and he could hear footsteps coming toward the door. He eased himself back to the lying position and pretended to be still out. Two men came through the door; one grabbed Sebastian by his feet the other lifted him up by his shoulders, and they carried him into the next room and sat him in a chair. "Mileo," one of the men said.

"You did not tell me this was a priest. I am not ready to go to hell for killing a priest."

"Relax," the other man said. "We are doing this job for his eminence the cardinal. He has promised absolution and a reward in heaven if we do this job for him."

"I was OK getting rid of this woman. She was a whore, but this is a priest," whined Mileo.

"While he is still out, just shut up and help me load her onto the boat and then we will come back and get the priest."

"I don't know about all this. My sainted mother said, 'Hell is not place you want to be.'"

"Look, Mileo, we are not going to kill the priest like we killed the woman. We are just going to throw him overboard, and who knows, God may save him, and if he doesn't, that's God doing, not ours."

"Well, if you put it that way, I guess it's all right."

"It better be, or our boss will not be so kind to us. You know what happens to those who don't obey him. Drowning would seem like a picnic, compared to what he would do to us. Get moving."

Sebastian could not believe what he had just heard. Cardinal Pulaski just had his girlfriend killed, and he was going to be next. He opened his eyes, just enough to watch as the two men carried out the woman. Her limp body hung between the men like a sack of potatoes. He could see her face; the eyes were open, staring back at him but he could tell they were seeing nothing. There was a wire around her neck, and her face was all bulgy and turning a blue color. He watched as they disappeared up a flight of stairs and disappeared from sight. He tried to stand, but whatever they had given to put him out still had an effect on him. He turned to his side so that he could rub the tape against the crate that was sitting next to him. The friction from rubbing had begun to blister his wrist, but he continued as fast as he could. The sound of footsteps coming down the stairs caused him to stop and try to get himself back into the position they had left him. He let his head fall to his chest and pretended to be still out.

The two men grabbed him under the arms and began to drag him across the floor. He was not a big man, but they were having trouble moving him like this.

"Mileo, drop him, and we will get him under the arms and around his knees. It will be easier to get him up the stairs." Sebastian felt himself being unceremoniously dropped to the floor. Then the men picked him up and carried him up the stairs and outside. It was night, and there was a mist coming in. He could feel the damp air on his face, and this helped to awaken him. Sebastian could not open his eyes for fear they would know he was awake. He heard the sound of water and the creek of wood that was old and water logged. He felt them carry him up the gangplank and onto a boat. There they dropped in on a pile of ropes near what he thought to be the front of the boat. Lying next to him was the dead woman. He could feel her lukewarm skin touching his cheek. The tape holding his hands together had begun to tear, he could almost get one hand loose. If what he heard was right, they were only going to throw him into the water bound so that he would drown. "Please God," he began to pray. "I must survive and warn your servant the pope."

The motor on the launch purred into motion, and Sebastian felt it being backed away from the dock. He also heard another boat also being started. Seemed like it was going to follow them into the bay. The water was smooth, and there was no wake this time of night because these were the only two boats leaving the dock. Sebastian could hardly tell that the boat was moving. Then suddenly they picked up speed, and Sebastian felt the woman's body roll heavily against him, and he was sickened by the smell of urine; she must have wet herself. The boat began to bounce up and down as it swept over the swells, tossing the two of them against each other over and over again. They had been in this boat for what seemed like forever when it began to slow down. Then the other boat began to circle, causing the boat Sebastian was in to rock crazily, making him feel sick in his stomach. He did no want them to know he was conscious, so he kept swallowing the bile that was rising in his throat. Sebastian wondered what was going on. Hearing footsteps, he closed his eyes again. He felt himself being pushed aside, and the men grunting as they picked up the woman, walked a few steps, and threw her overboard. There was a big splash and then he heard the boat—circling, revving its engines, sounding like it was plowing through something—and Sebastian knew what that something was. The woman's body was being ground up by the prop of the other boat like meat in a grinder. It would not be long for the sharks to smell the blood in this bay and get rid of the rest of the body. He did not hear the men returning. Suddenly, he felt himself being picked up, and they walked a few steps, and he had the feeling of being airborne and then the hard surface of the ocean hitting him. He knew that the other boat was close by, because he could hear the engine revving. Pulling as hard as he could at the tape as he hit the water, it tore, and using his free arms, he dove, kicking with his tied feet. It was like having a fin. Down into the murky dark water he went, and he could feel the vibration of the other boat's props passing over him with just a few inches to spare.

The tape was wrapped around his pants so Sebastian bent down and pulled off his shoes. His lungs were bursting, but he would not dare surface for air. They needed to think he was dead. Getting his shoes off was the easy part, but getting the pants off was another matter. Sebastian was on the swim team in high school, and he was comfortable in the water. Struggling to get the pants off began to wear him out. His lungs were screaming for air. He had not had time to get a good breath before hitting the water. Finally, the pants came off, and he began to swim underwater until he had to come up for air. He surfaced slowly, just letting his face come up above the water. He let out the air and took in a deep breath. Lucky for him, there was no moon out tonight. He could see the two boats not far from him. The smaller boat was still circling the larger one. As it quit circling, the water around the larger boat became alive and teaming with sharks. He needed to get out of there as quickly as he could, or he would end up being their next meal. Looking around as best he could, Sebastian saw what appeared to be the light of the city. They appeared to be about two miles away, which made his heart sink. He could swim but he was not sure he could do two miles it had been a long time since he had been in a swimming event. In the distance, he could hear the bell of a buoy. He could not see it, but he could follow the sound. He began to swim toward that sound. It took what seemed like all night, but he made it to the buoy and held on to it until a fisherman spotted him and picked him up. The fisherman gave him some clothes and a ride back to Rome. That was five days ago.

As he lay in the dark, he knew that he had to get back into his room and retrieve the manuscripts and get to the pope without the cardinal finding out that he was still alive. "Please, God, give me a plan. You saved my life, now help me help your servant Pope Leo." Uttering this prayer, he got up and lit a match, and finding a candle, he lights it. He stores his food, and the last of his water on a rock ledge. Taking the last candle, he begins to make his way to the entrance of the catacombs and his journey back to the Vatican. He does not think he will have any trouble getting through the gate dressed in the clothes the fisherman gave him. His only problem was the smell. It might attract some unwanted attention. But what choice did he have? He was sure at some point the cardinal would send Father Anton to search his room for the manuscript. He had not gotten to translate much of it but the part he had read frightened him and knowing the true nature of the cardinal made him afraid not only for himself but for the church.

Chapter 14

It had been a restless night for Patrick. He kept having the recurring dreams about what had just happened. He had woken several times in a cold sweat with the blackness of the night closing in on him. The ringing of his cell phone had jarred him into wakefulness. Forcing his eyes open, he looked over at the clock while the relentless ringing of the cell kept echoing through his head. Throwing the covers back, he reached for the cell, and answered the call. "Hello, this is Monsignor O'Rourke," he said in a hoarse voice.

"Monsieur, this is Mat Mason. I am Sister Judith's father. She said you wanted to talk to me this morning. How can I help you?"

"Thank you for calling. Would it be possible for me to return your call? It was an extremely tiring day, and I haven't gotten myself together quite yet."

"Yes, Father, I will free my schedule so that I will be available when you call."

"Thanks, Mr. Mason."

Patrick hung up and laid his cell on the nightstand. He reached down and pulled the blanket back up over him. He was not quite ready to get out of bed yet. There was something quite comforting about being in a warm bed with the covers pulled up. It reminded him of being a child in Ireland, sleeping in on a summer morning, safe and warm under one of his mother's quilts. He let his mind wander. How could the pope have died so quickly yesterday? Patrick had been with him nearly every day since he had become pope. Leo was not a big robust man, but he seemed to be in fairly good health until several weeks ago. And Patrick watched the decline, feeling helpless to do anything. He has asked Leo several times what was wrong, and Leo would not or could not tell him. He tried to remember what was going on when all this started. He could not think of anything thing unusual that was happening. The Vatican was always a busy place, and there was always a lot of intrigue going on around the pope. Cardinals vying for more power or better positions, and diplomats and people in general wanting time with the pope. But since the time he had asked Patrick to have Brother Sebastian to come and see him to do some translation on an old manuscript he had found Leo seemed distracted like he had a great weight pressed down on his shoulders. It seemed to get worse when the pope got a note from Brother Sebastian just before the monk was killed in a boating accident, which was still under investigation by the Rome police. What had a monk that was doing research work on the old papers of the original pope Leo doing out on A boat in the middle of the night so far from Rome? It was after this that the pope seemed to be going down in a hurry. This was also the time that Leo asked Mat Mason to come over and finish the work Sebastian had begun.

He was to have an appointment with the pope today to discuss what needed to be done and try to find out at what point Brother Sebastian was in his work. The note Leo had gotten from Brother Sebastian, was somewhat vague. It was almost like he had discovered something and was afraid to even tell this discovery to the pope.

Looking down at the chain around his neck with the key attached brought to mind just how important this key must be. He knew Pope Leo trusted him, and he was not about to let that trust be betrayed. He closed his eyes and began to pray. "Please, God, help me to be your servant, and use me in any way that will further your kingdom. Give me the wisdom I need to fulfill and understand what your servant Pope Leo wanted me to do. Amen."

Once again Patrick threw off the covers and this time got out of bed. Standing up he pulled off his boxers and walked into the bathroom for a shower. Turning on the hot water, he waited until he saw the water steaming before he stepped in. The feeling of hot water on his skin helped wash away the cobwebs from his mind. As he shampooed his hair, he began to make his plans for the day. First thing he needed to do was to touch base with Archbishop Valanti. He wanted him and his letter there when he met with Mister Mason. Patrick stepped out of the shower and toweled himself off and walked to the bureau to get some clean boxers and a T-shirt. Looking into the closet, he pulled out a clean shirt and clerical collar. Dressing quickly, he left for his office to call the archbishop from there.

Patrick was greeted by the Swiss Guard outside his office door; his office had not been sealed yet nor had the papal apartment. This would be happening very soon. The pope had been moved last night into the chapel before being taken into St. Peters. Leo would lie in state for nine days, so Patrick had this much time to use his office then he would have to leave. Once he was gone, his authority would also be gone. He opened his door, and to his surprise things look just like they did every other day since he became the pope's secretary. The difference was that there was not the usual crowd of people waiting to see the pope and that he could no longer go into Leo's apartment and find him there. His heart already felt heavy, like it was going to burst with grief for the man who had not only been his boss but also his friend and mentor. Patrick walked over and sat down behind his desk. It was filled with request from those who wanted an audience with the pope. Pushing these aside, Patrick reached for his phone. Dialing the archbishop's number, he waited listening to the ring.

"Archbishop Valanti's office," the voice on the other end answered.

"This is Monsignor O'Rourke. Is the Archbishop available?"

"One moment please" came the reply. "He will be with you in a moment. Please hang on."

"Hello, Patrick, how are you doing this morning?"

"I am all right, I guess. I got a call that woke me up this morning from Mister Mason, and I told him I would call him back and let him know when I could meet with him. I thought it would be best if we met with him together."

"That sounds good to me. How about just after lunch? The Camerlengo Cardinal Alveraz is on his way to interview me about what happed last night and why I was summoned to the pope's apartment. I have a feeling that you will be next. I do not think we should tell him about the letters or the key that the pope gave to you. Are we on the same page with this?"

"Yes, I think we should keep secret all that we know until we can find out what is going on. The fewer people that know, the better."

Patrick could hear someone knocking on the archbishop's door. "Got to go. I think he is here," said Valanti, and he hung up the phone.

Patrick picked up his telephone again this time dialing Mat Mason.

The phone only rang twice before it was answered, "Hello, this is Mat Mason."

"Mister Mason, this is Monsignor O'Rourke. Would you be able to come to my office in the Vatican this afternoon around one thirty?"

"Yes, that will be fine. Do I need to bring anything with me?"

"You may want to bring your laptop. We have a couple of things that need to be translated."

"I will do that. Anything else?"

"No. That will do it. See you at one thirty." Patrick hung up the phone.

Patrick thought about calling Valanti back to let him know that he had a time set for Mister Mason to come to meet them. He quickly changed his mind. It would not be wise for him to be calling while the camerlengo was in the process of interviewing the archbishop. The less they were connected, the better it would be for all concerned. He heard a quick knock and then his friend Jason stuck his head through the door. "Hi, Patrick, how are you feeling this morning?"

"I'm fine, Jason. The better question is how are you doing?"

"It's funny. Physically, I am OK, but for some reason, mentally, I feel like my brain is mush. It feels like something tried to get inside of my head. I just can't explain it. I have never felt anything like it before. Is there anything I can do for you?"

"As a matter of fact, there is. I am going to have a meeting this afternoon with Archbishop Valanti and a visitor. Can you post an extra guard outside my office and at the entrances to this part of the building?"

"Sure. Are you expecting any kind of trouble?"

"No. I just want to make sure that we are not disturbed by anyone while we are meeting."

"That should not be a problem, since Cardinal Alveraz has already begun the process of sealing off the papal apartments. Patrick, you do not seem quite yourself. Are you sure that you are all right?"

"Like you, I am OK. Just tired and heart sick to have lost the pope so suddenly."

"I will make sure you are not disturbed. See you later," said Jason as he closed the door.

Chapter 15

The constant drip of the water, the cold, the smell of rot, and darkness had done their work on Brother Sebastian. His nerves were already frayed from the ordeal of nearly being drowned. The only thing that was a bright spot for him was that he was fairly sure that Cardinal Pulaski and the mafia did not know that he was still alive. And as long as this was true, he was safe. He had no way of telling time, so he did not know whether it was day or night. Using one of his last candles, he began to wind his way back to the entrance that he had used to get into the catacombs. No matter what time it was, he knew it was important to get back to his room and retrieve the documents of the first Pope Leo he had been working on. He realized he was not the only one who was smart enough to figure out that there was a secret tunnel to the pope's private archives, and he had just begun to learn about the keys mentioned in the documents. He had told Cardinal Pulaski all that he had learned, so he knew that the cardinal had already been to the archives and taken the key. His untimely death would have left no one else with that knowledge. He only hoped that Pulaski had not been to his room and taken the documents, since he had not had time to hide them.

The candle did not give enough light for him to see more than just a step or two in front of him. Just as he rounded a corner, he stepped on something soft and slick and as he did, he heard and felt several small furry creatures he knew must be rats running away form where he was. He must have stepped on a dead rat that the others were feasting on. He continued on his foot, sliding on the blood of whatever he has stepped on, as he walked down the section of the tunnel. Overhead, he could hear the noise of bats as he and the light disturbed their sleep. Having them overhead told him that it must still be light outside. He now felt a slight movement of air and the flame on the candle began to flicker; this meant that he was not too far from the entrance. Coming out in the daylight was not what Sebastian wanted to do but he had no choice. It was of utmost importance that he retrieved the manuscript and hid it. He also needed to get a message to the pope and warn him about Cardinal Pulaski.

The pitch black of the dark inside of the tunnel had begun to turn to a gray, and the air no longer had a sour rotten smell. He could see the entrance about one hundred yards away, and he could also hear the noise from the city. It was comforting to hear voices and the sound of cars and children playing in the nearby park. Not wanting to be seen, he blew out the candle and placed it in a niche in the rocks where he could find it again. While he was out, he needed to find a better source of light and pick up some food that did not need to be heated. He was still wearing the clothes that the fisherman had given to him. He has gotten used to the smell of fish, but he was sure he reeked and others would smell him bringing attention to himself. He had to figure out a way to get into his room. With a little luck and the brothers being on schedule with their work and prayers, he may just be able to get in and out without being seen. Having a shower was another matter.

Sebastian got up on his toes and stuck his head out and looked around, before he crawled out into the full daylight. Pulling himself up and out of the entrance, he was still hidden behind the bushes that covered the area. He got down on his hands and knees and crawled out to the edge of the bushes. Looking up and down the street, he got up and brushed the dirt off as best he could. No one seemed to be paying any attention to him. Walking as much in the shadows as he could at the corner, he turned left toward the park. There were a lot of people milling around, so he figured it must be lunchtime. He passed several people eating, and mothers having picnics with their children. Careful to stay on the fringes, he made his way through the park without being noticed or seeing anyone that he knew. He was still about a mile from the Vatican, so seeing someone he knew would be rare. He began to pray that the other brothers would be busy finishing up the morning chores and getting ready for lunch, so that he could get to the house before the saw him. If his luck held out, he may just make it before anyone sees him.

Sebastian picked up his pace as he left the park. He noticed as he passed, if he was too close to them, people they would wrinkle up their noses in disgust at the smell of fish and the way he looked. Sebastian kept his head down and tried not to make eye contact with anyone. He also pulled the fisherman's cap he had on down lower on his head, covering all of his hair and most of his forehead. Up ahead, he could see the dome of St. Peters; it would not be far now. At the corner, he looked around and coming in his direction was none other than Cardinal Pulaski. All of a sudden he could not breathe. His heart began to pound; it felt like it was going to jump out of his chest. With the cardinal was his secretary Father Anton, and they were bearing down quickly on him. They were in an animated conversation and had not noticed him yet. Turning his back to them, he darted across the street nearly being hit by an oncoming car. Reaching the other side, he glanced over his shoulder to see both the cardinal and Father Anton staring in his direction. His saving grace was a transit bus pulling up to its stop blocking their view. Sebastian ran as fast as he could toward the garden, which was located just outside the Vatican walls. If he could get there before they crossed the street, he would be safe.

Sebastian dared not look back again. He just kept running. He reached the gate and had to wait, because a lot of school children from the local school were filing in, and it was just his luck he knew most of the nuns. Keeping his head down, he stood as close to one of the trellises covered in vines, trying to blend into the surroundings. As the last of the children entered the gate, he heard voices not too far behind him.

Father Anton was saying, "Isn't that the crazy fisherman who ran in front of the car down the block?"

"I believe you are right. Do you see one of the guards around? We don't want him coming into the garden area," replied the cardinal.

"I don't see one nearby. Should I say something to him myself?" asked Anton. "That might be a good idea."

"Hey, you," called Anton. Hearing this Sebastian turned from the gate and began to run as fast as he could down the street, pushing people aside as he ran. He could hear footsteps behind him, and they were just keeping pace with him. Being a swimmer he had strong leg muscles. He may not be fast but he had great endurance.

"Hey, you, stop!" Father Anton called again, but this time he was further back. Sebastian turned at the next corner and ducked into an alleyway, which he knew would bring him around to the back of the gardens. He kept running until he reached the end of the alley. Leaning against the building, he listened and did not hear anyone behind him. He was wet with sweat that mixed with the fish. It was a nauseating mixture which even he could smell. It was a fine spring day; the sun had knocked the chill off, and the temperature would have been in the midsixties. He shed the coat but that did not do anything about the smell. He had to get some clean clothes and take a shower. Even if he chanced being seen, he could not blend in smelling and looking like he did.

He slipped into the back gate. Looking around, he saw several people he knew, so he had to be careful. Standing at the other gate looking toward the way he had run was Cardinal Pulaski. Sebastian knew that he had to get through the garden and into the Vatican wall before Anton got back to the cardinal. Inching his way toward the entrance, he had to pass several of the nuns who worked inside. All turned to look at him as he passed, but none seem to know that it was Sebastian. Just a few more paces and he would be inside.

The Swiss Guard at the entrance was busy with a tourist, so he was able to slip pass. This was the most dangerous part of the journey until it was time to leave again. Sebastian turned and looked back toward the other gate and as he did, his and Anton's eyes met. Anton quit talking to the cardinal and began to run in his direction. Sebastian sprinted toward the opening that led to his quarters, and with any luck, he could be inside before Anton reached the entrance. Ducking around the corner, he headed toward the backdoor hoping everyone would be at lunch.

Reaching the door, he turned the handle only to find it was locked. He reached into his pocket to retrieve the key only to find an empty pocket. His pants were somewhere at the bottom of the ocean. There was a spare key hidden under one of the flowerpots; he began tilting the pots up, trying to find the right one. Finally, after what seemed to him like an eternity, he saw the key. Reaching under the pot, he retrieved it and unlocked the door. Carefully stepping inside, he looked up the stairs and around the entry hall, and all were empty. There were sounds of the brothers laughing and talking coming from the dining room. Carefully, he crept up the stairs toward his room.

The door to his room was closed as were all on the hallway. Sebastian opened his door and stepped in. Glancing around, he noticed that someone had been looking through his things. He thought it maybe the police or maybe the cardinal had been here or sent someone over to get the manuscripts. His desk was a mess. He quickly looked thought the papers. Looking into the bottom drawer under the books and papers he had placed on top of it the manuscript was still there. He picked it up and put it in his briefcase and placed the briefcase on the bed. He went over to his closet and pulled out a clean shirt and black suit. He wanted to blend in and nothing blended in at the Vatican better than a priest or a penguin.

Opening his door, he looked out into the hall still not seeing anyone he got his towel and a bar of soap and walked down to the shower room. Before he opened the door to the shower, he stood there with his ear against it listening to see if there was anyone inside. Not hearing anything, he quietly opened the door and stepped inside. Sebastian undressed and placed the dirty clothes on the floor by the door. He knew he would have to get rid of them somewhere outside. He turned on the water and stepped into it. It was cold at first but soon began to get warm. He just stood there and let the water wash over him. He lathered up as fast as he could, wanting to get out before anyone found him there. Drying off, he stood at the sink and shaved the five days' growth from his face. Standing there nude, he noticed his body was much leaner. He had lost several pounds since his capture and hiding. His face was still tan and his black hair shone slicked back, and his deep brown eyes still full of life but somehow wiser and less innocent. Sebastian dressed and wrapped the wet towel over the fisherman's clothes and carried them back to his room. He pulled out his gym bag that was in the closet and put the dirty clothes inside. He looked in the top drawer of his dresser and got the envelope he kept his extra cash in. He had a couple hundred euros. This would tide him over for a day or two. Picking up the briefcase off the bed and taking the gym bag, he left his room. Carefully, he made his was back down the hall to the stairway. As he tiptoed down the stairs he heard footsteps coming his way. He was at the half waypoint he could not go back up in time so he just froze in his tracts. Brother John rounded the corner and started up the stairs; he was caught off guard at the sight of Brother Sebastian standing midway down. Both just stared at each other for a moment, neither saying a word. John was the first to speak, "Sebastian, we thought your were dead. I am so glad to see this was not true. Where have you been? The police have been here looking for you several times. We heard you drowned out in the bay."

"John, I don't have time to explain right now. Will you trust me?"
"Yes!"
"Thank you, John. I am in grave danger and so is the pope I must warn him."
"You don't know? The whole world knows. Leo is dead."
"Leo dead! When? How?"
"We are not sure. It is all very mysterious."
Sebastian just stood there in shock, wondering just who he could trust now. "John," he said. "I need you to go to the Vatican and get a message I have written to monsignor O'Rourke that I am still alive and will get in touch with him tomorrow. Tell him not to tell anyone. You must do this right away. Will you do this for me?"
"Yes," answered John.
Giving John a warm embrace, Sebastian went down the steps and out the backdoor. He made his way over to the entrance of the gardens and

as he is passing the guard, they made eye contact, and there is a sign of recognition in his eyes. It is Olson who normally guards the archives. He has seen Sebastian many times coming and going as he worked there. Turning into the garden, Sebastian never looked back.

Chapter 16

Cardinal Pulaski left his office; he was heading into Rome for lunch. His driver was going to meet him in front of St. Peter's office complex. His phone was ringing, and he did not want to answer it and get tied up. Anton was coming through the outside door, and he motioned him to get the phone.

"Cardinal Pulaski's office," he answered. The cardinal brushed past him and as he did, Anton grabbed him by the arm. This did not set well with the cardinal. He did not like being touched especially by an underling. Struggling to get loose, he turned and frowned at Anton. The expression on Anton's face made him stop. The color had drained out of his face, and his hand was shaking. "Are you sure? Could it have been someone who looks like him? Thank you! I will pass this information on to the cardinal." With this, he hung up the phone.

Turning to the cardinal, he told him what he had just heard, "That was Olson the Swiss Guard who usually guards the archives. He was on duty at the entrance to the gardens this morning, and he said that Brother Sebastian passed him going into the gardens."

"Is he sure?"

"Yes." He has seen Sebastian many times coming and going from the archives. All of a sudden, Pulaski felt dizzy. How could this be? He had been assured that neither the woman nor Sebastian survived being thrown into the harbor and being run over by the other speedboat. Even if the boat had missed him, surely he would have drowned being thrown into the bay tied up. They had told him there was a swarm of sharks thrashing around in the water after the woman had been thrown in. If

Sebastian had not drowned, surely the sharks would have finished him off. If that was truly Sebastian, he had to be found, and this time they needed to make sure the job was done right. "Call Olson back and find out who else he has told."

"Yes, Cardinal," answered Anton.

Pulaski went back into his office and reached for his phone. He now was going to have lunch with a new partner. "Anton! Call Cardinal Lewis and tell him we will have to reschedule our lunch. Then call my driver and tell him I won't be needing him after all."

"Yes, your eminence," answered Anton.

Dialing the number of his old friend Don Vincenza Amato, head of the Rome mafia family, he waited for someone to answer. "Salva."

"This is Cardinal Pulaski. I would speak to the don."

"One moment please" came the reply.

"Ah, Cardinal. It is good to hear from you. Are you calling to tell me that you have completed your part of the bargain and released my family from purgatory?"

"No! Don, what I am calling to tell you is that you blotched the job I gave you to do. Brother Sebastian was seen leaving the Vatican this morning."

"But, eminence, that is not possible. I have assurance that both were drowned and then run over by the speedboat."

"My best people said they saw the blood and shredded clothing floating on the surface and the sharks. There was nothing left but shreds of clothing. So how can this be? It must be a mistake. All priests in Rome look alike. Are you sure?"

"Yes! The guard at the gate knew Sebastian very well. He saw him nearly every day as he passed him going in and out of the archives."

"Don't worry, your eminence, I will get my best people on it immediately. If he truly did survive, he will not be able to hide in Rome. We will find him before the sun sets tomorrow at the latest."

"I hope for your sake and the sake of your family this is true. Let me know as soon as he is found."

"Yes, eminence."

"Anton! Did you get Olson back on the phone?"

"Yes, sir, and he assured me that he has not told anyone. I have told him to keep this to himself."

"Good."

Cardinal Pulaski got up from his desk and goes over and shuts his door. As he does, he tells Anton that he does not want to be disturbed. He needs some time to plan. Things are not going as he thought they would. Soon, the rest of the cardinals would be arriving for the pope's funeral and then the conclave to elect the next pope. He had to get things in motion if he was going to be elected the next pope. He did not have time to search for Sebastian or to worry that he was still alive. He wondered if his newfound power could help in find Sebastian. He has used the one demon he has released to torment Leo. But it had not been as effective as he thought it would have been. Leo was a man of faith, and he had been able to keep it from inhabiting his body. The demon could only battle with him mentally, thus wearing the old man down. To use the demon, the cardinal had to direct it to the pope. He did not know if the demon had the power to seek out people, but he would soon find out. Getting the demon back had also been a problem; once let loose, they did not want to go back into the pit or purgatory or wherever the door opened into. Pulaski was not quite sure he wanted to use this demonic power again, but he knew this might not be an option.

He leaned back in his chair, placing his hands behind his head and closed his eyes. He could envision his election as pope and all of the power he would have. He relished the thought of having all of the cardinals bowing before him and kissing his ring. He would be one of the wealthiest and most powerful men in the world and beyond. Sebastian had to be found. Sebastian also had the manuscript with all of the information about the passageway and the other keys. What a fool he had been. He should have sent Anton immediately over to Sebastian's room and picked up the manuscript. He could have had anyone of the people in the archives finish the work Sebastian had begun.

Then the thought came to him that Sebastian must have come back to his room to get the manuscript and taken it with him. He had to find out immediately. Pressing the intercom button, he waited for Anton to answer, "Yes, may I help you?"

"Come in to my office." In a moment, Anton opened the door and stepped in. "How may I be of service?"

"I need you to go over to Sebastian's room and search it for the manuscript and anything else that might lead us to him. Also find out if any of the other brothers saw him coming or going."

"Yes, eminence, I will leave right away."

While Anton was gone, Pulaski thought he might just let the demon out and direct it over to the don's office. A little scare might just be what the don needs to make sure his people find Sebastian. The cardinal walked over to the door and went into the outer office where Anton's desk was and locked the outside door. He walked back into his office and also locked the door behind him. He wanted to make sure he would not be disturbed. Having done this, he reached up on the top shelf and pulled down a plain wooden box. Standing in the middle of the room, he opened the box, revealing a key that is in two pieces. He reached into the box and took out the pieces and carefully fitted them together. He pulled out the old piece of papyrus from the manuscript, which came from the book of the key of Solomon and carefully unfolds the page. Taking some powder out of pouch made from the bones of dead saints, he began to draw a circle and then the pentagram that is pictured on the page. Laying the key in the middle of the pentagram, he began to say the words that were written on the page calling on the angels whose names are written around the edge of the symbol. He intoned in Hebrew, "Come and serve me." Around him, the room began to shimmer and glow in an eerie opaque light, and as he watched, a door began to form right before him. It looked like it was made out of bronze and had an inscription across the top that Pulaski could not read. As the door became clearer, it had a handle in the form of a serpent coiled up ready to strike, and below this was a keyhole. Around the perimeter of the door were many symbols, some Pulaski knew because they were also on the key. He reached out and touched the door. It felt cold to the touch and gave him a feeling of foreboding. He placed the key into the lock hole and turned it. Reaching for the handle he pulled, and the door began to swing open. A bright reddish-orange light came from the door. Pulaski stepped back, allowing it to open all the way. He was not anxious to meet what is on the other side again. Just inside, the door looked like a deep chasm spiraling down into a bottomless pit. He dared not step any closer, pulling the key out of the door and holding it in front of him, he intoned the words written on the old manuscript page, and then cried out in Hebrew, "Come and serve me." Out of the crevice came a dark and foreboding shape billowing toward the cardinal. Holding the key toward the demon, it knelt before the cardinal. Pulaski spoke to the demon and told it to go to the don's office in Rome and torment the don. As he watched, the demon seemed to evaporate as it slipped under his office door and disappeared. Pulaski could see other demons gathering at the entrance of the door wanting to get out, but he did not have the commands to release them.

Taking the key in both his hands, he pressed the key on the papal symbol engraved in the center of the key, and it once again broke apart into two pieces. As the key broke, the room began to shimmer once again, and the door closed. He watched as it began to fade. The circle he had drawn and the pentagram instantly burst into flames and they too disappeared. The flash from the circle reminded him of the old flash power magicians used when creating an illusion. Feeling like he had been drained of all of his energy, Pulaski staggered back to his desk and fell into his chair. He hoped Anton would be a while. He would have to open the door once again when the demon returned from its task, and he did not need an audience when that happened. He needed the rest of the manuscript; he had tasted its power, and now he wanted all of it.

Chapter 17

It had already been a long morning. Patrick felt like he had been run over by a truck. He had just finished calling all of the people who had been on the pope's appointment list to tell them of the pope's death. The newspapers would be having a special addition, and the rest of the media would be airing the story today at noon when the Camerlengo Cardinal Alveraz would be making the official announcement. He had waited until all of the other cardinals from around the world had been notified. That had been happening all night. Alveraz's office would have notified the last one this morning.

Patrick needed to get a quick bite of lunch before Mat Mason and Archbishop Valanti arrived at his office in forty-five minutes. Closing his door, he headed down the hallway to the stairs. It would be quicker than the elevator. The only bad thing about going this way was that he had to pass the office of Cardinal Pulaski. Patrick noticed that the sun was shining brightly over the plaza as he came out of the door of the office building. There was always a crowd of people here, most of them tourists. There was almost a carnival air about the place—vendors selling sweets and coffee and others hawking their souvenirs of the Vatican. It amused him, thinking that in the gift shop across the street from the square you could purchase a rosary, like the one the pope gives to his special visitors. All this would be over soon as the news of the pope's death was announced. He knew of a small café just outside the walls of the Vatican where he could get a salad and small bowl of pasta. Crossing the plaza, he ran nearly headlong into Father Anton, Cardinal Pulaski's secretary.

"Good afternoon, Anton. We both seem to be in a hurry. I am on my way to lunch. How about you?"

"On business, Patrick," Anton replied as he brushed past Patrick without stopping. Patrick turned and watched Anton hurrying past the tourists. *Something is going on,* he thought as he turned back toward the café.

Entering the café, Patrick looked around for a table; the place was full of tourists and staff from the Vatican. Patrick spotted his friend Captain Jason Spitzer sitting at a corner table. "Hello, Jason," he said as he walked over to where Jason was sitting. "Mind if I sit with you?"

"Please sit, Patrick. Always good to see you."

"What's going on with you this morning? Don't misunderstand me, but you look beat."

"It has been a rough night. You don't look so good yourself."

"Did you ever figure out what ran into you in the pope's apartment?"

"No! And I hope I never see or feel anything like it again. It is hard to explain but my insides feel just like they have been run through. Everything inside of me is sore."

"I guess you were lucky not to have been killed," said Patrick.

"Sir, may I help you," interrupted the waiter. He was one of the typical waiters you would find in small café's—long on sneers and short on patience. As the waiter tapped on his pad and shifted back and forth from foot to foot, Patrick looked at the day's specials. "What are you having?" he asked Jason.

"I am having the pasta primavera with a small salad and a glass of the house wine," he replied.

Looking up into the dour face of the waiter, Patrick told him that he would have the same. With a quick turn, the man was gone. "Have you spoken with anyone about what happened last night?" Patrick asked Jason.

"I spoke briefly to the Camerlengo Alveraz last night, and I have been told that Cardinal Pulaski wants to have a talk with me sometime today."

"How about you?" asked Jason.

"I talked to Archbishop Valanti last night, and we are going to meet right after lunch today. We wanted to meet before I am called in by the camerlengo."

The waiter returned with Patrick's wine, both the salads, and a basket of warm bread. Patrick did not know how hungry he was until he smelled the warm bread. He and Jason bowed their heads, and Patrick blessed the food, and they both dove in with abandon. Patrick looked around to see if anyone one he or Jason knew were close by and could overhear their conversation. Looking over his shoulder, he saw Hans Olson coming through the door, who was one of Jason's Swiss Guards. Patrick had passed him a little while ago as he came through the gardens into the square and now to the café. Hans usually guarded the archives, so Patrick was well acquainted with him. He looked like a man on a mission. Not looking around for a table, he came straight to where he and Jason were sitting. This was a table for two, pushed up against a wall. Hans squatted down next to his commander and whispered something into his ear. At this news, Jason looked up in surprise. "Are you quite sure?" he asked. His bobbed his head up and down in rapid succession. "When was this?" asked Jason. He bent down again so no one could hear and whispered again into Jason's ear. "Get some of the guards to go over to the chapter house and see if anyone else has seen him." Hans got up and walked to the door in a hurry and was gone.

"What was that all about?" asked Patrick.

"You know Brother Sebastian who was drowned last week, and we never found his body. We assumed that it was so mutilated by the boat that anything left would have been eaten by the sharks."

"Yes!"

"Hans saw him this morning coming through the gate into the garden with a briefcase. He was coming from the direction of the chapter house."

About this time the waiter came back with the bowls of pasta and laid them in front of Patrick and Jason. The feeling that something was not quite right washed over Patrick. He had a feeling that what they thought was the murder of Brother Sebastian had something to do with the pope's death. Patrick could not put his finger on it, he just had a feeling. Both he and Jason ate their meals in silence and both were lost in deep thought. Glancing at the clock that hung over the cash register, he saw that he would not be able to finish his lunch and get back to his office in time to meet Mat and the archbishop. Folding his napkin, he picked up his ticket, pushed his chair back, and got up to leave. "Aren't you going to finish?" asked Jason.

"No, I've got to meeting back at my office in ten minutes, and I need to run. How about giving me an update after you meet with Hans after he and the other guard get back from the chapter house. And if I were you, I would keep this under wraps. On second thought, don't tell anyone until we have a chance to talk."

"OK," replied Jason.

Patrick threw a couple of euros on the table and went to pay his bill. Leaving the café, Patrick had to work his way through the crowds of tourists that were packing the gardens and the Vatican. He worked up a sweat, walking under the noon sun. He would be glad to be in the air-conditioned offices of the Vatican. It took Patrick longer than he thought it would. There were several people waiting at the elevator, so he decided to take the stairs. Running late, he took two stairs at a time, reaching the first landing in record time. Opening the door to the second floor, he turned right and headed toward his office. Rounding the corner, the guard came to attention. Patrick thought this was a little strange. It had not happened before. Then he heard footsteps behind him. Turning he saw that the archbishop was coming up behind him.

Patrick turned and greeted his old friend warmly. Putting the key into the lock on his door, he opened it and held it for Archbishop Valanti to enter ahead of him. They moved through the reception room and into Patrick's office. Patrick walked around his desk and motioned for the archbishop to have a seat in one of the two leather chairs facing the desk. Out of difference to his guest, he waited for the archbishop to be seated before he did. Looking at his friend, he could see stress and anguish written all over his face. "How did your meeting go this morning?"

"The Camerlengo Cardinal Alveraz had many questions," replied the archbishop. "I did not want to give him anymore information than I had to. He will be coming to see you today. I did not tell him about the letters or the key the pope placed in your care. I did tell him that you hold a letter for the next pope. Some camerlengos will ask for that letter; others let the pope's secretary hand it over to the next pope. I do not know what he will do."

"Have you spoken to anyone?"

"I had a call from the head of the curia, Cardinal Pulaski last night. I think he will be calling again today," answered Patrick. "I also had some interesting news today at lunch. Hans came into the café and told Jason that he had seen Brother Sebastian this morning going through the gate that leads from the courtyard inside the wall into the garden."

"How can that be?" asked Valanti. "He was drowned in the harbor last week."

"I don't know. Jason is sending Hans over to the chapter house to see if anyone has seen him, and he will let me know. I asked him not to tell anyone about this yet. I have a feeling the disappearance of Brother Sebastian and the pope's death are somehow connected. He was working on some papers for the pope that even I was not privy to."

They were interrupted with a knock on the door. The guard opened the door and told Patrick that there was a Mat Mason who wanted to see him. "Have him come in."

Chapter 18

Brother Sebastian tried as best he could to get through the gate without Hans getting a look at him. This was the second time he had to pass Hans. This morning he had been lucky there was a group of nuns also going through the gate and a lot of tourists coming in. Hans had looked up, but Sebastian thought he had made it through. It was just his luck this time that as he passed they met eye to eye. Sebastian looked away as quickly as possible, but he saw a sign of recognition in Hans's eyes. Walking as quickly as possible, he tried to blend in with the crowd of tourists and other Vatican employees as quickly as he could. Lucky for him, the plaza was filled to capacity today, all hoping to see the pope. Little did they know that this would not happen. The announcement of the pope's death had not yet been made. He clutched the briefcase close to his side. He did not want to loose it.

He needed to get through the gardens before he ran into anyone else that he knew. He also needed to find a place to hide until the message his Brother was going to deliver to Father O'Rourke was safely in his hands. He ducked into one of the trellis areas and sat down on a bench, which gave him a hidden view of the gate he had just left and the exit going into Rome and the exit to entrance to the Vatican offices.

Across the garden, he saw Father O'Rourke entering the garden from the Vatican offices. Sebastian stood up and started over toward him through the crowd. This must be fate. He needed to get to O'Rourke and share the information he had with him before someone else caught him. As he made his way through the crowd, out of the corner of his eye, he saw Father Anton also coming from the Vatican offices. He and Father

O'Rourke almost ran head on into each other. Father Anton looked like a man in a hurry and barley acknowledged Father O'Rourke. Father Anton was not going to lunch because he was headed toward the gate that Brother Sebastian had just come from. That meant that someone had seen him and called Cardinal Pulaski's office.

He quickly turned around and headed back toward the trellis where he had been hiding. Sitting back down on the bench, he was covered in sweat. He could feel the droplets running down his face and down his back. Keeping his eyes on Anton, he watched as he disappeared through the gate toward his chapter house. He saw that Father O'Rourke had left the garden and was headed into Rome.

It was nearing lunchtime, and he noticed that Hans's replacement had just arrived. Leaving his post Hans was heading in his direction toward the exit that went into Rome. He would have to pass directly in front of where he was sitting. Sebastian quickly stood up and crouched behind one of the posts holding up the trellis. Hans passed without even looking his way. Relief washed over him as he once again moved back over to the bench.

One thing was sure, he needed to get out of the garden and back to his hiding place in the catacombs. The cardinal's people had tried to kill him once, and now that they knew that he was alive, they would try again. He was not sure how long he could survive in the catacombs, but his chances were better there than out in Rome. The Mafia was like a Hydra with many heads. Once the word was out, he was a good as dead. Before this happened, he had to get to Father O'Rourke and share what he knew and give him the manuscript, because if something happened to him, someone else could finish the translation.

He got up from his bench, and once again tried to melt into the lunchtime crowds. He kept his head down and walked as quickly as possible toward the gate that led to Rome that Father O'Rourke and Hans had left through.

Reaching the street, he turned toward the entrance to the catacombs that was several blocks away. The thought of going back into that dark space with the bats and rats made a shiver go up his spine. But he could not think of a safer place at the moment. He had several hundred euros in his pocket that he had picked up and a flashlight. He needed to get something to eat and some candles and matches, and it would be nice to have a sleeping bag. Up ahead was a small grocery he had passed earlier; it was one he had never been in, so it should be safe. He also needed a change of clothes. He needed to keep what he had on clean so that he could come back into the Vatican unnoticed. His head ached, and he was still sore from being tied up and knocked unconscious and being thrown into the sea. Walking in the hot sun did not help the headache at all. That was the only advantage to the catacombs being underground; it had a constant cool temperature.

Sebastian had been so lost in thought; he had not been paying attention to those around him. He looked over his shoulder and noticed two shabbily dressed men walking not far behind him. They seemed to be keeping pace with him. The store was just ahead, so he picked up his pace a little and ducked into the doorway and made his way to the back of the store as quickly as he could. Getting behind one of the shelving units, he saw that the two men had stopped just outside the front door of the store and were leaning against the sidewalls. He watched as they glanced inside and on seeing him, they began to converse. Sebastian's heart began to beat faster, and he could feel his body temperature rise. This along with the headache made him nauseous. Looking around, he spotted what looked like a storeroom. While the men talked, he ducked down and made his way over to the door only to find that it was locked. Keeping low, he spotted a bathroom, and the door was open. Once inside, he quickly locked the door. Feeling dizzy, he went to the basin and splashed cold water over his face. There was only one stall, a basin, and a small window. Sebastian reached up and unlocked it and tried to raise the window, but it would not budge. Using all of his strength, he tried again and it still wouldn't budge. Using the briefcase, he swung it as hard as he could, breaking the window. The noise was thunderous, and he was sure everyone in the store heard it and he was right. He could hear the sound of footsteps running from the front of the store where the cashier was located. There was pounding on the door.

"Open up in there," someone was shouting.

"Open up, or I will call the police" came another voice. He could hear the door handle rattling. Sebastian threw the briefcase out of the window and climbed up on the sink. He stuck his head and one shoulder and arm out and worked the other shoulder and arm though the small opening.

He was looking out onto a narrow alleyway that opened onto a parking lot and loading dock. *It looks like it is about ten feet to the ground,* he thought as he dangled from the window ledge. He could see the briefcase lying on the pavement under the window. More knocking and shouting was coming from the door, and someone was screaming if he did not open up now, they would break it down. He had to hurry.

Pulling his trunk through, he could feel the jagged glass cutting into his stomach and side. He could feel something warm running down his chest as he hung out the window. Using the window frame, he managed to pull himself out of the window and as he did, he began to fall headfirst toward the ground. He caught himself on the lower ledge with his knees. Carefully, he pulled one leg out so that he was hanging upside down by his left leg. Once again, he could feel the glass cutting into his leg behind his kneecap. Pulling himself up using the brick on the side of the building, he was able to grasp the top of the window frame again. Supporting his weight, he pulled his leg free. Now he found himself hanging by his fingertips on the window frame letting loose he hit the ground landing on his feet. He did not stop to see how badly he was cut. He picked up the briefcase and begun to run down the alley toward the parking lot.

Over his shoulder, he could hear someone shouting at him to stop from the window he had just escaped from. Looking down, he could see a red stain spreading across his shirt and could feel a warm liquid running down his leg. He had to get to safety at all cost. He did not have time to stop. Now he was sure the word was out and the mafia was looking for him again.

Chapter 19

As Mat Mason entered his office, Patrick and the archbishop stood and turn toward the door to greet him. Mat Mason was a typical American professor, dressed in tan slacks, a blue blazer, white shirt, and regimental striped tie. He had close chopped gray hair and twinkling green eyes. There was an air of energy and life about him.

"Come in, I am Monsignor Patrick O'Rourke and this is Archbishop Valanti. Please come in. We have been looking forward to meeting you."
"Thank you. My daughter told me about the tragedy that happened last night. I am so sorry. I had looked so forward to working with the pope."
"Thank you," replied Patrick. "Please have a seat. We know that the pope had trust in you because of your daughter. She was one of the pope's favorite nuns."
"Why did the pope ask you to come to Rome?" asked Valanti.

"I was to do some translations on a manuscript that the pope had. The monk who had been working on it disappeared and later it was reported that he had been killed. The pope said it was important that the work be finished."

"Did the pope tell you what the manuscript was about?" asked Patrick.

"No. He just indicated it was of utmost importance to the well-being of the church."

"Mr. Mason, we do not have a lot of time. The pope gave me two letters—one addressed to me and the other to the archbishop. We opened the letters, and we have been unable to read them. The last thing he said was that we needed both letters together to understand what the message would mean. In one of the letters was a key to the archives that the pope wore around his neck. It is very similar to the one the archbishop wears. We need you to try to decipher these letters," said Patrick.

Both Patrick and the archbishop handed their letters to Mat Mason. He opened Patrick's first. Looking at it, it was obvious that it was not a language he knew. He laid down Patrick's letter and opened the archbishop's letter and could not read it either. "These are not written in any language that I know or have seen," he said, putting down the letters. "May I see the keys?" he asked.

"Sure," said Patrick as he handed over his key. The archbishop also handed over his. Mat looked carefully at the first key and then the other. "Both the keys are very similar, but I notice the difference is the Papal symbol on the one Patrick has and a sign on the other one that represents a guardian that belonged to the archbishop. There are many symbols that I recognize—Greek, Hebrew, and some Egyptian. But these letters are not written in any of those languages. The letters are written in an English alphabet, and you don't write most ancient languages in any other than their alphabet. You said the pope told you that to be able to understand his message you needed both letters?"

"Yes, that is correct," answered Patrick. "Right after college, before I entered graduate school, I served in the military. I was attached for a while in the decoding office for foreign affairs. This looks more like a code than an ancient language. Do you have a computer that I could input this information and send it to a friend in that department?"

"That can't be done. Whatever is written in these letters cannot leave this office or our possession," answered Patrick. "We will have to figure it out on our own."

"That may take a while," said Mat.

"We don't have a lot of time. This has to be done before the next pope is elected, and the cardinals will be coming to Rome beginning today. At the most, we will have about twelve days.

"How long did it take the pope to write these letters?" asked Mat.

"It would have happened in the time it took me to go and get the archbishop, not more than an hour."

"That's good news. This code must not be very difficult." Laying the letters out on the desk side by side, Mat began to study the letters. One thing that was apparent was that there were no vowels in either letter.

Also, the signature on each was different. One was signed just GS and the other was TV. "Does that mean anything to either of you?"

"No. The pope always signed Leo II, which is the name he took on becoming pope?"

"What was his name before that?"

"Gustav!"

"That's it. This is the key. The pope left out the vowels like he was writing in Hebrew. He also wrote the beginning half of a word on your letter, Patrick, and the ending half of the word on yours, archbishop. There is also no punctuation used in either letter. I would not be surprised if he wrote from left to right. One of the founding fathers for my country used a code similar to this when he wrote in his journals. The pope must have heard about this and used it from time to time. Father O'Rourke, get a piece of paper and write down the letters as I call them out."

Patrick reached into his draw and pulled out some paper and a pencil and began to write as Mat called out the letters.

"DRFRNDSHVBNTRMNTDBYWHTTHNKSDMN."

"Let's stop here and see what we are on the right track. I read them off to you from right to left, and you have written them down left to right. Assuming he was using a letter format, we can make out DR as 'Dear' and FRNDS should be 'Friends.' I will assume some vowels. I have been tormented by what I think is demon."

"That makes sense. Something has been tormenting the pope for several days," said Patrick.

"Now that we have the hang of it, I think it will go much quicker. Father, do you have a ruler in your desk? It will help me if I can place it under each line to keep my place," asked Mat. Getting a ruler out of his desk Patrick handed it to Mat, who continued to read much more quickly.

"As the tormenting became worse, I knew something was wrong. Someone must have found the key that was hidden in the archives. Brother Sebastian must have told someone what he had found out in the manuscript. What is written in the Bible about Jesus giving Peter the keys to the kingdom is not a just a legend. There are three real keys. I knew that one was hidden in the archives and went down to see if it was still there. I discovered that both the hidden parts of the key were gone, when I opened the book for the first part and felt in the secret door of the bookshelf for the other part. The missing key is the key to Hades. I was being tormented by a demon. The key is also known as the key of Solomon. The key can only be used along with the book of magic that belonged to Solomon. The book and the key were given to Solomon by the angel Gabriel as a gift from God. Legend has it that the book was lost when the temple was destroyed. One page of the book must have survived for the key to still work. The old manuscript must have led Sebastian to this page from the book and told him where the two parts of the key were hidden. You must find the key and this page before it is too late. Sebastian's last report to me said that the book had not been found but was still hidden. Clues to the location of the book were in the old manuscript he was working on. This also must not fall into the wrong hands. Whoever has the key and the page have only limited power. They must not get their hands on the rest of the book or they will be unstoppable. The location of the other two keys will be revealed in the manuscript. One is the key of destiny and can lead one into the presence of God, and the other is the key of illumination leading to a storehouse of untold knowledge and wealth. Leo the first is the last one to have all three keys. My predecessor Leo knowing the great power that they held decided that they were too powerful for one man to control, so he hid them. I found the manuscript by accident last year and asked Brother Sebastian to see if he could translate it for me. May God be with you, my friends."

Chapter 20

With the sounds of the people in the store yelling at him through the bathroom window still echoing in his brain, Sebastian made his way through the narrow alley dodging the trash cans and bags of garbage strewn about. The red patch of blood was getting bigger, staining his shirt, and he could feel the blood running down his leg where the glass cut his thigh. The odor rising from the open garage cans became nauseating under the hot sun. He could feel his stomach tighten with each wave of nausea. His legs felt like he had lead weights tied around them. He could see the end of the alley just up ahead. He kept looking over his shoulder to see if the two men were still following him, but he saw nothing.

As he rounded the corner, he could see the front of the store he just escaped from and the two men were still standing outside looking in. In the distance, he could hear the blare of a police car coming his way. The people who owned the store must have called them. He saw two men coming out of the store, waving their arms and a crowd had begun to gather. The two men who were following him began to look up and down the street.

Walking down the street, he noticed people were beginning to stop and stare at a priest who was bleeding.

"Father! You are hurt," someone close to him was saying.

"No, no I am fine," he said pulling his case up close to his chest, trying to cover up as best he could the spreading red spot on his chest. Pushing his way through the gathering crowd, he turns toward the opposite direction from which he had come. He knew that he had to get as far away from here as he could. He began walking as fast as his legs would let him. Up ahead, he could see a drug store. He needs some bandages to stop the bleeding on his chest and on his leg.

It was his lucky day, since the drug store was nearly empty. He found the isle where the bandages were. Then he got a tube of ointment for the cuts that had an antibiotic in it. Keeping the case close to his chest, he paid for his purchase and headed for the toilet. Sebastian quickly stripped off his coat and shirt. The cut on his chest consisted of several long and narrow slits. Thankfully, they were not too deep. He covered the cuts with the ointment and brought the slits together with the bandages and tape.

He took his shirt and washed the bloodstain with cold water. To his delight, the blood came out. He still had the rip in the shirt, but if he buttoned his coat it would cover most of it. Sebastian loosened his belt and carefully took off his pants. He could see that the cut on his thigh was deep. He knew enough to realize that it needed to be sewn up. Using just the tape, he pulled the cut together as best he could. Then he wrapped gauze around his leg as tight as he could without cutting off the circulation. Once again he tried to wash the blood off his pants. Being black, the stain did not show too badly. Using the hand dryer, he dried the pants off, and using the tape on the inside, he was able to pull the torn material back together.

Sebastian redressed, looking into the mirror. He looked pale but his clothes were passable. Leaving the toilet, he looked around for a drink case. Seeing one at the back of the store, he picks up a couple of sports drinks and finds some the aspirin for the pain.

As he checked out and left the drug store, he kept close to the storefronts, trying to blend in. It was a long way to the entrance to the catacombs. He stopped in a doorway and opened one of the sports drinks and the aspirin bottle and downed two with a big swallow. As he continued walking, he found that the sports drink and the aspirin helped to ease the pain in his leg and head. He saw an alley up ahead and decided to step inside. The sun was hot, and the alley would provide some shade for a moment. Stepping inside, Sebastian leaned against the cool wall and took a deep breath. The wet shirt felt good against his skin. He took the last gulp of the cold sports drink and dropped the empty can in an open trash can that stood beside him.

Even though it was a little cooler in the alley, the day was hot. He edged close to the corner of the building, leaned against it, and peered around the corner. Out of the corner of his eye, he saw the two men coming this way. Sebastian's heart began to pound, and he broke out into a sweat. Quickly, he turned and looked down the alley only to see that it was a dead end. Looking again, they were too close for him to run, and he had no strength anyway. About half way down the alley, he spotted a dumpster. The top was open which meant that it may have been empty. Picking up his briefcase, Sebastian ran to the dumpster. Peering inside, it was only half empty. The stench of old rotting meat and other food wafted up toward him; he threw his briefcase in and climbed in after it. Not wanting to close the lid, he crouched in the corner and pulled several garbage bags up around himself, leaving only his head out.

Sebastian heard voices. It sounded like two men discussing whether or not to search the alley. Hearing footsteps getting louder echoing off the pavement, he knew that they had decided to come in and have a look around. As they get closer, he took a deep breath and ducked down under the bags he had pulled around himself. He heard the footsteps stop in front of the dumpster where he was hiding. He heard the two men arguing as to who will reach in and pull out the garbage bags and get into the dumpster. One of the bags near his head began to move.

"Hey! What are you doing?" came a loud voice.

"Nothing" came the reply from one of the men. "Just throwing away a couple of drink bottles."

"Well, that is not a public dumpster. You two need to move along before I call the police." Sebastian still not breathing heard the two men turn and head back out of the alley.

Chapter 21

The don was sitting in his office. He had been on the phone getting all of his men out into the street looking for this monk, Sebastian. He was sure that he was dead. How could he have survived tied up with duct tape and thrown into the bay and then run over with the speedboat? With all that blood flood coming from him and the prostitute from the boat props what the props did not cut to pieces the sharks should have take care of. He sank back into his soft leather chair. He enjoyed his office. He liked the smell of leather on his chair and the sofa facing his desk. He liked the way the light shone on the paneled wood on the walls. All of this looked expensive, and it was. All of this made him feel important.

The low sofa facing his deck served him well. It made his employees and his guests sit well below him, making them have to look up to him. He took off his shoes and dug his toes down into the deep thick Persian carpet that ran under the desk, sofa, and chrome coffee table. Twenty thousand euro, but he was worth it. "Yes!" he thought to himself. He had reached the top. He was someone to recon with. How dare the cardinal call and threaten him. There must be some mistake. This Brother Sebastian was dead. Don't all of the monks look alike? Someone had made a mistake, and he was sure it was not him.

Threats, threats! What could this cardinal do? Threaten to excommunicate him? I don't think so! He thought. *I give too much money to the Holy See for that to happen. Refuse to get me out of purgatory? But I am not dead yet, and there are many priests one could pay to do that.*

The don was startled out of his thought by knocking on his office door. "Come, come," he called. The door opened, and Sofia came in.

She had long black hair parted in the middle and flowing down over her shoulders and down her back like many Italian women wore their hair. She was dressed in a short black skirt that showed off her long shapely legs, white blouse unbutton down the front, her ample breast pushing against the material, causing the shirt to look like it was going to pop open even further. Just the look the don liked. Her hips swayed as she walked toward his desk keeping his full attention.

"Pardon," She breathed in her husky voice. "You have a visitor. Shall I show him in?"

"Yes, thank you, Sofia." The don smiled. He enjoyed the view as she turned and walked back to the door. *Not much between the ears, but a hell of a lot of sex appeal through the tits and ass where it counts*, he mused.

The don rose to meet his guest. It was Carlos, one of his top men. The don had sent one of his own to the Vatican to learn if the news from the cardinal was true. Carlos was a big man standing over six four and weighed over two hundred pounds of pure muscle, and close chopped, curly black hair framed his face. His dark brooding eyes seemed to be twin dark holes in his beautifully chiseled olive face. His white teeth shone between cruel thin lips in a permanent snarl. If it were not for the scars on his forehead and along his right cheek, he would have been thought of as a pretty boy.

The don watched Carlos walk in. He had the swagger of someone who was very sure of himself and his abilities. "Have a seat," the don invited. Carlos came around the end of the sofa and sat down, facing the don's desk. Sitting down, the don was eye level with Carlos, which irritated the don a lot. He always wanted to have the appearance of having the upper hand. "What did you find out?" he asked.

"Sebastian has been seen by a guard. The guard at the gate just beyond the priory saw him leave the Vatican and reported it to his boss, then to one of the fathers he saw in the gardens and reported it to your friend the cardinal."

"How can this be?" demanded the don. "It is all your fault. You were in charge of this operation, and you assured me things went as we planned. Do you want to take Sebastian's place in the bay as shark food?" yelled the don.

"I don't know how this happened," pleaded Carlos. "But I will take care of it immediately. I have the city covered. He cannot breathe without one of my people hearing it. I will have him before the day is out."

"You better." Glared the don. "Now get out and find him." Carlos rose from the sofa and headed for the door. Turning as he opened it, he looked the don in the eye and said, "I have never failed you, and I won't now!" Carlos closed the door quietly behind him as he left.

The don sat staring at the closed door, reflecting on Carlos parting words. He seemed to relax a little and settled back into his soft leather chair. Carlos was right. He had never failed to deliver on any assignment. The don had every reason to believe him.

There was knocking on his door again. It was Sofia just coming in without him inviting her. She looked pale and was very upset. Seeing her distress, the don rose and went to her. "Sofia, what's the matter?" he asked.

"Have you seen the news? Did Carlos tell you?" she asked.

"Tell me what?" he replied.

"It's the Holy Father. He is dead." The don just looked at her in stunned silence. Sofia walked over to the bookcase and slid aside a panel revealing a TV set and switched it on. There on the screen was Vatican square. The flag was at half-staff, and the pope's balcony was draped in black. There was somber music being piped onto the square. The place was filled with people just standing and looking toward the balcony.

The sound of a voice was coming from the set but it was too low for him to hear what was being said, "Turn it up, Sofia" he said.

"This is Malcolm Aims of the BBC. We have just had news that the pope died last night of unknown causes. We got the news just moments ago as the flag was being lowered and the balcony was being draped in black around 2:00 p.m. Vatican time. All of the cardinals from around the world are on their way to the conclave and the pope's funeral. Mourners, as you can see, are gathering. Some are weeping openly. Both nuns and priests have knelt before the pope's balcony to lead the faithful in prayer. We will continue to broadcast and keep you informed as the day continues. Once again Pope Leo had died, this is Malcolm Aims reporting for the BBC."

Both the don and Sofia just stood unable to take their eyes off the TV screen. *This will certainly make it more difficult to find Sebastian especially if he mingles with the crowds at the Vatican,* the don thought.

Chapter 22

As Mat finished reading the letters, Patrick and the archbishop sat in stunned silence. *This is the twenty-first-century magic, and demons are just for fables, stories, and fiction out of the past,* thought Patrick. *With all of our modern technology how could any of this be true?* Patrick lifted his head and looked at the archbishop with a question in his eyes. Seeing his disbelief, the archbishop looked back at Patrick and said, "Patrick, my son, there are more things in heaven and earth than man can ever comprehend."

"But, Archbishop, how can that be?" he asked. "I know the Holy Father has been sick for most of this year. He was under much stress last night. He was not himself. Surely his mind was playing tricks on him. Come on! Keys, magic books belonging to Solomon? I am a fairly good Bible student, and I don't recall Solomon practicing magic."

"Patrick," the archbishop said in a gentle voice, "I was chosen to be the guardian. Only the pope and I have keys to the papal secret archives. When I received my key, my predecessor told me that I must guard the archives with my life. It contained many secrets—some wonderful, some fearful. Within the archives are books that hold knowledge only a few have been privileged to see. Some date back to Solomon and before. I have heard that some are from the library at Alexandria before it was burned down. Don't be so quick to disbelieve." Patrick sat back in his chair, looking back at the archbishop letting the words wash over him. He looked down at his desk and the two keys lying there. Mat had not said a word; he just listened to the exchange. "Mat, what do you make of all of this?" asked Patrick.

He leaned back in his chair, thinking how to best answer Patrick. Feeling cramped, he pushed his chair back with his knees and stood up and walked over toward the sidewall which held a credenza. On it sat a flat screen television set and a tray, which held a container of ice and bottles of water. He picked up a bottle and opened it, taking a big swig. He turned back toward Patrick and the archbishop. "Monsignor O'Rourke, the more I learn, the more I find out. I don't know. People are cured from cancer or other terminal diseases after praying, and we cannot find a scientific reason for this. In my research of ancient writing, there is much written on the key of Solomon. All you have to do is 'Google it.' I have found that within every myth we find a bit of truth of fact. I did not know the Holy Father except what I heard about him from my daughter and the correspondence we shared. From this information, I would say, 'Yes, he was under much stress and having health problems but his mind was still sharp.' So I would take as truth what he has written. We know from the Bible gospels that Jesus endowed Peter with much power. He gave him the keys to the kingdom. Who are we to say what the keys were and what power they held. Without a lot of power, how could eleven men spread the gospel throughout the known world and literally change the course of human history? We can send a man to the moon, and we can send pictures over the airwaves, but we still have no idea how the ancients built the Colossus of Rhodes, the Hanging gardens, stone hinge, or the pyramids. So I agree with the archbishop. There is more unknown on heaven and earth than our finite minds can comprehend."

Patrick looked from Mat to the archbishop. Angels, demons, magic keys, and books—it was more than Patrick could comprehend. His mind was reeling. He was good in math and science. *He had an analytical mind, but what he needed was proof,* he thought, but he was also a priest. He had seen faith in action. The scientist in him was saying, "No way," but the priest was saying, "Have faith and trust in your friends." The holy father had been like a real father to him. If this was what he thought was happening, he would have an open mind.

Patrick reached over and took hold of the key the holy father had given him, and he took the letter, folded it, and placed it back into the envelope. He put the chain over his head and tucked the key under the collar of his shirt. He could feel the key resting on his chest, and it gave him great comfort. Following Patrick's lead, the archbishop also placed the key around his neck, but he let it hang down the front of his cassock. He then took his letter and placed it back in the envelope and tucked it into his red sash.

Mat walked back to his chair, facing Patrick's desk. Holding the bottle of water, he sat down keeping his eyes on Patrick.

Looking up, Patrick said, "OK, where do we go from here? How do we fight this evil?"

"We must first find Brother Sebastian and get the manuscript into safe hands," said the archbishop.

"When Hans saw him, he was dressed as a priest. He was not wearing the brown alb that the brothers normally wear. He also had a briefcase."

"Wearing the black suit with the cleric collar would make you almost invisible in and around the Vatican. That is why he must have dressed that way," said Patrick.

"What time was Sebastian seen by Hans?" asked the archbishop.

"A little after noon," replied Patrick.

"That would have been lunchtime followed by prayers for the brothers in the chapter house. Sebastian chose a good time to return. It could be that he got in and out without being seen," observed the archbishop.

"I nearly ran headlong into Anton, Cardinal Pulaski's secretary, as I was going to lunch. He looked like a man on a mission, and to think about it, he was headed in the direction of the chapter house," said Patrick.

"Someone must have alerted our head of the curia," said the archbishop. "Let me call the west guardhouse and see if Hans answers, and I will find out," said Patrick.

Patrick picked up the phone and dialed the extension for the west guardhouse. He listened as it rang then he heard Hans's voice, "West guardhouse!"

"Hans!"

"Yes, monsignor, how may I help you?"

"Did you tell anyone other than your captain about seeing Brother Sebastian?"

"Yes, sir, we have to report anything we think is important to the office of the head of the curia. So I told Cardinal Pulaski's secretary, Father Anton, that I had seen Sebastian. I made that call before I came to the café to find Captain Sitzler."

"Thank you, Hans. That will be all." Patrick hung up the phone and relayed what he had heard to Mat and the archbishop. "Now we know where Anton was going," said Patrick.

"Patrick, you still have papal authority for the next several days. You need to use that to get Jason to go over to the chapter house and find out if anyone has seen Sebastian," directed the archbishop.

Once again, Patrick picked up the phone and dialed the extension for the office of the Captain of the Swiss Guard. The connection was made, and he listened as the phone on the other end began to ring. After several rings, he heard Jason's voice, "You have reached the office of the captain of the Swiss Guards. Please leave you name and a message, and I will get back to you."

"Jason, it's Patrick. Please call my office as soon as you get this message. It is very important." Patrick hung up the phone.

"Mat and Patrick, we need to keep in secret what we have learned here today. We need to swear and oath to do this," said the archbishop.

"We swear," they all said.

"If there is nothing else for me to do, I will go and spend some time with my daughter," said Mat as he rose to leave. Patrick came around the desk and shook his hand. Mat bent down and shook the archbishop's hand, and Patrick led him to the door.

Patrick walked back to his desk. "What are we going to tell Pulaski?" asked Patrick.

"Nothing," said the archbishop. They both sat in silence, lost in their own thoughts.

Chapter 23

The sun was beating down on Father Anton as he headed toward the chapter house. He hated this Rome heat. He wished he was back at his old assignment in the cool German mountains. Having to wear black with this tight collar did not help his humor anyway. He was never really cutout to be a priest. He only did so to please his father, and as usual, this did not please him either. Anton had always had a dark side. Being pious was not his nature. He found his niche in the church, working for this cardinal who shared and appreciated his dark side. It had been bad luck that he had run into Monsignor O'Rourke. He did not want him to know where he was going. He passed though the gate and noticed that Hans was just leaving and his replacement waved him through. Being the secretary of the head of the curia, he was well known and showed much difference. It was nearing one thirty and lunch should be over and prayers following should be short. As he rounded the corner, he could hear the bells calling the brothers to chapel. *That's fine with me,* he thought. *It would give me time to search Sebastian's room without being disturbed.*

He climbed the steps; nearing the top, he noticed that the door was ajar like someone had left in a hurry and was trying to be quiet. Entering the hallway, it felt good to be out of the sun. He could feel droplets of sweat running down his back. Letting his eyes adjust to the darkness, he headed toward the stairs. In the distance, he could hear the brothers intoning the ancient chants. Climbing to the second floor, he found Sebastian's room. He had been here on several occasions to pick up notes for the cardinal.

The room was stark. It was painted in the original white, which had aged to the color of vanilla ice cream. The cot was made up and the chair pushed up under the desk, which was clean, unlike the last time he was here. At that time, it was covered with reference books and writing paper. In the center was an old document with Sebastian looking over it. No paper, no books, just empty and clean. The closet door was standing open. Anton walked over and began to look through the clothes that were hanging there. In the bottom of the closet was a footlocker. He opened the lid and started to empty the contents onto the floor. Underwear, socks, family pictures—the same meager possession that most of the monks kept but not a book or the manuscript. Leaving the contents on the floor, Anton walked to the desk and opened the drawer. In one, he found paper and pens, in another were the reference books, but no notes or anything pertaining to the manuscript. *Sebastian must have taken everything of importance with him,* he thought. Turning, he left the room and the mess behind him. Going down the stairs, he heard voices and the sound of steps resounding on the wooden floors below. Anton paused at the end of the stairs and looked toward the sounds coming down the hall. The first person he sees is the Abbot of the chapter house. Seeing Anton, the Abbot said, "Father Anton, what brings you to our house?"

"The cardinal got a call earlier today saying that Brother Sebastian was seen coming toward the house."

"How can that be!" the abbot exclaimed. "He was killed out on the bay two weeks ago."

"We are only following up on the information we have."

"The Lord be praised if what you say is true."

"You are saying none of the brothers have come to you with this news?"

"No! This is the first I have heard of it."

"We were told that he was here at lunchtime today. Were all of the brothers present in the hall?"

"As far as I can recall, there were all there, with the exception of the ones assigned to cook and serve, and they were in and out."

"I want to talk to them. Have them come into the waiting room."

"I will do this right away," said the abbot as he turned to leave his brown robe trailing behind him, stirring up the dust that had been tracked in from the outside.

"Abbot!" Anton called, "don't let them know why I am here." Anton walked the short distance to the waiting room. The door stood open. It was a fairly large room with two sofas on either side of a fireplace—several overstuffed leather chairs and beautiful murals on the walls. A colorful Persian carpet covered the floor between the two sofas. It was a warm inviting room. Anton sat in one of the overstuffed chairs next to the fireplace.

It was not a long wait. Four brothers came through the door. They were dressed alike in brown-hooded albs tied at the waist with a plain rope. They stood side by side each brother having his hands stuffed in the sleeves of his albs lined up before Anton. Anton stood up and faced the line of brothers. "You were serving lunch today." Each brother looked Anton in the eye, and all nodded their heads. "Did any of you see Brother Sebastian?" he asked.

"No!" they replied in unison.

"How could we? Our dear brother was killed two weeks ago?" said Brother John.

"That may not be the case," answered Anton. He watched their faces for a reaction. All seemed surprised except Brother John whose face remained unchanged. "Are you sure?" Anton asked again. All of them shook their heads no. "All right, you may leave, all except Brother John." Anton watched as the other brothers left the room. He turned his full attention to John. "You did not seem surprised at the news as the others did. Is that because you saw Sebastian today?"

I cannot betray Sebastian, he thought. *Please God forgive me this lie.* Brother John prayed. "I just do not show emotion as the others. But I too was surprised by what you have said," he answered Anton.

"Don't lie to me." Anton glared. "You know it is a mortal sin to lie to a Father," he threatened.

"I am telling the truth. I have not seen him."

"If I find out that you are lying, I will see to it that you will be excommunicated. Now, go!"

Brother John turned and left the room. His heart was pounding, and his knees felt weak. He had never lied to a father before. He could feel Anton's eyes boring a hole into his back. He tried to keep his head up and his gait steady, all the while breaking into a cold sweat.

Anton walked out of the waiting room and down the hall to the front door. He watched John walk down the hall, back toward the kitchen. He knew he was lying, so he must be watched in case Sebastian tried to contact him again. *We will meet again soon,* Anton thought as he walked out the door and into the hot summer sun on his way back to report to the cardinal.

Chapter 24

Sebastian lay still daring not to move. He did not know how much longer he would be able to do this. He felt the slimy rotten meat against his face. Things he did not want to think about were crawling up his legs. The smell was almost more than he could bear. He knew if he breathed in this smell again, he would not be able to keep from vomiting.

He listened as the two men walked away. His heart was pounding, which caused his head to throb worse. He carefully moved the garbage bag he had rolled up to cover himself. He was thankful it had not leaked on him. He pushed away the rotten meat from his face. He knew that he must smell like the garbage he was sitting in. He checked his shirt, and it was still wet but there was no blood seeping through the bandage. He knew that would not be the case with his leg. The voices had faded into the distance so he felt like he could raise himself up at least to the edge of the dumpster and see if it was safe to climb out.

Edging up, he placed his hands on the greasy sides and pulled himself up far enough to get a view of the alley. The alley was empty with the exception of a couple of stray cats tearing at the bags of garbage that had fallen from one of the many cans lining the alley. Rooting around in the garbage beside him, he found his briefcase. He pulled himself up so that he was standing in the dumpster up to his knees in garbage. Using the sides of the dumpster, he hefted himself up and over, landing hard on the alley's driveway.

Retrieving his briefcase, he tries as best he could to brush his clothes off, but he couldn't brush off the smell. Looking in both directions, he picked up his briefcase and opted to leave in the opposite direction he came in. This meant climbing over the wall at the end of the dead-end alley. He had no idea what was on the other side. This would also throw him several blocks out of the way, but he felt like the men would be somewhere out on the street he had just left still looking for him.

Looking up toward the sun, he thought it must be between two and three o'clock in the afternoon. The sun was still riding high, and the temperature was on the rise. The wet pants and his shirt felt good. He needed to stay out of the sun; the heat would zap what strength that he had left.

Reaching the end of the alley, he stacked up several garbage cans and climbed up on them. Peering over the fence was the backyard of a house. He quickly threw over his briefcase and the sack he was carrying and heaved himself over the wall. Landing in the soft dirt, he looked around, and seeing no one, he quickly made his way to the street. He looked in both directions. He did not see anyone who he thought might be a danger to him.

The street was filled with residents and tourists. It was a pleasant tree-lined avenue with a center divider also planted with trees. The street was a mix of residences and small cafés with some shopping. He noticed it was a somber crowd. Some of the women were crying. As he passed a café, he noticed that the patrons were crowded around the TV mounted above the bar. He could see the picture but could not hear what the commentator was saying. The camera panned away from the commentator and into what must be Vatican square. It was filled with people, which was not unusual. Maybe they had not heard the news yet about his death and were waiting for the pope to bless them as was his custom. As he watched, the camera zoomed in on the papal balcony. Sebastian seeing the black caused his knees to become weak, and he caught himself on the back of a chair. Although he knew the pope was dead, seeing the balcony draped in black made it seem so final.

One of the patrons came out, and while passing Sebastian and seeing that he was a priest, some discomfort vanished.

"Are you all right, Father?" he inquired. Sebastian nodded and sat down in the chair.

"We are all so sorry to hear of the Holy Father's death," he said. Hearing the news again that Leo was dead, crashed liked the tides against the beach smashing into his mind. Now he must be more careful than ever. His mind was filled with one nagging question, "How did Leo die? What part had the cardinal or the don played in this?" Sitting there in a stupor, he tried to clear his mind. He needed help. It would not be long before the cardinal sent Anton to the house in search of the manuscript.

Would Brother John be able to get his message to Monsignor O'Rourke now?

Taking a deep breath, he forced himself to get up and continue down the avenue toward the catacombs. He still needed matches, some candles, and a sleeping bag, if he could find one, and something to eat and drink.

He tried to stay close to the storefronts as he could and in the shade. At an open air deli, he stopped, got in, and grabbed a sandwich and a drink. The TV was on in there also, and they were rerunning the announcement by Cardinal Alveraz the Camerlengo of the pope's death. He was saying Leo died in his apartment last night and asking for prayers for the pope and all of the cardinals on their way to Rome for the funeral and the conclave to elect the next pope. That was the end of the announcement. Sebastian finished his sandwich and drank and left the café.

He kept his attention on the people around him and was on the lookout for a store that might have what he needed. If he was thinking correctly, he needed to turn left and that would put him on the street that led to the catacomb's entrance. As he reached the corner, he spotted out of the corner of his eye, a back sedan cruising slowly, the two occupants were looking at the crowd. He stooped down, pretending to tie his shoe, allowing him to be hidden by the passing people. He stayed down until the car had passed. Rising, he hurried down the street. At the next corner, he saw a grocery store. Slipping into the store, he let himself take a moment to have a deep breath of the cool air and a look around.

The store was nearly empty, just a few older people buying what they needed for the day. Grabbing a cart, he moved down the isles, filling the cart with several bottles of water, some candles, matches, and some bread and cheese. Over in the corner were some of last year's merchandise; among the items were several blankets and a pillow. It was not a sleeping bag, but it would do. Looking into the cart, he decided this was about all that he could manage to carry. There was no one standing in the checkout line. The woman working at the checkout had the tired look of someone who had worked long hours and carried a heavy burden. She greeted Sebastian with a forced smile. "Good afternoon, Father," she said.

"Good afternoon," he replied. "Would you try to get all of this in one bag for me?" he asked. Sebastian watched as she scanned and bagged his purchases.

"That will be five euros, Father." Sebastian pulled out the money and paid the bill. She lifted up the bag and handed it to Sebastian.

"I am saddened to hear of the Holy Father's death," she said.

"Thank you, my child. We all are!" he replied, taking the bag. Reaching for her hand, he said, "Bless you, my child." Stooping down, he picked up his briefcase and left the store.

He carefully looked both ways. He no longer saw the black sedan or anyone that might be looking for him. The crowd on the street had thinned out, so he did not have as much cover as he needed. He crossed the street at the corner and started walking past the cemetery wall. This would be where he was the most exposed. He had walked about a block keeping close watch on the people and the oncoming traffic.

Up ahead, he could see the niche in the wall, and behind the bushes planted along, it was an entrance to the catacombs hidden from the street. He had to force himself to keep a steady gait and not to panic and run. In the distance, he could see a black sedan at the traffic signal. He began to pray that the light would hold long enough for him to reach the entrance.

Carlos, one of the don's men was sitting at the wheel of the black sedan at the traffic light on the street that ran by the cemetery. He had been cruising the streets on this side of town, looking out for Sebastian. The crowd on the street had become fewer as the tourists and residents were headed down to the square from of St. Peters to mourn for Pope Leo. His foot was getting itchy to get moving. He felt like he had been sitting at this light for an eternity. At least, it was cool inside the car. The air-conditioning was going full blast. He glanced up at the light. Still red. He leaned over to change the station, and while he was fiddling with the tuner, he heard the blast of a horn. Looking up, he saw that the light turned green, and he gunned the car. He was going much faster than he needed to. He kept moving his head right and left turning to look at every person on the sidewalk. His cell began to ring, and he leaned over to pick it up; doing so, he swerved causing it to slide across the seat. Looking down toward the passenger seat, he saw the cell, but out of the corner of his eye, he saw a figure dressed in black carrying some sort of packages, but he was going too fast to see if it was Sebastian. Finally, getting his hand on the cell he answered; it was the don.

"Carlos, do you have anything to report?"

"No, sir," he said while checking his rearview mirror. The person was still back there, but he couldn't turn around until the next corner. "I will call as soon as I have anything," Carlos reported.

"You better and soon," Carlos heard, and the cell went dead.

Sebastian's heart was racing; he was out of breath, and the sack he was carrying felt like a lead weight. His leg was throbbing, and the tape must have come loose in this heat. He could feel the blood once again running down his thigh. He turned his head toward the wall and pulled the package close to his chest and face as the black sedan passed by. He kept his pace steady; it was less than a block to the entrance. He dare not take time to look behind him. *Keep praying,* he kept thinking over and over. He could see the niche just ahead. Unable to restrain himself, he broke into a run. He stepped into the niche and pulled the branches aside. Try as he could, he could not seem to get between the bush and the wall while holding onto the bag and briefcase. Putting the briefcase and bag down, he squeezed past the bush to the opening of the catacombs. Stretching as far as he could, he was unable to reach either the bag or the briefcase. The limbs at the bottom of the bush are not as thick as the ones in the middle or at the top. Getting down on his hands and knees, he broke off some of the lower limbs just enough of them so that if he lay on his stomach and inched forward, he may be able to reach the bag and briefcase. Throwing the broken branches behind him, he wiggled through the hole he had made until he could feel his briefcase. Carefully, he backed out, pulling it with him. Once again, he forced his body thorough the hole between the bush and the wall. He must get in further this time to reach the bag. He felt the jagged lower limbs ripping into his face and neck and the hard dirt digging into his chest and thighs. Stretching as far as he could, he got the tips of his fingers touching the bag. Giving a push with his leg against the wall, he finally got hold of the bag and began to pull slowly. He was crawling backward, moving the bag an inch at a time as the bag reached the bush. It snagged on one of the broken limbs and begins to tear. One of the bottles of water rolls out and into the clearing in front of the niche. Sebastian kept crawling and pulling. Finally, the bag cleared the bush. He pulled himself into a sitting position stretching out his legs before in. Through the bush, he watched as the big black sedan drove slowly by on the opposite side of the street.

 He dared not move. He held his breath as it passed by. When it was out of sight, he quickly edged out behind the bush and retrieved the bottle of water. Gathering up his briefcase and the torn bag, he stooped down and crawled through the entrance of the catacombs. For the first time today, he felt safe. Sebastian failed to see the torn piece of the black bag hanging at the bottom of the bush.

Chapter 25

The don slammed the telephone down after speaking to Carlos. It had been four hours since Sebastian had been seen leaving the Vatican. It was now 4:30 p.m., and he had promised that Cardinal Sebastian would be found before sundown. He knew Rome was a big city with lots of places to hide. He understood that but he was not sure the cardinal would. He was hoping to have some news before he left to go home. He leaned back in his chair, letting his mind wander. Sophia stuck her head through the door, "Don, do you need anything?" she asked,

Yeah, he thought, *you leaning over my desk with my hard dick buried deep between your legs.* "No!" he answered. *But maybe later,* he thought. Sophia nodded and closed the door.

The don switched off the TV and closed his eyes. He suddenly felt the hairs on the back of his neck stand up. His eyes popped open. The room was beginning to feel uncomfortably warm. The temperature in Rome was hovering around ninety degrees, but the air-conditioning in the building had always kept his office cool. Not only was the hair on his neck standing out, he could feel something crawling over his skin like he was covered in ants. He got out of his chair and walked over to look at the thermostat. *That's funny,* he thought. It was showing it was seventy-five degrees in his office. He could feel sweat running down his chest and underarms. It felt like it was ninety degrees in here. He crossed the office to the bookcase that held the TV; there was a small refrigerator hidden behind a wooden door. Reaching inside, he pulled out a cold bottle of water. Unscrewing the top, he lifted it to his mouth and gulped it down. He walked back over to his desk and rubbed the cold bottle over his forehead and cheeks. He just did not feel good. He sat back down and lay his head down on the desk and closed his eyes.

Something was just not right. He raised his head and opened his eyes and saw what appeared to be black smoke. *Oh my god!* he thought. *The building must be on fire that is why I am so hot.* His mind was saying, *Get up and run,* but he could not move. He opened his mouth to scream but no sound came out. The black smoke was enveloping him. He could feel it in his mouth and going up his nose. It was seeping in through all of the pores of his body. He could hear voices, but could not understand what they were saying. Surely, it was the fire department or the police.

All of a sudden, every muscle in his body contracted. He was thrown out of his chair and onto the floor. The voices grew louder, and the don realized they were not outside; they were inside his head. His body convulsed, snot came from his nose, and urine ran down the front of his expensive suit as his bladder emptied. Another convulsion racked his body, and his bowel emptied; the smell made him gag, and he vomited his stomach contents.

The voice in his head grew louder and louder. He felt like he was loosing his mind. The voices were reminding him over and over of every evil deed he had ever done, and the list was endless. He felt himself thrashing around on the floor. His hand clawed at his shirt, tearing it off, the crawling sensation on his skin had changed to a stinging fire. He began to slap at his legs, trying to put out the pain, tearing off his pants with his fingernails. He clawed his legs until they were bloody. Pulling himself up, holding on to the desk, he ripped off the remainder of his clothes. Standing nude, he took his belt from his pants and began to flail his back and chest with the heavy buckle on the end of the belt, trying to beat off whatever was stinging and burning his skin. His blood splattered over the desk and walls. The pain on his body did not equal the pain he was feeling in his mind. A feeling of emptiness, hopelessness, dread, abandonment, and helplessness; he had no control over his body or his thoughts. It was totally controlled by whatever evil that had entered it. He was trapped inside his body. He had never felt such terror and hopelessness, nor had he endured such pain.

Without warning, his mouth was forced open, and he heard screaming filled with terror like he had never heard before. From his mouth poured forth something black, and he felt like he was being turned inside out. His knees buckled, and he felt the floor rising to meet him, and he realized the screams he was hearing were his own, and then there was silence, and he felt everything going black.

A scream brought him back to consciousness, he did not know if it was his scream or if it was coming from someone else.

"Don! Don! Can you hear me?" floated through his semiconscious mind. Then silence again. Way off in the distance, he once again heard voices; not the ones he had heard before. Different somehow; he felt hands touching his body. Someone was pounding on his chest. He felt a bolt of lightning shoot through his body and then his eyes popped open. At first, he could only make out light and darkness, then shapes began to take form. The shapes became people dressed in uniforms.

"Don Vincenza Amato, can you heard me?"

"Yes" came a whisper from his lips.

"Can you tell me what happened? Who attacked you?"

"No!" once again came from the don in a whisper.

He felt himself being lifted up off the floor and placed on something soft, and he was covered with a blanket. The people were close now. He was on a stretcher.

"We are going to take you to the hospital. Do you understand?"

"Yes!" came the same whispered response. As he was being taken out, he heard the phone ringing. Sophia let it ring as she watched the ambulance crew take the don out. She herself was in shock. She had not been gone that long, and when she returned, she found the don sprawled in the middle of his office nude and bloody. The office was a wreck. Things were broken and knocked to the floor and blood was over the desk and the walls behind it. The phone continued to ring. Finally, Sophia walked over and picked it up. "Hello," she mumbled.

"Sophia, it's Carlos. Let me talk to the don."

"Carlos, he is on his way to the hospital." And she told him how she had found the don.

"Which hospital?"

"They are taking him to the one close to the Vatican. I don't remember the name."

"I know which one," Carlos replied. "I will have to go over here," he said and pressed end call on his cell.

He was making his fourth trip down the avenue where he thought he had seen Sebastian. How could he have just disappeared while he went to the next block to turn around? There was nothing on this side of the street; just the wall to the cemetery. There was not a gate into the wall that he could see, and there was not a store or shop anywhere around. The wall was over six feet tall. He would have seen him climbing over it even from a distance. A man in a black suit climbing over a stucco wall would surely be visible from the corner.

I will check it out later, he thought. Besides, it would be getting dark soon, and he did not want to be in the cemetery at night. *Not that I am sacred,* he thought to himself.

Chapter 26

Another day had passed. His friend now had been gone for two days. Yesterday seemed like a bad dream. Today did not promise to be much better. The sun was coming through the blinds of his room. He could see the dust floating in the beams of light.

Patrick rolled over and swung his legs over the side of his bed. It had been a long and restless night. His sheets and blanket were twisted. It looked like he had been in a wrestling match. He ran his hand through his thick blond hair, getting it out of his eyes. It was five forty-five according to the clock on his bedside table. And it was around midnight last night before he had gotten into bed.

Yesterday had been a long hard day, especially considering his meetings with Cardinal Pulaski and Cardinal Alveraz. Patrick and Archbishop Valanti met quickly last night to compare notes on their meeting with the cardinals. Cardinal Alveraz was the easiest. He just wanted to know the facts surrounding the pope's death. Patrick had told him he had a letter for the next pope from Leo and he had the key Leo wore around his neck. The cardinal made notes of this and told Patrick to hold onto both of these until the election was over, and then he could present them to the new Holy Father.

The meeting with Pulaski was not so easy. He kept pressing both Patrick and Valanti about the details of Leo's death, and he was particularly interested in what happened to Jason. He had talked to Jason and not gotten much from him. He wanted to know what Jason had told them. He also questioned Patrick at length as to what Leo had said just before he died and if he did he leave any instructions or correspondence behind. The only thing Patrick told him was about the letter to the new pope. Pulaski also showed a lot of interest in knowing if Patrick knew what Brother Sebastian was working on for the pope. He wanted to know if Patrick had had any communication with Brother Sebastian since he had been seen that morning leaving the Vatican by the gate Hans guarded.

Both Patrick and the archbishop had kept silent about the personal letters and the meeting they had with Mat Mason earlier in the day. Patrick was sure Pulaski would find out about Mat being in town and their meeting, but he felt that would come to light soon enough.

Patrick could not believe that it was only two days ago that Leo had died. From the light coming into his room, he could tell the sun was rising quickly. Glancing at his clock, it was already six thirty. He had been lost in thought for forty-five minutes. Getting off the bed, he stood up, stretched, and headed to the bathroom for a shower. Patrick kicked off his boxers and turned on the shower. While the water was getting hot, he got out his razor and started shaving. The steam from the shower began to cloud up the mirror. Patrick stepped into the hot shower; the water running over his body helped him relax. He felt like it was washing away some of the sorrow he felt. Getting out, he toweled off and quickly dressed. He was anxious to see what Jason had found out. He had returned Patrick's call last night, and Patrick had asked him to go down and find out if Sebastian had really been at the chapter house.

Leaving his room, he went down the hall past Leo's apartment. There was still a Swiss Guard posted at the door. He knew the apartment had been cleaned and was now sealed, waiting for the new pope.

Patrick arrived at his office, feeling somewhat refreshed. It was going to be another long day. Outside the door waiting for him was Jason. "Good morning, my friend," Jason greeted Patrick. Jason was dressed in his kaki Swiss uniform that he wore when not on official Vatican guard duty.

"How are you today?" asked Patrick. "You certainly look better," Patrick commented.

"I am much better, although my insides are still sore."

"Come in to my office and let's have some coffee and talk," Patrick invited as he opened the door to the waiting room. Jason followed Patrick inside, closing the door behind him. Patrick walked through the room to his office door, unlocking it, and held it for Jason to enter. Patrick walked around behind his desk and picked up the phone and dialed the number for the Vatican coffee shop. Motioning Jason to sit down, he waited for an answer. "May I help you?" said the voice on the other end of the line.

"Yes! Please send up a pot of coffee and a tray of sweet rolls to my office. This is Monsignor O'Rourke," said Patrick

"Thank you, Father. They will be right up." Patrick hung up the phone and sat down facing Jason. "Sorry, I missed your call last night. What did you find out at the chapter house?"

"Several things," replied Jason. "Father Anton had been there before I was, and he caused quite a stir. He searched Brother Sebastian's room, or I should say tossed it, leaving a mess. He had the abbot bring all of the brothers who were serving in the dining room to him, and he questioned them. None of them said that they had seen Sebastian, but he must have been there at lunchtime. Some of his clothes are missing along with his briefcase. There were no papers found in his room either. Anton has special interest in one of the brothers."

"Which one?" asked Patrick

"It was Brother John."

"Did you talk to him?"

"No! He was gone when I was there. I will go to see him today. Why do you think Anton was so interested in John or Sebastian?"

"Well, Cardinal Pulaski and Sebastian go back a long way. Sebastian may have told Pulaski what he was working on for the pope," said Jason.

"That would explain the cardinal's interest in what the pope said to me and the archbishop the night he died."

"I was questioned at length also about what I encountered that night by the cardinal, but I have no memory after being knocked to the floor," said Jason.

"Did the pope ever tell you what Sebastian was working on for him?"

"No. They always met in the private papal apartment or in the archives. I never was privy to any of their meetings." There was a knock on Patrick's office interrupting their conversation. "Yes, come in," called Patrick. Paulo, one of the employees came in with a silver tray holding the order Patrick called in. "Just set it down on the credenza, will you?" asked Patrick.

"Will there be anything else?" Paulo asked as he set the tray down.

"No, thank you." Patrick answered. Patrick motioned Jason to follow him over to the credenza for coffee and sweet rolls.

"Where were we?" asked Patrick as he returned to his desk and sat down, sipping his coffee.

"You were saying," responded Jason. "That you were never in the meetings with the pope and Sebastian. I know you and Leo were close.

He never gave any indication what was going on? Even on the night he died?"

"No!" answered Patrick, hating that he was lying to his friend.

"Has anyone contacted the Rome police concerning Brother Sebastian?"

"Not that I know of," said Jason. "I have close contacts with Inspector Remeta. I will call him later on today. What do you want me to say if anything about the pope's death and the mystery surrounding it?"

"As far as anyone outside the church is concerned, the pope died quietly in his apartment."

"I understand that is for the best," answered Jason.

"Do you think that the inspector can be trusted with the knowledge that Sebastian was working on a secret project with the pope and that he is still alive and has those documents still with him?"

"Yes, he has been very helpful and discrete in the past. He is also a deacon in the church and very loyal."

"Good. Then give him a call. We need to find Sebastian as soon as possible."

"Do you think Sebastian will try to contact Pulaski or Anton? Should I have them watched?"

"Yes, but be very discrete," answered Patrick.

Rising to leave, Jason placed his cup on the credenza and turned back to Patrick. "I have to be at a staff meeting in ten minutes. I will get back with you this afternoon after I speak with Inspector Remeta."

"Thanks, my friend," says Patrick as he rose and ushered Jason out into the waiting area.

Patrick returned to his office. He crossed over to his desk, and before sitting down, he took his cell phone out of his pocket. He had forgotten to charge it last night, so it was dead. He reached into his desk and took out his spare phone charger and reached down under his desk and plugged it into the outlet. Plugging in his cell, he watched as the icon of the battery changed from red to green as it began to charge. Patrick slided the arrow to the left to turn on his iPhone. He saw that he had a missed call and several e-mails. Pushing the phone icon, he touched recent calls, and he did not recognize the number that came up. They had also left a voice mail. The cord was not long enough to lift the phone to his ear, so he bend down his chin touching his knees, and he pushed the voice mail button. A recognized the voice came on.

"Monsignor O'Rourke, this is Brother John. I have an urgent message for you, concerning Sebastian. We need to meet. I can say no more."

Patrick sat up, and for a moment, just stared at the screen. Quickly, he touched the recent call icon at the bottom of the phone. When the call came up, he touched the number on the screen and leaning down again, he heard it begin to ring. After what seem like a week, he heard, "Hello"

"May I speak to Brother John please?" asked Patrick.

"Is there a Brother John around," Patrick heard the voice on the other end of the line ask.

"No Brother John here" came back the reply.

"Are you sure?"

"Look man, this is a public phone in a bar, got no Brother John here!" There was a clunk as the phone was hung up and the line went dead. Patrick sat up, placed his phone on the floor, wondering what he should do next. Wait on Jason to go to the house and talk to Brother John or should he try to contact him?

John's message sounded urgent. Maybe he should call the house and talk to John this morning or arrange a meeting with him later today. Patrick pulled out the Vatican phone book and looked up the number for the Vatican's private service. Dialing the three-digit number for the brothers of mercy chapter house, he waited for an answer. "Brother Pablo speaking" came a heavily Spanish-accented voice.

"This is Monsignor O'Rourke. I would like to speak to Brother John."

"One moment please" came the reply. Patrick was put on hold. Over the phone came the voices of many brothers singing one of the chants he had heard so often at chapel services.

"Monsignor," a voice broke in, "Brother John will be with you in a moment" And the chanting came back before Patrick had a chance to reply. Several minutes passed, he could tell because the chant started over.

"Monsignor, this is Brother John" came the familiar voice. "I am so glad you called this morning I have an urgent message for you from Sebastian."

"What is it?" Patrick interrupted.

"I don't know. It is a note in a sealed envelope."

"Can you open it and read it to me?"

"No! Not here. There are too many people around. I am not sure Sebastian wanted me to know what is written here or he would have told me. He said I should make sure I gave it to you personally."

"OK, when can we meet?" asked Patrick.

"That is up to you, Monsignor. I will come whenever you tell me." Patrick thought a moment.

"Meet me in the square by the obelisk. There will be a large crowd and that should be safe. Meet me at 2:00 p.m. today."

"I will be there" came the reply from Brother John. Patrick hung up the phone and sat back in his chair, thinking about what he should do next.

Chapter 27

The smell of antiseptic was strong to his nose as he tried to open his eyes; they felt like they had lead weights on them. The sound of beeps coming in a steady rhythm broke through his consciousness. Then the sound of hushed voices began to register with him. He did not know who the person talking was, but he recognized the voice of his wife Maria. They were talking about him, but he could not understand all the words yet, and they seemed far away. He concentrated with all the strength he could muster and finally got one eye open.

The room was semi-dark. He could tell he was lying down. He tried to focus on his surroundings. He felt like he was seeing things through a dirty glass, all cloudy and dull. His wife's voice seemed very close now, and he could make out her shape standing by his bedside. He tried to speak but no sound would come out. He strained hard again and was able to get his other eye open. He could see the monitor where the beeping was coming from, and he could see tubes from the bags on the stand by the monitor, trailing down toward his body. His wife was speaking to a nurse, and while he watched, she turned toward him and took his hand. She looked toward his face, and seeing that his eyes were open, she called to the nurse who was leaving. "He's awake! Come quickly. See his eyes are open."

"Don Amato, can you hear me?" the nurse asked. He tried to form the words, but they would not come. Using sheer willpower, he was able to move his head enough so she would see.

"Good," she said. "You are at St. Vincent's hospital near the Vatican. You were babbling and restless and appeared to have been beaten. You were not making any sense, so you were given a sedative to help you sleep. We have found no broken bones but a lot of bruising, both internally and externally. These appear to be nothing serious. The sedative is wearing off slowly. You should be fully awake shortly. We will be keeping you here tonight for observation, and if all goes as expected, you can go home in the morning. Do you understand?"

Once again, he moved his head, yes. He found it was easier this time.

Bella was still holding his hand. He gave her a little squeeze and she bent down and kissed his cheek. She smelled of lilac soap, fresh and clean. Her long black hair fell across his head and shoulders. When she stood up, he could see the tears in her eyes. It was at times like these that he felt like a bastard for treating her so carelessly.

"I have been so worried about you, Vincenza. Who could have done this to you?" He lay there looking up at her, trying to remember, but his mind was still too fuzzy.

"I don't know," he managed to whisper.

"Close you eyes and sleep," Bella said. "I will be right here with you." The don closed his eyes. The sound of the monitor and the noise coming from the hospital was enough to keep him awake. The cobwebs that were clouding his mind began to fade. He began to remember what had happened to him. The memory jarred his eyes wide open and a low groan escaped his lips. He used the rails from the bed to pull himself up to a sitting position. Cold sweat popped out on his forehead, and he began to shiver. "Vincenza, what is it?" Bella asked, rising from her chair, coming to his side.

"Raise the bed up for me," he gasped. "I need to sit up." Bella raised the bed as he requested.

"You have only been asleep for a couple of hours."

"What did you say? I have been asleep for two hours? I have just closed my eyes."

"It's all right," Bella cooed, trying to comfort him.

"While you were out, Carlos came by to see you. Something about a missing priest."

"Some water, if you please," he asked. His throat felt like it was full of dust. Bella poured him a cup of water and held it to his lips. He reached up and took the cup and downed it all, holding it out to her to be refilled. They both turned toward a nurse who was coming in with what looked like a dinner tray. Vincenza glared up at the clock; it was twelve ten. He had been asleep for a while. He felt hungry, and the food did not look too bad. There were some flowers in the room. White lilies. Looking at them gave Vincenza a chill.

"Who are these from?" he asked, motioning toward the flowers.

"Why, they are from your friend Cardinal Pulaski," Bella answered. "While you eat your dinner, I am going out for a bit myself, if you think you will be OK."

"That's fine," he replied. Bella gathered up her things, giving him a quick peck on the cheek, then she left. He was right; the food was not bad, and he ate it all with relish. When the nurse came back, she looked pleased that he had eaten well.

"I will call the doctor and tell him your vital signs are normal, and you are sitting up and eating. If he lets me, I will come back and remove your IVs and the catheter. After this, you will be able to get out of bed and move around later today."

"Catheter? He felt like he needed to pee. He reached under the sheet and felt a tube coming out from the head of his dick. *O shit*, he thought, *that's going to hurt like hell when it's pulled out.*

He lay his head back on the pillow and just stared at the ceiling. He forced his mind to think back to yesterday in his office. All he could remember after Sofia left was something that looked like black smoke, searing pain in his head, and the feeling he had lost control of his body. Remembering caused his heart to race. He could hear the monitor beeping faster and faster. Fear bean to crawl up his back, and he could feel the hairs standing upon the back of his neck, and the sac holding his balls tightened up, making him feel nauseous. He felt like he was falling into a dark pit. The alarm on his monitor began to sound off, and he was immediately surrounded by several nurses; he could see someone shoving a needle into the IV line, then he felt nothing; everything went black.

When he awoke, Bella was in the room again. He was feeling much calmer. Standing next to Bella was someone dressed all in black. His back was to him so he did not know who it was. He and Bella were speaking in hushed tones, and he could not make out what they were saying.

"Bella," he whispered, trying to get her attention, but she was too far away and too deep into the conversation. The blinds in the room were partly closed; the sun rays played on the wall by his bed. He watched as it made patterns on the wall by the amount of light coming in; it must be morning. He had been out for a while. His uncovered breakfast tray was sitting on the table beside his bed. On it was a glass of juice. Reaching up to get it, he found that the bed rails were blocking his arm. He reached through the rails and pulled the tray closer to the bed. In doing so, a vase of flowers plummeted to the floor. Both Bella and the visitor turned toward the sound of the vase crashing to the floor. Water from the vase and glass fragments splashed all over the visitor's pant leg. Bella rushed over to Vincenza side.

"Vincenza, you are awake. Let me call the nurse. She wanted to know immediately." Looking back toward the visitor, Bella said, "Father Anton, let me get you a towel from the bathroom."

"Thank you, Bella" came the response. Anton caught and held Vincenza's eyes in a stare that sent tingles up Vincenza's spine.

"How are you, Vincenza? The Cardinal has been concerned about your well-being, since we heard what happened." Vincenza tried to reply but he could not get the words to form. He just lay there looking back at Anton. Bella brought Anton a towel, and he used it to brush off the glass and try to dry himself. Bella tried again to call the nurses station, pressing on the buzzer.

"While you are here, Father, visiting with Vincenza, I will walk down the hall and find a nurse."

"That will be fine, my child. I have a prayer to say for Vincenza, and the cardinal has him sent message," Anton replied. Vincenza began to shake his head back and forth, not wanting Bella to leave him alone with Anton. Anton quickly stepped between Vincenza and Bella, blocking her view. He reached down and began to squeeze Vincenza's hand against the rail. He beckoned to Bella, "Go, my child, it will be OK until you return." Bella gave a half smile and hurried out of the room. Anton leaned over the bed so close that Vincenza felt like he was being drowned in a sea of bad breath. The odor of garlic and onions made him gag. "You had better find the missing Brother Sebastian and in a hurry, if you don't want another visit from the cardinal's friend," Anton whispered. The eyes looking down at him were cold, and the mouth was turned up in a cruel smile. Just looking at him made Vincenza's heart race. "I am sure you would not want it to visit Bella or one of your children," he sneered. Heat swept over Vincenza's body, and he broke out in a sweat. He closed his eyes, blocking out Anton, but he could not hold in the scream that was forming in his throat.

"No!" he screamed and again and again.

Anton turned from the bed and headed toward the door. As he turned into the hall, he saw Bella and the nurse heading his way. Anton nodded and kept going toward the elevator and back to the Vatican.

Chapter 28

The morning has been very busy for Patrick. He had met with Jason first thing, and after the meeting, he had gotten in contact with Brother John and set up a meeting, and it was almost two o'clock. Patrick placed the papers he was working on in his center drawer and tidied up his desk. He wanted his office to be presentable if one of the arriving cardinals needed to meet him. It was strange passing through the empty reception room. Just a couple of days ago, it would have been packed with people waiting to see him to schedule an audience with Pope Leo. Instead of the sound of voices, there was only the sound of his shoes bouncing off the floor and walls, making an eerie hollow sound with each footfall.

Patrick quickly made his way through the hallways nodding to those who knew him. There was a crowd of people waiting for the elevator, so he decided to take the stairs. He was wearing a cassock today over his shirt and pants, which made it difficult to take the customary two steps at a time.

Reaching the ground floor, Patrick exited the door leading to the street that ran parallel to the square in front of St. Peters. As Patrick thought, the square was filled with mourners, including many nuns and priests all kneeling in prayer. The obelisk stood nearly in the middle of the square. It took Patrick a lot longer than he thought to reach that point. He had no problem moving through the crowd, which stepped aside to let him pass. The problem was they always didn't have room to move. Nearing the obelisk, there seemed to be several men dressed in monk's robes. They all had their hood pulled up over their heads so that their faces were hidden.

Patrick began to circle the obelisk slowly, trying to see which one of these monks was John. Suddenly, Patrick felt a hand on his shoulder. He turned to see the face he was looking for. Brother John looked relieved to see Patrick. "Monsignor O'Rourke," he said. "I am so glad to see you."

"And I you," Patrick replied. Patrick noticed that he seemed to be walled in by a living, brown fence, as the other monks circled around them.

"I thought it would be safer if some of the brothers came with me," John offered. Patrick nodded in agreement. From the folds of his robe, John produced a white envelope with Patrick's name on it. He handed the envelope to Patrick, who quickly slipped it into the sash around the waist of his cassock. "Please let us know how we can help," John said.

"Thank you, I will. How did Sebastian look when you saw him?"

"His eyes had dark circles, and he had lost some weight, but other than that, he looked fine. He seemed scared and very upset at the news of the pope's death. He was most emphatic that he must see you, Monsignor. It is a matter of utmost importance. Hopefully his location will be in the letter."

Patrick reached out and embraced John saying, "May God bless you." The Monks broke rank, leaving an opening for Patrick to leave.

Patrick had not gone more than fifty yards when he ran head long into Father Anton. "Monsignor, what brings you out into the crowd?"

"I might ask you the same question," Patrick replied. Anton looked past Patrick in the direction of the obelisk.

"Aren't those monks from the chapter house? What are they doing out in the square?"

"I have no idea."

"But I thought I saw you coming from that direction. Did they say anything to you about our missing monk?"

"I am not concerned with that at the moment. Jason, captain of the guards, is working with the Rome police. I am sure Cardinal Pulaski will hear any news long before I do," said Patrick, pushing past Anton and heading back to his office.

On the way, Patrick stepped out onto the street and pulled out his cell phone and dialed the Vatican number for the archbishop. Valanti answered on the second ring.

"Patrick, I have been waiting for your call." Patrick quickly filled him in on his call to the house and the meeting with Brother John.

"Meet me in my office. I should be there in fifteen minutes."

"I will be there," answered Valanti.

Patrick hurried up the street and entered the Vatican office building. The halls were quiet only a couple of nuns waiting at the elevator.

"Good afternoon, Monsignor," they said. Patrick returned the greeting and stood aside when the door opened to let them enter first.

Anton watched as Patrick walked away then he turned his attention back toward the obelisk. The brothers he had seen were no longer there, and a crowd of tourists had taken their place. No need to pursue the brothers right now. He knew where they could be found, or he could order them to his office. He had another business more pressing. He needed to report back to Cardinal Pulaski on his visit with the don.

The nuns stepped aside to let Patrick off at his floor. He was always uncomfortable with the deference they accorded to him. It almost bordered on veneration. It was a short walk to his office. The Swiss Guard on duty came to attention as Patrick passed by them. Opening the door to the outer office, he saw Archbishop Valanti sitting in one of the chairs. He rose when he saw Patrick enter.

"Good afternoon," he said.

"Good afternoon," Patrick replied. Valanti followed Patrick into his office and sat down in one of the chairs facing Patrick's desk. Patrick walked around his desk and also sat down. He reached down into his sash and pulled out the white envelope Brother John had given him. Patrick opened his lap drawer and took out a letter opener and opened the envelope and pulled out a single sheet of paper.

Patrick unfolded the paper and read it aloud. "Monsignor O'Rourke, I have been hiding in the catacombs, since I escaped being killed by the mafia. I was able to weaken the duct tape binding my hands before I was thrown into the bay. Being a strong swimmer, I was able to swim deep enough to escape the bullets and the boat prop. I was able to swim to a buoy and was picked up by a fishing boat and made my way to the catacombs. I have the manuscript that Pope Leo gave me to translate. I must get it to you immediately. We are all in great danger. I made the mistake of telling Cardinal Pulaski what I had found out from the first part of the manuscript. I tried to warn the pope, but I guess it was too late. May God forgive me. The key he got out of the archives is the key of Solomon. He does not have its full power yet. He needs the rest of the book that goes with the key. I am going back to the catacombs. Please help me. I will try to call you soon. Brother Sebastian."

"So this confirms what we had already figured out yesterday when we read the pope's letters to us. This demon that Pulaski has let loose, no telling where it is and what it can do. No wonder the pope warned us to never be in the same place at the same time. I wonder how Jason survived its attack. He was only knocked to the ground and only sustained bruises from the force of the hit he took."

"I don't know, Patrick. I have done some research, and it appears that Solomon used these forces to help build his temple, so they must have great strength. The most troubling thing I found out was he also used these demons to control the people. It would not take many encounters like the pope and Jason had to cause fear and widespread panic, and nothing controls people like fear. Like we talked about yesterday, we don't think about demons or even consider them real, but we have both read the many accounts of Jesus casting out demons from people during his ministry here. They are also mentioned in the Old Testament and in many ancient writings and even other religions. I surmise since we very rarely hear of demons today, although we do an occasional exorcism, most of them may have been confined in purgatory until the end of this present age."

"What do you think we need to do?"

"First, we need to find Sebastian and the manuscript before the cardinal or the mafia does."

"Who do we know that we can trust?" asked the archbishop.

"I would trust Jason with my life," answered Patrick. "His loyalty still lies with Leo and the church. He and Pulaski have never been close, and he does not like Anton at all. Who knows the catacombs?" asked Patrick.

"There are maps in the archives telling where the tombs of Peter and the other popes are buried. We have other documents going back to ancient times before St. Peters was built when Christians met down there or hid there from the Romans. That research would be a good job for Mat Mason. I feel he can b trusted, or Leo would not have asked him to come here," said the archbishop.

"I will call Jason and you get in touch with Mat, and we will meet here tonight around nine o'clock. The offices should be empty by then, and we will not draw too much attention."

"I will go to the archives and call Mat," said the archbishop as he stood up and headed toward the door. Patrick smiled at his dear friend as he watched him leave. Reaching for the phone, he dialed Jason's extension. After a couple of rings, he heard Jason answer, "Captain of the Guards."

"Jason, it's Patrick. I need to see you right away."

"Be right up" came the reply.

"No, meet me in the square, and we will go and grab a bite of lunch."

Chapter 29

The darkness was oppressive. He could not see more than a few yards in the glow of the single candle mounted on the ledge. It was damp; there was a constant drip coming from the center of the passage way as the groundwater seeped through the rocks from above. It had formed a small pool where the erosion had worn a place on the floor.

All night, he could hear the scratching of feet scraping on the hard floor coming and going from the water. Once he had felt what he knew was a rat scurry across his legs, he also felt the cold nose of one as it smelled the blood on his leg and was trying to paw its way through the bandages to the raw wound on his leg.

It had been a long night. He was sitting on one of the blankets and had wrapped up Indian style in the other one. He took the flashlight and turned it on, so he could examine the cuts on his chest and thighs. The cuts on his chest had burned and hurt during the night, and he felt like he might have a slight fever. Pulling the gauze and tape away, the wounds looked angry and felt hot. It did not look infected, yet but he knew that he needed stitches.

Looking through his bag, he found a new tube of ointment, and he treated the wounds and replaced the bandages.

Feeling hungry, he pulled out the bread and cheese. He noticed that the bottom of the bag had a hole in it, and most of the cheese and bread was gone. He pulled out what was left of the bread and ate from the part that looked un-chewed. He picked up the bottle of water and had a long drink.

Sebastian looked at his watch; it was a little after twelve. The streets would be filled with office workers and tourists. Now would be a safe time to get out and go to a hospital. Maybe he would be able to use a phone at the hospital. *St. Joseph's was not too far,* he thought, *so he would go there.*

Sebastian pulled the blanket from his shoulders and struggled into his coat. The tape was still holding his shirt together. He had taken some water and washed most of the blood out.

He took the flashlight and his briefcase and walked deeper into the catacombs looking for a place for his briefcase. He came to a fork in the tunnel and went to the left, thinking most people would turn to the right. Soon it dead ended in what appeared to have been a door opening into a small room.

Over the lintel carved into the stone was what appeared to be a fish. This must have been where early Christians lived or prayed. Shining the light around inside, Sebastian saw several brick lying on the floor. Near the top was a hole where they had fallen from.

Standing on his tiptoes, he was able to reach the hole. He attentively stuck his forefinger into it. He felt nothing. The top row of bricks seemed to be loose, so he removed several of them. Shining his light into the hole, a white reflection shone back at him. Removing a few more, revealed a skull its jaws clenched together in a Macomb smile. This was a burial site or one of the graves from the cemetery above. Sebastian took the briefcase and shoved inside, moving the skull and other bones aside. He replaced the bricks he removed.

He stepped back and shined the light on the wall. He could tell the difference, but to a casual observer, it all looked the same. The telling signs that someone had been there were the footprints he had left on the floor in the dust.

He walked back out to the fork. There was a clear path on the dusty floor showing where he had been. He walked down the right side where the tunnel forked for about a hundred yards.

This passage seemed to be endless. There were several passages leading off it, so Sebastian walked down several of these back and forth across the passageway. When he got back to the fork, he walked round and round in a circle. He walked back down the left fork several times. By the time he was done, it was impossible to tell which way he had gone.

He made his way back up to where he had slept the night before. He folded up his blankets and placed them and his pillow on the ledge with his water, candles, and one of his flashlights. He picked up the torn bag and finished the bread, then stuffed the bag into his pocket. He would trash it at the hospital. He packed up the bandages and the tape; they too were placed with his other things on the ledge. Sebastian blew out the candle, turned on the flashlight, and headed toward the entrance.

As he got closer to the entrance the stale air began to freshen Soon the tunnel brightened and the light coming in lifted his spirits. The sun must be shinning. Soon he heard the sound of traffic and the roar of tires running on the asphalt.

He had to get onto his toes to reach the ledge to get out. Pulling himself up, he stuck his head out of the hole. There was no one hiding there waiting to grab him. He was looking out only at the bushes. He pulled himself through to the outside, and in doing so, his shirt caught on a jagged rock and split open again. He also got dirt on his jacket and pants. Standing up, he began to brush him self off as best he could with a bush on one side and the wall on the other.

There was a lot of traffic on the roadway. Pulling the bush aside, he was able to barely squeeze past it and into the niche in the wall. The light was holding traffic, so he waited for it to turn before he stepped out. There were people coming up the sidewalk toward him. Sebastian stepped out of the bushes just as they passed, joining in behind them. He was sure they did not notice him, although the people coming up behind them must have thought it was strange for a priest to appear out of the bushes. He could not worry about that now. No one seemed to be paying him any attention.

He continued to follow the crowd at least to the corner, where he would turn right toward the Vatican and St. Joseph's hospital.

Sebastian kept a close watch on the passing cars. There were no big black sedans to be seen today. At the corner, he picked up his pace. The hospital was still several blocks away.

He would be exposed walking these blocks, because there were not many people walking here. This was a residential area, and the people who lived here would still be at work on in school.

He began to breathe easier as he spotted the entrance of the hospital. He did not want to go into the main entrance. The emergency room would be better. He spotted a sign directing people to the side entrance for emergency services.

Opening the door, Sebastian moved toward the nurses' station. "May I help you, Father?" The nurse behind the desk asked.

"Yes, I had an accident, and I need someone to look at my chest and leg. I may need a few stitches," Sebastian said, opening his coat exposing his torn and the bloody shirt.

"Come with me," the nurse said as she came around the desk and took Sebastian by the arm leading him into a room.

"Please sit on the end of the examining table, Father and remove your coat and shirt. I will get you a gown to put on." Sebastian did as she asked.

"Father, you will also have to remove your pants so we can tend to your leg." Sebastian stepped off the table and kicked off his shoes and removed his pants.

The nurse returned with the gown, and he slipped it on. "Get back on the table and lie down, and I will get a doctor in here right away," she said as she left the room, drawing the curtain so Sebastian could have some privacy.

Sitting on the table, Sebastian saw a phone on the counter next to the wall. He got down and pulled the curtain back just enough to see down the hall. No one was coming. He picked up the receiver and dialed nine to get a dial tone. He called the main number at the Vatican. After a few rings, he heard, "Vatican city. How may I direct your call?"

"Monsignor O'Rourke, please."

"Thank you." The phone begins to ring.

"Monsignor O'Rourke" comes the voice on the other end. "Monsignor, it's Sebastian"

Patrick can't believe his ears. "Sebastian, where are you?"

"I am in the emergency room at St. Joseph's hospital."

"Are you all right?"

"I got cut, trying to get away from some men who were following me yesterday."

"Stay where you are. I will be right there," said Patrick.

"Yes, I will," replied Sebastian. Hearing someone coming, he hung up the phone and climbed back up onto the table. The curtain parted, and Sebastian saw a middle-aged man with a beard walk into the room.

"Good afternoon, Father. I am Doctor Jacopo. I understand from the nurse that you have a wound on yours chest and leg. Let me examine your leg first," he said, pulling the gown up so he could see the wound. "That cut will need to be cleaned and stitched." Reaching around Sebastian to untie the gown, he helped him lower it. Looking at his chest, he commented, "That is also a nasty cut also on your chest." Pulling on a pair of gloves, he took a swab and began cleaning his chest wound. "This one will not require many stitches, but you will need to be on antibiotics. It is infected. Let me call for a nurse, and I will stitch the leg first. Then the nurse can finish cleaning and bandage both for you," Dr Jacopo said as he left the room.

Sebastian could hear the doctor giving orders to the nurse, after which he came back into the room. "Why don't you lie back?" said the doctor, "while I stitch the leg." Sebastian eased back on the table.

The nurse came in pushing a cart on which were needles, dressing, and all that was needed. "This will sting a little," said the doctor as he injected a painkiller around the cut on his leg. Sebastian closed his eyes and clinched his fist every time the needle pierced his skin. But he thought this is the first time in weeks that he felt safe.

The doctor's pager began to go off just as he was finishing stitching Sebastian's leg. "I must get this," he said. Picking up the phone, he dialed into the switchboard "Yes, I will be right up."

Speaking to the nurse, "There is an emergency upstairs in the don's room. I am needed immediately. Sorry, Father, but I am finished here. The nurse can take care of putting on the bandages." The doctor pats Sebastian on the shoulder and leaves.

"Who is upstairs?" asked Sebastian.

"It is Don Vincenza. Everyone knows him." She looks around and seeing no one, continued, "He is head of the mafia in the city of Rome. No one dares cross him or fails to come when he calls." Sebastian had heard the name before in the warehouse and on the boat just before he was thrown into the bay. He had to get out of here as soon as possible. "Are you all right?" the nurse asked. "You are trembling, and your face is flushed"

"I'm fine. Just being stitched made me a little nervous," replied Sebastian.

"Can I call anyone for you? You don't need to be walking around in this heat."

"No, thank you. I called a friend while you were getting me the gown, and he is on his way to pick me up."

"You stay in this room until he comes. I will check on you periodically."

"Thanks."

Chapter 30

Carlos wheeled into the parking lot of St. Joseph's hospital. He had been to the hospital last night after he had talked with Sophia. The don was not conscious while he was there. His wife was going to stay with him, so he should be safe. He had stayed a while but seeing there was nothing he could do, he left. He spoke to the nurse on duty and the security guards to make sure the don was well protected. Using his usual tactics, a little money here and a threat there, always got the job done. He had spent the rest of the night driving around Rome and checking with his people. And still there was no news of that monk. The don's wife called him to come over. The don was awake, but he was still not rational. She had gone to get a nurse, leaving the don with a priest, and when she came back with the nurse, the don was screaming and incoherent. So Carlos had come right over.

Passing through the front door, he passed the reception desk and walked back to the elevators. Carlos hit the up button and the door came open. He entered and pushed seven for the don's floor. The ride was quick. The door opened in front of the nurses' station. Turning right, he walked down the hallway to the don's room. Carlos paused a moment straightened his coat then knocked on the door. He heard Bella say, "Come in." Carlos pushed open the door and entered. The don was lying on the bed with his eyes closed. "Carlos, thank you for coming. The nurse gave him a sedative. He will be out for a while. Do you know Father Anton?" she asked.

"Yes, I have seen him before, why?"

"He said or did something to Vincenza while I was out. He was OK when I left him," said Bella. The nurse walked in, interrupting their conversation. "Doctor Jacopo is in the emergency room. I called his pager and asked him to call me back, and he did so a moment ago. I asked him to come up here right away."

"Thank you," said Bella. She and Carlos did not resume their conversation until she had left.

"Carlos, what's going on between Vincenza and the cardinal?"

"Bella, I can't tell you anything. The don would have me killed if I told anyone and that includes you."

"But Carlos, how can I help him if I don't know?"

"Just stay close to him. That will help." The door to the room opened, and Doctor Jacopo came in.

"Bella, Carlos, good to see you. What happened? I would have been here sooner, but I was stitching up a priest who came in this morning with cuts one his chest and leg." Bella related what happened to the doctor. "Well, Bella, this is not unusual when someone has gone through a physical and mental trauma. We see this often in accident victims. They relive what has happened to them over and over. He will be OK, but it may take a little time," he said. Doctor Jacopo walked over and checked the don's vital signs and told Bella they were normal. "Try to get some rest yourself," he said to Bella. As he was turning to leave, the room Carlos touched his arm.

"Who is the priest you were stitching up?"

"I don't know."

"Then call and find out for me!"

"We don't give out that information."

"I said, call and find out for me!" Carlos said in a menacing voice.

The doctor hesitated, then picked up the phone in the room and called down to emergency.

"Let me speak to Angelina, the nurse who was assisting me as I was stitching up the priest."

"One moment, Doctor Jacopo, and I will get her."

"Angelina, what is the priest name we were stitching up?"

"One moment, Doctor, and I will ask him." She came back on the line, "His name is Sebastian Bantoleni."

"Thank you"

Turning to Carlos. "His name is Sebastian Bantoleni." Carlos was stunned. He could not believe he could have such luck.

"You did say his name was Sebastian? Is that correct?"

"Yes! Can I go now? I need to check on him before he leaves."

"So he is still here?"

"I am sure he is. The nurse just asked him his name while I was on the phone." Carlos pushed the doctor out of his way and burst out of the room and ran down the hall toward the elevator. There were several people waiting for it. When the door opened, Carlos shoved them aside and hit the button for the first floor.

Meanwhile in Sebastian's room, he asked the nurse, "Who wanted to know my name."

"It was the doctor who attended you up in the don's room."

"I need a pen and a piece of paper quickly, please," said Sebastian. Seeing the look of shear terror in his eyes, she got both out of a drawer and handed them to him. As quickly as he could, he wrote down the location of the manuscript and how to get into the catacombs and folded it and on the top wrote the name Monsignor O'Rourke. "Are you a believer?" he asked the nurse.

"Yes, Father," she said. "My sister is a nun." Sebastian handed her the note.

"Swear on your immortal soul and the soul of your sister that you will guard this note with your life, and you will not give it to anyone other that Monsignor O'Rourke." She just looked at him and the note.

"Swear!" Sebastian said forcefully.

"I swear," she said, putting the note into her pocket.

Carlos luck was not as good as he first thought. The elevator was stopping at every floor, letting visitors and staff on and off. He had three more floors to go. He pulled out his cell and called another of the don's men. Hearing someone answer, he said, "Marconie, meet me at St. Joseph's hospital now!"

"Will do, boss. I am about a mile away. Carlos, is there something wrong?"

"No, not wrong but right. Our buddy Sebastian is here in the emergency room. So hurry!" Carlos hung up. Several in the elevator were looking at him. Carlos pulled his coat open just enough so that his shoulder holster could be seen. "What are you looking at?" he asked.

The visitors and staff all got out at the next floor, leaving Carlos alone in the elevator. "One more floor, Sebastian, and you are mine," Carlos thought as the door closed, and he felt the elevator descend.

Chapter 31

As soon as he got the call from Sebastian, Patrick ran from his office. He passed the Swiss Guard and said over his shoulder, "Call your captain and tell him to meet me at St. Joseph's hospital."

"Yes, Monsignor" came the reply. Patrick passed the elevator and headed toward the stairs. Taking two at a time, he was running like he was being chased by Satan himself

He nearly knocked down on of the visiting cardinals as he hit the door at the bottom of the stairs. "Sorry, Eminence," he said as he sprinted to the outside door. There were always cabs near the Vatican. Running to the curb he held up his hand at a passing one. It did not stop, but the one behind it did. Patrick opened the door and jumped in. "St. Joseph's hospital, and this is an emergency," he told the cabbie.

Tires squealed as the cab pulled from the curb and merged into traffic. "Are you all right, Father," he asked.

"Yes, yes, it is someone at the hospital I know."

"We should be there in fifteen minutes," he told Patrick. Horns blared as the cab weaved in and out of the Rome's traffic; tires squealed as other drivers had to slam on their brakes. Patrick was thrown from side to side as the cab continued to weave in and out of the traffic.

"It is just up ahead, Father," called the cabbie. Patrick took our twenty euros from his pocket. As the cab came to a sliding stop at the curb of St. Joseph's hospital, Patrick leaned and dropped the euros over the seat. "Keep the change," he said as he opened the door and ran toward the hospital.

Patrick had been to St. Joseph's many times, so he knew exactly where to go. The cab had let him let him out at the front door, so he ran around to the side entrance where the emergency room was located. He went through the ambulance entrance doors, which would put him into the hall closest to the nurse's desk. Moving quickly, he approached the desk slightly out of breath, "Brother Sebastian," he panted. The nurse pointed down to a room on the right following close behind him. Patrick entered the room. Sebastian was just tucking in his shirt, "Sebastian," Patrick said as he walked over to him and embraced him gently.

"Monsignor, we are in great danger," he whispered into Patrick's ear.

"How so?"

"The don is on the seventh floor, and they know that I am here."

"Monsignor," said the nurse, coming up behind Patrick. "Here is a note for you." Patrick took the note and glanced at its contents. "Why are you giving me this, Sebastian?"

"It is the location of the manuscript. I left it for you, incase something happened to me before you arrived." Patrick put the note in his pocket and helped Sebastian into his coat.

As the elevator opened and Carlos was stepping out, he saw a priest hurrying up to the nurse's desk, then walk down to one of the rooms. It was the pope's secretary, Monsignor O'Rourke. Carlos had seen him many times at a distance accompanying the pope. He stepped into the hallway and hid behind the food cart holding the lunch trays. In a moment, he saw Brother Sebastian step out through the curtain and into the hallway. *Bad luck*, he thought, because their eyes met and he saw recognition on Sebastian's face. Sebastian stepped back quickly into the room, running into Patrick, nearly knocking him down.

"Sorry, Monsignor," he said.

"What's wrong?" asked Patrick. "Do you feel sick?"

"No, Carlos, one of the don's men, the one who tried to kill me is out by the elevator."

Turning toward the nurse, he asked, "Is there another way out of here, other than going by the elevator?"

"Yes, you can exit by the front door by turning right out of this room." Patrick took the note she had given him out of his pocket and taking his pin wrote Jason's name on the front scratching out his name with this message, "Jason, if we are not here when you arrive the don's men have taken us. This is the location to the manuscript. Get it to the archbishop," Patrick said.

Then turning back to the nurse. "Give this to Jason Sitzler. He is captain of the Vatican guard. He is coming here to look for me." Angelina took the note and put it back into her pocket. "God will bless you, my child," said Patrick.

Taking Sebastian by the arm, they exited the room, and turned toward the front of the hospital.

Carlos stepped out from behind the food cart and began to follow them. Angelina hid behind the curtain until Carlos had passed and rounded the corner.

Carlos kept pace with Sebastian and Patrick through the several twist and turns toward the front door. Pulling out his cell, he called Marconie. "Yes" came his voice after only one ring.

"Are you here?"

"Out front."

"Excellent! Sebastian and Monsignor O'Rourke will be coming out the front door. Be there with the doors open ready to receive our guests."

"Gotcha, boss"

Patrick held tight to Sebastian, moving him along quickly. He could hear footsteps echoing off the stone floors coming up behind them. He turned his head and caught sight of Carlos about twenty paces behind them and closing fast. Patrick could see the front doors just ahead. If he could get out and to the curb and get into one of the cabs located there, they just might get away.

As he came through the door next to the curb, right in front of them was a four-door black sedan blocking any chance of getting a cab with its doors open. As he turned to go back into the hospital, he felt a hand on his shoulder and a blunt object shoved into his side. "Just keep walking, Monsignor. I know that the threat of death means nothing to you, but see that mother over there and her children coming in? I know you do not want to be responsible for their untimely death, do you?" Patrick shook his head, no and continued toward the car. "You get in the back with me, and you, monk, get in the front seat with Marconie." Patrick and Sebastian did as they were told. "Marconie, head back to the warehouse at the marina, on second thought Amalfi is too far go to the one we use in Rome."

"Your favorite place, right, Sebastian?" he did not answer. He put his head down and began to pray. "You will tell me what I want to know, monk! And if I can't beat it out of you, you'll talk as you as you see your friend here having his skin peeled off a little at a time. I might just decide to cut off his nuts one at a time, that is, if priests have any," Carlos said with a sneer on his face. "We are going to have some fun with these too. Right, Marconie?"

"Yeah, boss," he replied as he speeded into the traffic, daring anyone to get into his way.

Chapter 32

Jason parked his car in a visitors' spot outside the emergency room. He came into the hospital through the visitor's door. Looking down the hallway, he spotted the nurses' station. He was still dressed in his camos with the pope's insignia on the sleeve. He removed his cap and approached the nurse at the desk. "I am here from the Vatican to pick up Brother Sebastian and Monsignor O'Rourke."

"I am sorry, but you are too late."

"What do you mean too late?"

"They left about ten minutes ago by the front door. You must have just missed them."

"Thanks," Jason replied and walked back down the hallway past where he had come in, going toward the front door. When he reached the front door, he did not pass or see Patrick or Sebastian in the lobby. He went outside. He looked both ways, and they were not where to be found. He did not like the feeling he had in the pit of his stomach. Something had to be wrong. Patrick would not have asked him to come and pick them up and then just leave.

Jason walked back into the lobby and made his way back around to the emergency room. Seeing the nurse he had spoken to coming out of one of the examining rooms, he caught her attention.

"I didn't see them anywhere. Are you quite sure that they left?"

"Yes, I watched them walking down the hallway toward the front door."

"Did they say where they were going?"

"Not to me. I was with another patient." Jason shook his head and turned to go muttering to himself. "Something is not right about this. Patrick would not have left, knowing I was on my way."

"Sir, just a moment please. I just remembered that the nurse who was with them. She went into the lounge to lie down because she is not feeling well. Would you like me to ask her if she knows anything?"

"Yes! Thank you." Jason watched as the nurse disappeared down the hall and through a door marked personnel only. Jason paced back and forth as he waited. "Angelina, there is someone asking about the two priest who were here."

Angelina stood up from the couch. "What does he look like?" she asked.

"Good-looking young man dressed in camos with a Vatican insignia on his sleeves and captain's bars on his lapel."

"Would you go back and ask what his name is, and if it is Jason, will you bring him back here? I need to speak to him in private, and please do not tell any one I spoke to him. Promise!"

"Yes, I promise," she said as she walked back down the hall. Coming up to him, she asked, "Is your name Jason?"

"Yes, it is. Why do you want to know?"

"Just come with me," she said. Jason followed her down the hall to the lounge door. "The nurse you need to see is Angelina. She is waiting for you inside." Jason opened the door to find standing in the middle of the room, a young nurse, and by her appearance, she looked like she had seen a ghost. "I am Jason," he said.

"I have a note for you from Monsignor O'Rourke," she said, handing the note to him. He read the outside and quickly scanned the inside. "Do you know who took them?"

"No!" she said, tearing up. "One of Don Vincenza men was standing in the hallway and one of the priests the one who was hurt recognized him and stepped back into the room. They asked if there was another way out, and I told them by the front door. The monsignor gave me this note for you, and then they left. I saw the man following them."

"What floor is the don on?" asked Jason.

"Seven I think, but please don't tell anyone I told you or that I let you know one of his men was here following the priest. He will think nothing of having me or some of my family killed."

"I will keep your secret." Jason assured her as he left.

Jason found the elevator and took it the seventh floor, checking with the nurse on duty. He got the don's room number. He made his way to the don's room and began knocking on the door.

"Come," he heard a woman's voice say. Jason opened the door. Bella rose from her chair and walked toward him.

"I am Captain Jason Sitzler from the Vatican. I need to speak to the don," Bella motioned toward the bed.

"As you can see, he has been sedated since the last Vatican visitor," she said.

"And who would that have been?"

"Father Anton. He upset the don so badly he had to be sedated."

"How long will he be out?"

"Several hours, I understand."

"Thank you, and you are?"

"I am Bella Amato, the don's wife."

Jason took out one of his cards and handed it to her. "Please have the don give me a call when he wakes up. It is very important that I speak with him."

"I will do my best," said Bella, taking the card.

Anton, the don, and Cardinal Pulaski—that certainly makes up an unholy trinity to say the least, thought Jason as he made his way back to the elevator.

When he got back to his car, he decided to call the archbishop. "Vatican city, how may I direct your call?"

"Connect me with Archbishop Valanti's private line. This is Captain Jason Sitzler."

"Immediately, sir." After a few rings, Jason heard the line pick up and the filmier voice of the archbishop, "Valanti here."

"Archbishop," said Jason. "I am just leaving St. Joseph's hospital."

"Are you all right, my son?"

"I'm fine. I came to pick up Patrick and Sebastian, but they are gone. The don's men picked them up before I had a chance. Patrick left me a note for you and me. See if you can get a hold of Mr. Mason and have him come to the Vatican and meet me in my office. I should be there in about fifteen minutes."

"That should not be a problem. Mat is here with me in the archives. On second thought, Jason, why don't you come here?"

"Sounds good. Don't tell anyone about our meeting," said Jason as he hung up started his car and headed back to the Vatican.

Jason called Inspector Capleno on his way back to the Vatican. "Lorenzo, I need your help, and this must be kept quiet," Jason said to his friend, when the inspector picked up the phone at his office in the central Rome police department. "Carlos, one of the Don Amato's men may have taken Monsignor O'Rourke and Brother Sebastian."

"So the monk really is still alive?"

"Yes. This has a lot to do with Pope Leo's death, I think. I am on my way to the Vatican to give Archbishop Valanti a note that Patrick left at the hospital before he and Sebastian left. Can you meet me in my office and if you have some way, put a lookout for Carlos and any of his men."

"I have a couple of matters that I need to take care of, but I will meet you as quickly as possible."

"Thanks, Lorenzo," said Jason and hung up.

Parking in his reserved spot, Jason made his way to the papal private archives. He had only been inside twice while on his tour of duty. Normally, only the keeper of the archives and the pope were allowed to enter. The pope's archive was located on the ground floor of one of the original building that made up the Vatican City. The guard at the door snapped to attention as he approached but did not move baring his access to the door. "Sorry, sir, I cannot let you pass."

"It's OK. I am expected. Call the archbishop, and he will allow me to come in." The guard made the call, and the door opened from the inside, and the archbishop came out and escorted Jason into the archives. Mat was seated at one of the long library tables, and he rose to greet Jason and shake his hands.

Jason took the paper out of his pocket and read what was written on it to them and then he filled them in on what he had found out at St. Joseph's. He then handed the note to the archbishop who read aloud what Sebastian had written. "It is imperative that we get the manuscript before anyone else does, and find Patrick and Sebastian," said the archbishop.

"We agree," the other two chimed in.

"I have called Inspector Capleno of the Rome Police who is a friend of mine. We have worked together many times. I am expecting him shortly. Let's get to work on finding the entrance Sebastian talks about. What do you know about the catacombs?" asked Jason.

"Not too much," said Mat.

"I have many maps and manuscripts that will tell us what we need to know, but it will take some time. Let's begin with the current plan of the old cemetery and the wall running beside the road Sebastian described." Valanti walked over to a large cabinet with a glass cover with what looked like a lot of pigeon holds in it and started pulling out rolled up documents. Some were maps, others were hand drawings of different parts of the catacombs.

Valanti began to unroll several and lay them on the table. "This one is the current map of the cemetery. It may or may not show any entrances to the catacombs below. Some of the tombs are actually down inside the catacombs. There are a few maps from the middle ages that may show places to enter the catacombs but many homes, offices, stores, and churches have been built in Rome over the years, blocking some of these entrances. Our glimmer of hope is that the street Sebastian talks about is one of the oldest in Rome. The name has changed over the years many times under many rulers, but it is the same road. This document is the oldest one I have. It dates back to the first century, showing where Christians hid and worshiped down there. Let's get started."

Jason stood back and let Mat and the archbishop pour over the maps. He was a solider not a historian. Several hours passed with no success. "We need to take a break and have something to eat," said Valanti.

"I am a bit hungry and am running out of steam," observed Mat.

"I will call and have something delivered. Sandwiches and coffee OK with you two?"

"Fine," they replied.

As Valanti called in the order, Mat asked Jason to read Sebastian's note once again as he looked over the current cemetery map, hoping that something would click with him. "Look, here is the road and the wall running parallel to it, but the map does not show any breaks where an entrance would be."

"Archbishop, you said the road has been here a long time. Just how long is that?"

"Well, it is part of the Appling way paved with stones so it would date back to before Christ." What is the date of the earliest document you have?" asked Mat.

"It would be a couple of centuries after the death of Christ."

"What was here before the cemetery? asked Mat, pointing to the map.

"Houses, a gym maybe, mostly anything, I guess," Valanti answered.

Do you have access to a copy machine that makes transparences?" asked Mat

"They should be able to that for us up in the Vatican library. Why do you ask?"

"We could take the oldest map we have that shows the entrances to the catacombs and overlay it onto the recent map and that may give us a clue as to where to look."

"That is a good idea, Mat." Valanti walked over to the shelves holding the maps and pulled out the oldest one he could find, showing what Mat asked for. "This is the oldest, but you see, it does not match up in size."

"Yes, but we can have it blown up to scale."

"Jason, would you take this map up to the library. I will call ahead, and they will be expecting you." Valanti called the head librarian and told him what he wanted.

Mat carefully rolled up the map and placed it in its protective covering. This being done handed it to Jason.

"I will hurry back as soon as the transparency is ready," said Jason, taking the map and leaving.

"Wait a moment please," said Valanti, crossing the room to his desk and taking out a piece of paper with the papal seal on the top. "You will need this to get past the guards here and in the library. It is an authorization for you to have this document. If you have any problems, call me on my private line."

"I will," replied Jason, taking the document and leaving.

"This appears to be the best chance we have in locating where Sebastian entered the catacombs," said Mat. They both sat down to wait. Not long had passed when there was a knock on the door. The archbishop got up and pressed the switch that electronically unlocked the door. One of the monks came in, pushing a cart with the food that had been ordered.

"I'm glad to see that," Mat said, getting up and coming toward the cart. "Should we wait for Jason?" he asked

"No, but we will save him some." They filled their plates and sat down at the archbishop's desk and ate in silence. They both jumped at the sound of the phone ringing on the archbishop's desk. Picking up the phone. "Valanti here," he answered.

"Archbishop this is Dominique in the Vatican lab at the library. At this time, we do not have a sterile lab available in which to unfold this ancient document and make the copy you requested."

"This is important, and time is of the essence," replied Valanti.

"But, your eminence, I am not allowed to do that. Only the head of the lab has such authority."

"Well, get him on the line so that I may speak to him."

"He is in a staff conference right now and cannot be disturbed."

"Dominique, just go and tell him, the head of the papal archives is on the line, and I believe he will talk to me."

"Yes, eminence." After about ten minutes, Valanti heard a male voice.

"Archbishop, how may I help you?"

"Have your people made the copy of the document I requested."

"It will be done immediately by me personally."

"Thank you" and Valanti hung up the phone. "Bureaucrats and their red tape, but hopefully, I have cut through it," he told Mat.

Chapter 33

"Hey, monk, put on the seat belt and then place your arms behind your back!" Sebastian did not move. Carlos slid up the seat, grabbing Sebastian by the ear, turning his head toward him, "Monk, do as I say, or your friend back here will get a bullet in his knee." Sebastian slowly fastened his seat belt. He knew if his arms were behind him, he would be helpless, but he knew Carlos would have no problem shooting Patrick. So he did as he was told.

Patrick watched Sebastian comply; he would rather have taken a bullet and seen Sebastian put up a fight. Traffic was heavy this afternoon, and he wondered if he opened the door and jumped out if he would survive. He was fairly sure that he would be run over at least once while they were in this center lane. He decided he would try if Marconie would get into the curb lane or at least stop at a traffic light.

Carlos had once again settled down in the seat beside him. Patrick could feel the blunt end of the barrel of Carlos's pistol pressing against his ribs. "Just sit back and relax, Monsignor, you are going to need all of your strength when we get to the warehouse."

"Step on it, Marconie. We need to get out of the city quickly."

"Right, boss," he said as he accelerated weaving in and out dangerously. Neither Patrick nor Carlos were wearing seat belts; they had been removed for some reason from the backseat of this sedan so they were in constant motion crashing against each other. Patrick hoped that the jostling would not cause Carlos pistol to go off accidentally.

"I'm going to hang a right in a couple of blocks from here near the forum. I know a short cut to get us out of this traffic."

Patrick thinking this may be his chance began to slide closer to the door, bracing himself against Carlos. He could just see the forum up ahead through the front window between Sebastian and Marconie. He took a deep breath, thinking this just may be his only chance. Marconie swung wide to make the turn without loosing any of his speed. There was a car double-parked right at the corner, so he veered left to avoid hitting it. Patrick pulled the door handle just as he made the left swing and the momentum of the swerve pulled the door open pulling Patrick with it.

Suddenly, there was a deafening explosion, and Patrick felt a fiery pain shoot through his chest and again on his right side as the bullet passed through his body. He was hanging onto the open door, watching as the pavement rolled by underneath him. Out of the corner of his eye, he saw the surprise on Carlos face that he was still hanging on the open door. He saw Carlos straining against the centrifugal force that was holding him down in the seat. Carlos had grabbed the top of the front seat and was pulling himself toward Patrick aiming the pistol this time at his head.

Patrick knew he had to let go. He forced himself to release his grip on the door, and the next thing he saw was the pavement coming up to meet him. He felt himself bouncing along for what seemed like eternity. The coat sleeves and pants knees he had on were soon worn away from being scuffed on the pavement. He could feel the skin being torn from his body. He could tell that his body was keeping up with the speed of the car, and he could see the door swinging above him before it slammed shut. The last thing he remembered was the acid smell of exhaust fumes and the odor of burning rubber then he felt himself hitting a stationary object and not moving any longer. The sudden stop jarred every bone and organ in his body, and then there was only blackness.

"What the hell just happened?" yelled Marconie.

"The priest jumped out of the car but not before I put a bullet in him first. If the bullet didn't kill him, the fall on the pavement will at this speed," said Carlos. "Get us out of here!"

The tourists, who were double-parked, stood looking on in horror as they watched as Patrick bounced down the street. He came to rest against one of the cars parked by the curb. His coat and shirt were in shreds as were his pants. Blood began to pool under where he lay. "Call 911, Willard," the woman screamed as she ran toward Patrick.

"I don't know if they have 911 here," he replied as he pulled out his cell phone. "It's 113 for the police," another passer by yelled.

Kneeling down beside Patrick, she placed her two fingers gently against his neck to feel for a pulse. "He is still alive," she hollered. "Bring me those napkins out of the glove box." Willard came up to her, handing her the napkins. "Did you get anyone?"

"Yes, the police. They are on their way."

"That must have been a gunshot we heard instead of a tire blowing. He is bleeding badly." A crowd began to gather.

"It's a priest," someone said.

"Who would be evil enough to shoot a priest?"

"Do any of you have any medical training?" The woman asked. No one moved or said anything.

"Willard, go back to the car and get me my coat to put under his head." She saw the blood was still coming fast from his side. She looked around and called out to the crowd, "Someone, anyone, I need a rag of some kind to apply pressure to his wound. If I can't stop the blood flow, he will soon be dead." A runner took the towel from around his neck and handed it to her. She folded it into a square and lifted up Patrick's shirt and placed it over the hole in his side and applied pressure. Where his clothes had been torn away so was the skin on his hands, arms, and legs. These wounds also seeped blood. *Thankfully,* she thought, *at least he is unconscious.* The pain she was sure would be severe.

In the distance above the sound of the traffic, they could hear the uneven sounds of the sirens heading their way. "Willard, did you also get an ambulance?"

"I just got the police, but I told them what had happened."

A police car came around the corner and slid to a stop just past where Patrick lay. Both officers jumped out and came and knelt beside Patrick and began to ask the woman questions.

"I don't speak Italian," she said.

"No problemo, madam," one of the officers said. She told them what had happened. She moved her hand holding the blood soaked towel. "He was shot here," she said once again applying pressure to the wound. One of the officers got a first-aid kit from his car. He opened and placed a pressure pack into her hand, and she removed the towel and put the pack into place still holding it firmly.

"He is also loosing a lot of blood from the other side." The officer used scissors to cut away the rest of Patrick's shirt and the top of his pants. Pulling them aside, revealing another whole seeping blood. The officer applied another pressure pack to this one.

One of the officers reached into Patrick's jacket pocket and found his wallet. Looking inside, he was surprised to learn from his driver's license just who Patrick was. "Call Inspector Capleno. He has ties with the Vatican and has a friend who is the captain of the Swiss Guards there, and tell him we have Monsignor O'Rourke, the late pope's private secretary here and that he has been shot."

The ambulance arrived and came to a stop behind the police car. A medic came to where they were kneeling over Patrick. Seeing all of the blood, he proceeded to cut off the remainder of Patrick's sleeves. Cleaning his arms with alcohol, he started an IV of ringer solution. He could tell by his blood pressure and his pulse that he would soon be slipping into shock. "Renaldo, get a stretcher over here now! He needs to be transported to the hospital immediately."

Catherine moved aside as they lifted Patrick up and onto the stretcher. She went over and stood beside her husband, watching as they loaded Patrick into the ambulance, and they watched as it left. One of the officers came over. "We may need to get a statement from you. Where are you staying in Rome?"

"The hotel Calone. We will be there until the end of next week."

"Thank you both. You may have saved his life."

"What name are you registered under?"

"Willard and Catherine Phillips."

"Thank you again. We will be in touch."

Willard and Catherine walked back to their car. Catherine glanced back to where Patrick laid his blood still pooled on the pavement. Something caught her eye, something shining in the late afternoon sun; she walked back over and picked it up. It was a gold key on a chain; the chain had been broken. The key had symbols on it, one which she recognized from the tour of the Vatican they had that morning. The priest must have had it around his neck. She went back to the car and climbed in beside her husband showing him what she had found. She put it into her purse for safekeeping. They would try to find the priest and return it later. Now, they decided that they must go back to the hotel; she needed to shower and change because she was covered in blood.

The inspector was just leaving the office when the call came in about Monsignor O'Rourke. He returned to his desk. He had just talked to Jason earlier and was on his way to meet him. They had talked regarding the pope's death yesterday. This was indeed strange, considering what Jason had just told him. Now the pope's secretary being shot along with the mystery of the monk's resurrection from the dead, all of this was very strange indeed. He took out his cell and hit redial on the number Jason had called him from. "Captain Sitzler's office" came the reply.

"This is Inspector Capleno of the Rome Police. May I speak to your captain?"

"He is out of the office at the present time. Would you like to leave him a message?"

"No! This is of utmost importance. Find him for me."

"Sir, he is in the papal archives with Archbishop Valanti. Let me give you his personal cell number. This will be the best way to contact him. It is 3337129465."

"Thank you." The inspector dialed the number and waited.

"This is Jason Sitzler" came the answer.

"Jason, this is Lorenzo. I was on my way over when I received a call. Sorry to be the bearer of bad news, but it is about your friend Monsignor O'Rourke. Some tourists saw him either being thrown or jumping from a car near the forum not long ago. It looks like he has been shot." Hearing this, Jason nearly dropped his phone. Stooping down to retrieve it, he managed to reply, "Is he alive?"

"Just barley. They are taking him to Metro Central Hospital. I am on my way over there."

"I will meet you as soon as I can get away," Jason replied as he hung up his phone. He did not realize he had sat down during the conversation.

"Captain, here is the document that you need and the original." Jason took both and headed back to the papal archives.

"Captain!" called someone behind him. "You forgot your paperwork."

"Thank you," he replied.

Chapter 34

The sound of the shot still echoed in Sebastian's ears. The smell of gunpowder and seared flesh made him sick. He pulled his arms out from behind himself and started to unbuckle his seatbelt. He felt an arm going around his neck and choking him.

"Settle down, monk!" said Carlos, tightening his arm and cutting off Sebastian's air supply. "I know that you are not afraid to die, and I assure you that you will be meeting up with your friend soon enough. But I know you don't want to cause the death of some innocent person, do you?" asked Carlos. Sebastian stopped struggling, and Carlos loosened his grip. Sebastian took a deep breath. "Pull over in front of that store," he told Marino. "If you don't do as I say, monk, the next person who comes out will die. Now lean forward." Sebastian did as he was told.

"Marino, take these plastic cuffs and tie the monk's hands together behind his back." Marino pulled Sebastian's arms behind him and did what Carlos ordered.

"Now, monk, sit back and behave for the rest of our ride."

Marino pulled the sedan back out and into the afternoon traffic. "No need to hurry now," said Carlos. "We don't want to be stopped by the Rome police. You will have a short reprieve from what I have planned for you, monk. I need to speak with the don first."

Sebastian had no fear of Carlos or what lay ahead; his heart was filled with sorrow at the loss of the pope and Monsignor O'Rourke. His only hope was that he could hold out until Jason and the archbishop found the manuscript. He was already in pain from the cuts on his chest and leg. *The body is weak*, he thought, but his mind and will were strong.

Through the fog of pain and stress, Patrick felt what his mind conceived to be motion. The bright light he had seen as he leaped from the car quickly changed to blackness, and he felt nothing. Now the blackness was turning to light like a morning fog lifting and through the fog was pain; pain like he had never felt before. With each sensation of motion and movement came a sharp jolt of pain flashing through his body like a burst of lighting. With that last jolt came the blackness again.

"Ahhhh!" he heard someone screaming, and he felt hands touching his body, and everywhere they touched on his arms and legs, it burned like fire. He heard muffled voices all around him and then the bright light was back, but it was different this time. Behind the light seemed to be a face, and it was calling his name. Was this heaven or had he landed in purgatory? He tried to open his eyes, but they would not open. He tried to speak and that didn't work either. Then he felt hands again, and they seemed to be all over him feeling, probing it felt like the hands were now inside of him and then he heard the scream again, but this time he realized it was his screams. Then there was a bee sting feeling on his arm, and he felt a warm sensation crawling up his arm and then he felt nothing.

"Nurse, the sedative is working. Continue cutting the rest of his clothes off, and let us begin to clean up the concrete burns on his arms and legs. Give him another pint of plasma. He has lost a lot of blood.

"Doctor, here is the MRI. It shows that the bullet entered his left side near his rib cage and was deflected by his breastbone and exited on the right side just passing through the outer layer of skin. He was very lucky other than a few busted ribs and a broken sternum and the holes in both sides, but there is was no other internal injury. What he sustained is very painful but not life threatening."

The ride through Rome to the warehouse was uneventful. Sebastian recognized the warehouse immediately. And his mind was flooded with memories from his first visit here. "I will get out and open the big door, so no one will see us getting out of the car with the monk," said Carlos exiting the vehicle and going to the door. He punched in the code, and the door slowly began to rise. It was pitch black, inside so Carlos went in ahead of the car and turned on the lights. As soon as Marino was safely inside, Carlos closed the door.

The door next to Sebastian opened, and Carlos loosened his seat belt and grabbed his right arm and pulled him from the car. This way, his arms had been tied behind him, and Carlos pulling him out caused several of the stitches to break loose, and the wound on his chest came open. Sebastian felt warm liquid running down his chest and puddling around his waist where his belt was.

"Take him back down to the basement and tie him to a chair and lock the door." Marino took Sebastian by the arm and led him toward the stairs. It was damp and cold down there just like he remembered. the dank musty smell assailed his nose, and it began to run. Marino flipped the switch, and one single light came on in the hall at the foot of the stairs. Marino pushed Sebastian along. The door where he had been jailed before was still standing open. Marino led him inside and forced him into the metal chair against the wall, and after tying him to it, he slammed and locked the door, leaving Sebastian in total darkness. Sebastian lowered his head and began to pray.

"All done, boss," Marino reported when he returned.

"You stay here with him and make sure he is here when I return."

"Will do."

"I am going back to the hospital to see if the don is awake yet. I will take the small Scion and leave the black sedan here just in case the Rome police are looking for it."

Carlos left by the office entrance at the front of the building. The Scion was parked in its usual space. Carlos got in, backed out, and headed toward St. Joseph's hospital.

Chapter 35

Jason made his way back to the archives in a daze.

"Captain, are you all right?" the question startled Jason back into reality.

"Yes."

"You look like you have seen a ghost."

"Just some bad news. Call the archbishop to unlock the door." The guard made the call, and in a short time, the door opened, and the archbishop came out.

"Jason, my son, are you all right?" Without answering, he took Valanti by the arm and guided him back inside.

"Archbishop, I have grave news," and he told him and Mat what the inspector had said.

"O my God, please help your two beloved children," Valanti whispered a prayer.

"The inspector is on his way over there. I told him I would meet him as soon as I could."

"I will come with you," said Valanti.

"No! It is more important that you stay here and work with Mat. That is what Patrick would want. I will call as soon as I know anything."

"You are right, of course, but I will have a hard time concentrating until I know whether he is alive or not."

"I promise I will let you know." Jason handed Mat the two documents and started for the door.

"Buzz me out. I want to be there close to the time the inspector arrives."

"God go with you, my son," said Valanti as he unlocked the door.

Jason returned the guard's salute as he passed, hurrying toward his office on the first floor near the main entrance of the office complex. He heard his cell ringing.

"Jason here."

"Jason, this is Lorenzo. Wait for me at your office. I should be there in ten minutes."

"I'll be here." Jason took the steps instead of the elevator. Coming out of the stairwell door, he ran face-to-face with Father Anton.

"Captain Sitzler, I was just on my way to see you. The cardinal wants to know if you have seen or talked to Monsignor O'Rourke today. As far as we can tell, he left early this morning and had not returned."

"No, I have not seen him today."

"Do you know if his absence has anything to do with the missing Brother Sebastian? I saw him yesterday talking to a group of the brothers out in the square."

"He has not mentioned any of that to me."

"Well, if you see him, tell him that the cardinal is anxious to talk to him about several things."

"I will be sure to do that," answered Jason as he continued on his way down the hall toward his office. He could feel the eyes of Father Anton boring into his back. He hoped his lie had not been detected.

He entered his office space, and the duty officer told him that the inspector had just arrived and was seated in his private office. Jason thanked him and walked down the hall and entered his office. The inspector was seated in one of the chairs, facing Jason's desk. "Lorenzo, it's good to see you again," said Jason, extending his hand.

"And you also," said the inspector, taking Jason's extended hand and shaking it warmly.

"Do you have any further news on Patrick or Sebastian?"

"Patrick is in Metro central. I have one of my detectives guarding him. He called to say that Patrick is resting comfortably, and his injuries are not life threatening. As for Sebastian, I have no word. I have as you requested made some discrete inquires around Rome to some of my informants asking if they have seen Carlos and have heard nothing so far."

"Thanks, I am relieved to hear the good news about Patrick."

"Are you available now to go to the hospital with me?" the inspector asked.

"Yes! I want to be there when he wakes up."

"Jason, are you armed?"

"No, why?"

"I think it would be a good idea in case of trouble."

"OK, give me a moment." Jason went to his closet and pulled out his shoulder holster and reached into his desk draw for his Beretta. Checking the clip, he shoved it into his holster. "Let's head out." He said and led the inspector through the door. Stopping at the duty officer's desk he called the archbishop and let him know that Patrick was OK. "Do you want me to drive?" asked Jason.

"No! I have my official car and a driver at the curb."

"Sounds good," said Jason.

The inspector climbed into the front seat beside the driver and Jason settled into the backseat. "Fill me in on what is going on," said the inspector.

"I think I should wait until we are in private," replied Jason, nodding toward the driver.

"This is Sergeant Remetta, one of my most trusted detectives. You may speak freely in front of him. He has many underground contacts which may prove very helpful." Jason filled them in on most of what had happened, beginning with the night of Pope Leo's death. He left out the part about the catacombs and the hidden manuscript. He let them think that it was still lost.

"Seems like the cardinal and the don have a vested interest in Sebastian and whatever is in that manuscript. But I don't see how the pope's death figures in on what happened to you that night."

"I know, but I have a gut feeling it is all connected." The Sergeant wheeled the car into the hospital parking lot.

"Park in the reserved police space, Sergeant, near the front door."

"Yes, sir" came the reply.

"Stay with the car and call me if you hear from any of our people."

"Yes, sir."

"OK, Jason let's go in." They both exited the car and entered the hospital.

"Man, this is a big place," Jason commented.

"Yes, it is. This hospital has the best trauma center in Rome. We bring most of the accident victims here and all the police who are injured. We have a secure floor just for our use. That should keep Monsignor O'Rourke safe."

"This makes St. Joseph's look like a clinic. I have passed it many times, but until you see it up close and come inside, you have no idea how big it really is," commented Jason.

The inspector led the way up to the main information desk. It appeared to be made out of solid marble and was manned by four people sitting at computer terminals. One of the people greeted the inspector. "Good to see you this evening, Lorenzo."

"Thank you. And how are your husband and the children?"

"Fine, thank you for asking. What brings you here tonight? There are no officers as patients at this time."

"I am here to see the priest who was in the accident today. Is he still in emergency?"

"Let me check. Do you have a name?"

"No! He was admitted as a John Doe."

"Oh yes, you have a detective with him I see. He is in room 904 in the east tower on the secure floor."

"Thanks," he said, leading Jason toward the bank of elevators.

The hospital was unusually quiet at this time of the night, so there was no one else on the elevator with them. They exited on the ninth floor and looked at the signage to figure out which way to go. Jason spotted it first. "This way," he said, heading down the hall to the left. "Here it is," he said, knocking on the door. A man in a dark brown suit opened the door, seeing Inspector Capleno. He stepped aside and let them pass. "Jason, this is Detective Gillespie, one of my team."

"Pleased to meet you," he replied, extending his hand. Jason walked over to the bed. Patrick was lying under a blanket and wearing the standard hospital gown. An IV line ran from his arm up to a bag on a pole attached to the bed. His face looked peaceful and unharmed. Both of his arms were bandaged. "What's the report on him?"

"The nurse was just in. He is doing remarkably well."

"Would you get her for me?"

"Yes, captain."

"Until he wakes up we will not know much."

"I agree," answered the inspector.

There was a knock on the door, and the nurse came in. "What can you tell us about his condition?" asked Jason. She gave them an update on his treatment and the prognosis.

"How long will he be out?"

"He was given protocol, which is a fast acting but short-term anesthesia. He should be coming out of it in about an hour."

"Let's go down and get something to eat while we wait," said Jason.

"There is a café in the lobby that is not bad. Salvatore, we will not be too long. As soon as we get back, you can take a break for a couple of hours. But stay close, in case I need you."

"Thank you, Inspector," he replied. Jason and the inspector left.

"If he begins to awaken, call me," said the nurse. "I will return immediately."

Jason and Lorenzo went down to the café and ordered some coffee and a couple of sandwiches. "I know this will be on the news. Do the reporters have his name?"

"No, but they do know where we transport accident victims."

"Will the hospital switchboard have his name?"

"Not unless we release it. It is standard procedure to hold all information until next of kin is notified. In Patrick's case, all permission has to come directly from me."

"That's good," said Jason.

The inspector's cell began to ring. "Inspector Capleno here. Yes, thank you." "Carlos has been seen heading toward St. Joseph's driving a two-door red Scion. My people will follow him when he leaves. I had sent a couple of detectives over to watch the hospital where the don is a patient, after I got your call that the monsignor and Sebastian had been taken."

Chapter 36

Carlos gunned the four-cylinder engine of the Scion and merged into traffic and turned right heading toward St. Joseph's hospital. It was a good forty-minute drive even in the light early evening traffic. He had good news to give to the don, although he also had some bad news. Shooting the monsignor, a priest of the church, was not ever good. Carlos turned on the radio, hoping to get a local Rome news cast that was giving current events other than just broadcasting funeral music or updates on the plans for the funeral for Pope Leo or the arrival of some cardinal or another. He was having no luck so far. There was much speculating on who would be the next pope. He switched to yet another station, and this caught his attention.

"In local events today, there was a priest shot and thrown from a car near the Forum. A couple of tourists witnessing the event could only say that it was a black sedan with Rome plates. The priest was taken to Metro but as of this hour we have no report on his condition." Carlos turned off the radio. He called the number for Metro.

"Metro Hospital, how may I direct your call?"

"I just wanted to ask about the priest that was brought in. What room is he in?"

"Sorry, sir, I cannot give out that information without a name."

"Monsignor O'Rourke"

"Sorry we don't have a patient by that name."

"Are you sure?"

"Quite sure."

"Thank you." *That was strange. Either he is dead of they don't know who he is,* Carlos thought. *I will have to go over to Metro after I leave St. Joseph's.* The rest of the drive to St. Joseph's was uneventful. Carlos turned on the radio again, finding a station playing American soft rock and settle back enjoying the music. St. Joseph's loomed up ahead.

It was one of Rome's older hospitals being build after the Second World War. The nuns and the nursing staff were the best in Rome for care. Carlos parked in the front lot and climbed the marble steps toward the front door. The lobby was bustling with people leaving for supper. He had no reason to stop at the information desk. He knew where the don's room was located. He pushed the up button, and the doors slowly opened. There was something about old bronze doors and wood paneling in an elevator that relayed strength and reliability. Carlos pushed seven and leaned back against the side of the car as it rose slowly but did not stop at any floor. He heard a *ding* and glanced up to see seven on the floor register. The doors opened, and he stepped out into a recently cleaned floor; a pleasant odor of pine lingered in the hall. He proceeded down the hall to the don's room, knocking before he entered.

"Come" came the muffled voice of Bella from inside. Rising to greet the visitor she said, "Carlos, I was just about to call you. Vincenza is awake and has been asking for you."

"Carlos come over to me," called Vincenza.

Carlos approached the bed. The don was in a partial sitting positing but still looked pale and drawn. "What news do you have for me?"

Carlos leaned close. "It would be better if Bella were not here to hear what I have to say."

"Yes, of course. Bella, could you give us a moment alone my angel?"

"Yes, if you wish. How long will you be here, Carlos?"

"I will stay with him until you return. Take as long as you wish."

"I will go down and get a bite to eat and take a short stroll," she said, walking over to give Vincenza a kiss. Vincenza and Carlos watched her leave.

"Well?" said the don, giving Carlos a questioning look. Carlos pulled up a chair and sat beside the don.

"First, we have Sebastian. He is tied up back at the warehouse. Marino is watching him."

"That's good news," said the don. "I must call Cardinal Pulaski right away" reaching for the phone on the bedside table. Carlos reached out and grabbed the don's hand.

"What are you doing? How dare you touch me!"

"Sorry, sir, but you need to hear something else first."

The don cradled the phone. "OK, Carlos, what else is more important than this?" Carlos filled him in beginning with finding Sebastian downstairs in the emergency room up to and through shooting Patrick. The don looked paler than before.

"You killed Monsignor O'Rourke and left the body on the side of the road near the Forum? Are there any witnesses that can tie this to you in any way? Are you sure he is dead or could he have survived?"

"I listened to the news on the way over, and they reported the incident, but did not name Monsignor O'Rourke, only that a priest was shot and taken to Metro. I called, but they do not have him as a patient."

"If it is a police matter, the desk will not have that information. You need to go there and check it out for yourself. If he survived and is still alive and unconscious, you need to finish what you started, before he tells them where to look for Sebastian and who has him. Do you understand?"

"Yes, Don, I do."

"I still need to call Cardinal Pulaski and tell him we have Sebastian. I will just omit the rest until you finish your part. Now Go!"

"But I told Bella I would stay until she retuned."

"Carlos, you answer to me not to Bella, and I said go." Carlos put the chair back where it was and left the room.

Seeing the nurse, he asked, "Where would the don's wife go to get a bite at this time?"

"There is a coffee bar just off the lobby." Carlos took the elevator back to the first floor. When he stepped out, he looked around, searching for the coffee bar. He walked to the center of the lobby and turned slowly looking. In the far corner, he spotted the bar.

Walking over, he saw Bella sitting in a corner booth. "Bella," he said, "the don has sent me on an errand. You may want to take your coffee and sandwich back up to the room."

"Thank you, Carlos, for finding me. I will do as you say." Carlos smiled at Bella and turned and left. It had gotten dark quickly tonight. The lamps in the lot were already on. The parking lot was just about empty. Visiting hours would soon be over. Carlos spotted a familiar face looking at him from a passing car. He gave him a curt nod in recognition.

Carlos climbed into his car. Metro was a good hour from here, and he had not eaten yet. Pulling out of the hospital lot, he decided to go a few bocks back and eat at Mama Leonie's. Some of her good pasta would hit the spot. The drive there was pleasant and soothed his nerves after his visit with the don. His stomach began to growl. *It won't be long now,* he thought, patting his belly. *A little pasta washed down with a bottle of Vino will do just fine.* Mama's was busy; there were several people waiting. Carlos pushed his way through the crowd, causing a few angry stares. Mama's always kept an empty booth toward the back for Carlos and his crew. He settled in it, and one of the staff came over with a bottle of his favorite Vino and a menu. He had an hour or so to kill. He wanted to be sure visitors' hours were long over. *I don't need any witnesses,* he thought. *I will be there during shift change.* The police may not know that one of the don's contacts within the department tipped us off long ago that the ninth floor at Metro. It is where they kept prisoners, accident victims, and the wounded police. All I have to do is put on a white smock and carry a clipboard, and I can go into any room I like without being bothered. Getting rid of the monsignor should be a piece a cake as they say. It will look like he died in his sleep. Carlos poured himself another glass of wine.

Don Vincenza picked up his cell and found Cardinal Pulaski's personal number and hit the send button. After a few rings, he heard the cardinal's voice. "Don Amato, you must be feeling better. Anton said you were not doing well when he came to visit."

"I am somewhat better, your eminence. I called to let you know that we have captured Brother Sebastian. He is, as we speak, locked in the basement of my warehouse just outside of Rome."

"Well, well, Don, that is good news. Does he have the manuscript with him?"

"No, he must have hidden it somewhere while he has been on the run. But do not worry, I will get that information out of him."

"Do what you must, but do not kill him. He is of use to me. If you are unable to get the information, call me back, and I will send my messenger over and it will do the job. You are familiar with it, aren't you?" The thought made the don's skin crawl. "Just to make sure you do your job, I am going to send over Anton to watch."

The phone in the don's hand went dead. A feeling of dread crept over him as his mind replayed the events of the last couple of days.

Chapter 37

Sebastian strained against the ropes that held him securely to the metal chair. The ropes were cutting into his wrist. His chest gave him sharp pains with every breath where Carlos had ripped the wounds open when he had Marino pinned his arms behind his back. Being tied in that position kept pulling the wounds open more and more. The blood continued to run down his chest matting the hair on his stomach and pooling at his waistline. He could stand the pain, but the darkness, dampness, and cold were beginning to get to him. He felt like he was drowning as the wet cold crept into his bones.

He had no idea how long he had been down here, but it was probably nightfall by now. There was no sound coming down to him. He was cloaked in silence except for the sound of his breathing. He began to pray that God would give him the strength to hold onto the information or let him die before they broke him. Carlos was cruel. He could expect no mercy, nor could he expect the cardinal to protect him once he gave them the location of the manuscript; he was as good as dead. The cardinal could find someone else to do the translation.

"Oh God, forgive me," he cried from the depths of his soul. "How could I have been so blind as to trust in a man I knew to be filled with so much ambition? Who has sought his whole life to sit on the throne of Peter since I have known him? He was an archbishop when we first met, and I was only a student. I was assigned to him as a novice, just beginning my training in the brotherhood. I was always a quick learner and eager to please. Pulaski took an interest in me and in my abilities to learn languages quickly, and almost immediately, I began working for him as a translator. I should have known then by some of his dealing and the people they were with that they were evil people. On several occasions, I suspected what I was doing for him was illegal, but by then, I was in too deeply to get out, and I had also involved my two brothers in one of his schemes.

"On that night things had gone horribly wrong, the police were tipped off, and one of my brothers was wounded, and the other shot and killed one of the police officers. Pulaski and his men got my brothers to safety.

"Pulaski kept the pistol with my brother's fingerprints and blood on it and has held that over my head making me do his bidding, and he still does. I thought I had to protect my brothers and their families at all cost, but the cost has become too great.

"My mistake was underestimating how evil Pulaski was. Once he got into the archives and found the key and used its power on Leo, I knew he had to be stopped.

"He became suspicious when I quit giving him additional information from the manuscript. I knew time was running out so I ran. I should have gotten out of Rome quickly, but I wanted to warn the pope first.

"That was a mistake, because I knew that Pulaski had the web of the mafia on his side. Carlos found me not once but twice. I had been lucky the first time, but I think my luck is fast running out."

Sebastian heard footsteps coming down the hallway, the scratching of a key being fitted into a lock. The door hinges screeched as it was pushed open. The light from the hall was for Sebastian as bright as the sun, temporarily blinding him. In the doorway, he could make out the shapes of two men but that was all he could see. They entered the room.

"Sebastian, I have a visitor to see you." The voice was Mario.

"Well, Well, Brother Sebastian, how good of you to see me." Sebastian also recognized that voice, and it sent chills up his spine.

"Father Anton, what brings you here to see me? If I had known you were coming, I would have left."

"Sebastian, I would not have missed this meeting for the world. The cardinal sends you his blessings."

"You can tell him for me to keep his blessing. He will need them more than I will."

"You can end this now and save yourself much pain and suffering. Just give me the manuscript, and I will have Carlos end your life quickly. Then if we need you again, our beloved cardinal can summon you from purgatory using the key you so graciously provided to him."

"I would rather die than give him anymore power than he already has."

"Why let your death be in vain? Once he is elected pope, he will have full access to all of the Vatican's secrets."

"No, he will have only the one he has now. The first Leo hid the other keys, and only the one who has the manuscript will be able to find them. Besides, they will never elect him pope."

"I would not be so sure of that, my dear Brother. Things are progressing rather well from what I hear. It would take something big to happen to stop him getting the votes he needs."

"One thing, Anton, you have not taken into consideration. I am not the only one who knows what he has done. God knows and will not allow him to sit on the throne of Peter."

"You really do have some faith. We will see how long it lasts once Carlos gets back here and begins to work on you. Mario, have you heard from Carlos?"

"He called to tell me he is on his way to Metro to get a report on Monsignor O'Rourke's condition, and if he is not already dead, he soon will be."

"You see, Sebastian, we have everything under control. Now tell me what I want to know."

"I will tell you nothing."

"We will see about that when Carlos returns."

Mario and Father Anton walked out of the room, and Mario slams the door. Sebastian hears the lock click shut and is once again in total darkness.

Chapter 38

Jason and Inspector Capleno stepped out of the elevator and were met by Detective Gillespie. "The nurse just left after checking his vital signs. He is doing much better than they expected."

"You can take some time off while we are here, but stay close by. On your way out, tell Detective Remetta I said to stay put. Tell him, I have been told that Carlos is on his way over here. It is important that I know the moment he arrives."

"Yes, Inspector, I will do as you say."

"Jason, you go ahead into Monsignor O'Rourke's room. I need to speak to the security office here in the hospital and make some arrangements to have him moved." Jason proceeded down the hall to Patrick's room.

He knocked on the door before he entered.

"Come in," he heard Patrick say. Jason entered the room.

"Patrick, welcome back from the dead. I knew I was to pick you up at the hospital, but this is the wrong one."

"Very funny, Jason."

"You look better than I thought your would." "I am not up to par yet, but I'm getting there. Have you had any word about Sebastian?"

"The only thing we know is what you told me in your note. Sebastian is still missing. Do you remember where they were going to take the two of you?"

"Yes, he was to have taken us to a warehouse outside of Rome. It was the same one he used to keep Sebastian before."

"There are over a hundred warehouses in that area. It will take weeks to search all of them. Did he say anything else that might narrow it down?"

"No, just that he was taking us back to the same warehouse."

"Did Sebastian say anything?"

"No, not a word. Carlos had him in a choke hold just before I jumped and was pinning his arms back behind his back and putting plastic cuffs on him."

"The road you were turning onto, will it give us any clue?"

"Marino, the driver said it was a shortcut that would get us out of the traffic and the city quickly."

The inspector came in the door. "Monsignor O'Rourke, I am Inspector Lorenzo Capleno. I have worked with Jason on several cases involving the Vatican."

"Thank you for coming, Inspector."

"Patrick had been filling me in on what happened and a possible location for Sebastian." Jason filled in the inspector on the information Patrick had provided.

"We have been aware that the don has several warehouses he used from time to time down by the docks. You were telling Jason that the road where you jumped out was a shortcut. As a matter of fact, it is. But it will still give us twenty to thirty warehouses to search. Once we begin the search, he will soon figure it out and smuggle Sebastian out or kill him. I was just meeting with the hospital security. We have a tail on Carlos, and he is headed this way. Someone called earlier asking for you by name to see if you were a patient here. The operator told them that you were not. Then they asked if the priest in the accident was a patient. She said she could not give out information. She reported the call to security, which alerted Detective Gillespie who I have guarding you. Monsignor, if the, Don, thinks you are dead, they may leave Sebastian where he is, and Carlos will lead us there."

"Inspector, how can we do this?"

"We will need to get you out of the hospital and back to the Vatican after Carlos sees you are dead."

"What do I need to do?" asked Patrick.

"You will just have to lie still and hold your breath. Oh by the way, you will have to lie on one of the tables in the morgue. I will take care of the rest."

"I am in yours and God's hands."

"Jason, stay here with the monsignor, and I will make the arrangements. We will have to move quickly with as few people involved as possible. We know that Carlos has some contacts within the hospital staff, but we have never found out who they are." The inspector left.

"Patrick, are you up to this?"

"I will do what I need to do to stop Carlos and Pulaski. Have you been in touch with Archbishop Valanti?"

"Yes, I called him from the hallway. He knows that you are all right."

"Get back in touch with him and tell him our plan."

Patrick's nurse came in. "Monsignor, I will need to take out your IV and redress your wounds."

"Do you have my clothes?"

"Yes, they are in the closet. What is left of them, but you can't put them on. I am sorry to say you can't have anything on."

"What!"

"Sorry, but in the morgue, you will have to be totally nude covered by a sheet."

"Jason, will you get my clothes and see if my billfold is there and the key," Patrick said, running his hand over his chest where it had hung. Jason walked over to the closet. Patrick's clothes were hanging on a hook. His coat had his billfold in the breast pocket where the police officer had replaced it after finding out Patrick's identity. His ripped shirt and pants were also there. Jason went through the other coat pockets and his pants pockets but did not find the key.

"It's not here," he said to Patrick.

"Nurse, I had a key on a chain around my neck. Have you seen it?"

"No, Father, it was not on you when your were brought up to the floor. I will call down to the emergency room and see if it is there." She left to make the call.

Jason was on his cell with Valanti. He ended his call. "All will be ready when you get to the Vatican. We will bring you in through the tunnel, and you will stay in the Swiss Guard guest quarters where I will be sure you are safe. Valanti will be there to meet you."

The nurse returned to finish dressing Patrick's wounds. "Sorry, Father, both the nurse and the doctor who attended you said there was not key around your neck when you came in."

Patrick's face fell at the news. "This is not good. It must have come off at the accident scene where I jumped. Jason, go and find the inspector and ask him if he can send out a car and search the scene and talk to the officers who were there. We have got to find that key."

"Will do," Jason said heading for the door. Seeing the inspector at the nurse's station, he headed over to him.

"Lorenzo, we have another problem," he said. Jason told him what was needed. The inspector's cell began to ring. "Yes, I see."

Turning to Jason. "We have more pressing problems. Carlos has just pulled into the parking lot."

"What do you need me to do?"

"Get that gurney over there, and take it to the monsignor's room. I have one more call to make." Pressing in a number into his cell in a moment, he heard Detective Remetta's voice answer. "When Carlos enters the hospital, I want you to drive around back and park where the hearses usually pick up the bodies from the morgue."

"Will do." The Inspector put his cell in his pocket and walked down to Patrick's room.

The nurse had Patrick lying on the gurney covered in a sheet all but his head. "Sorry, monsignor but we will have to cover your face for the journey to the morgue."

"I understand, Inspector. Do what you must do."

"Nurse, go and get me the two orderlies, we will need. It will look better if they are pushing the gurney down to the morgue. Jason and I will accompany you."

The nurse came back with the orderlies. She pulled the sheet up over his face. He felt the gurney moving out of the room and into the hall. Patrick could see the hallway lights through the sheet flashing by as he went under them. He closed his eyes because the motion and the lights moving past was making him sick. He was jolted as they stopped at the elevator.

The ride down to the basement left his stomach hanging somewhere on the ninth floor. He did not think he could continue to swallow the bile that was coming up from his stomach. Coming out of the elevator, there was a temperature change. It was cold down here. He heard an electric door sliding open, and the smell of death and antiseptics filtered down to him through the sheet, causing him to heave. The bile was now all over him and the sheets.

Jason pulled the sheet off Patrick's face and body and began to wipe the vomit off his face and neck. "Sorry," Patrick said to Jason.

"It's all right. Get me a couple of clean sheets" Jason yelled to the orderlies. He helped Patrick sit up and pulled the dirty sheet out from under him and threw it in a bin.

The orderlies slid Patrick over onto a clean gurney and rolled the other one against the wall. Patrick lay back down, and Jason covered him up with a clean sheet.

"Monsignor, we are going to roll you into an autopsy room that has a window opening to the hallway. This is the one we use for identification of bodies by families. You will be in there with a doctor acting like he is prepping you for an autopsy. Jason and I will be just outside the door. Are you sure you feel up to this?"

"I'll be fine," Patrick lied. They rolled Patrick into the room. "Just lie still. We will signal the doctor to tell you when to hold your breath." Having said this, Jason and the inspector left.

The inspector's cell rang. *I need to put this on vibrate,* he thought to himself as he answered, "Capleno here."

"Carlos has just taken the elevator to the ninth floor. His inside contact has given him a smock and stethoscope. He looks just like a doctor. I am going to my assigned position just outside the morgue."

"Thanks. Carlos is here and is dressed as a doctor. I will notify Gillespie," the inspector said, ending the call.

Detective Gillespie had barley closed his cell, when he saw Carlos step out of the elevator and cross over to the nurse's desk. He watched the exchange. "Nurse, I have been asked by the Holy See to check up on the priest you have here as a patient."

"I am sorry to inform you that he passed away a short time ago."

"Is his body still in his room?"

"No, he has just been taken to the morgue. You missed him by a few minutes."

"I need to see his body for identification."

"You will find his body in the morgue, Doctor, located in the basement of the hospital."

"Thank you," said Carlos as he started back to the elevator.

Gillespie called the inspector, "He is on his way." The inspector turned to Jason. "Signal the doctor. Carlos is on the way, and tell him to make sure the door to the hall is locked."

Carlos rode the elevator to the basement. He followed the signs to the morgue. As he passed through the sliding door and into the morgue, he approached the orderly manning the desk.

"I am here to identify the priest for the Holy See. Where can I view the body?"

"He is in autopsy room A down the hall, but you can't be admitted once the autopsy has begun. You can watch through the window." Carlos made his way down the passageway. Autopsy room A was brightly lit. He tried the door; it was locked. He pressed the bell button. The doctor on duty in the room answered through his headphones.

"Yes!"

"I need to come in and identify the body."

"Sorry, doctor, that is against the hospital's rules."

"How can I do my job of identification?"

"I can roll the gurney closer to the window if you like. That is how most identifications are done."

"Yes, yes, do that," Carlos said.

"OK, its showtime," the doctor whispered into Patrick's ear.

"When I pull the sheet from your face, do not breath," he warned.

Patrick felt the gurney slowly moving. His eyes were closed. When it stopped, he felt the sheet being folded down off his face. Now his face and feet were showing. He had a tag on his toe that had him listed as John Doe.

"How is that doctor? Pull the sheet all the way off him"

"That is a bit unusual."

"I want to make sure it is Monsignor O'Rourke. I am told that he has a small birthmark on his left shoulder. Lift him up and roll him over so I can see it." The doctor pulled the sheet down to Patrick's waist and lifted him up showing his birthmark. Suddenly a sharp pain from being lifted shot through Patrick's body, causing his right leg to jerk. The doctor laid him back down.

"His leg just moved."

"Doctor, you know that it is not unusual as rigor sets in for muscles to contract. I have had a corpse sit up on the table before." Pulling the sheet back over Patrick's body, he fans it a couple of times, giving Patrick a chance to breathe.

"What was the cause of death?"

"As far as I can determine, he bled out from the wound on his side. But I will not know for certain until the autopsy is complete. Is that all?"

"Yes," said Carlos, turning to leave. A smile curled up his mouth. *One down and one to go,* he thought. *There will be no question as to the cause of the monk's death.*

After about fifteen minutes, the inspector's cell rang. "All clear, Carlos has left the parking lot with the tail on him."

"It's clear. Let's get the monsignor ready and get him back to the Vatican."

Chapter 39

Cardinal Pulaski sat in his office, going over the schedule for the public viewing of the pope's body in Saint Peters Basilica. The cardinals had escorted his body there yesterday and celebrated a Mass in his honor.

It had been a busy few days since Leo's death and talk about Leo's successor were rampant. Although he could not openly campaign for the job until they were sealed in conclave. Ah, but his good friend Cardinal Lewis was heading up a team of cardinals doing it for him. He would at this point be a shoe in. He had enough votes to be elected, but the conclave was ten days away and a lot could happen in that length of time. There was no one else who could be considered a frontrunner. Several other cardinals were being talked about although none of them had as many votes as they needed; the votes were equally spread out among them.

The phone began to ring; Pulaski ignored it. "Anton, why don't you answer the phone?" There was not answer, and then it dawned on him Anton had not returned from the don's warehouse. The persistent ringing caused him to pick up the phone. "Cardinal Pulaski," he answered.

"Joseph, it's Martin."

"I hope you are calling with good news, my friend."

"I just lined you up with two more votes. These two are our insurance for success. By the way, Joseph, there was on the news a story about a priest being shot near the Forum this afternoon. By chance, have you been contacted by the Rome police yet?"

"No, not yet."

"I went to see Monsignor O'Rourke this morning, and he was not in. The guard said he had not been seen since last night. You don't think it could be him. That would certainly cause a stir among the cardinals since he was Leo's secretary. Some of the cardinals are uneasy already about the mystery surrounding Leo's untimely death."

"I will let you know immediately when I learn something. Thanks for the good news. After I am elected, you will take my place as the head of the curia. Together, we will be unstoppable." Pulaski hung up and continued his work on the funeral plans. *Leo,* he thought, *your funeral will be something to be remembered.* Once again, the phone began to ring. "Cardinal Pulaski speaking."

"Cardinal, I am just leaving the warehouse. Carlos is on his way back here. I have news. Monsignor O'Rourke is dead. Carlos just viewed his body and made a positive identification."

"Where is the body?"

"In the morgue. They are performing an autopsy as we speak to determine the cause of death."

"This needs to be kept as quiet as possible before the elections. I understand some of the cardinals are a little nervous. Did you see Sebastian?"

"Yes, and he refused to give me any information. But do not worry, I think Carlos will make him talk."

"Go to the hospital and have the body sent to the Russoleni funeral home. They are the ones who handle all the arrangement for the Vatican. I will call them and make sure he is buried quickly and quietly. Make sure the hospital does not give out any information to the press. Call me from the hospital when you finish there. I may have another errand for you to do for me."

"Yes, your eminence."

Pulaski picked up his phone and called his friend Cardinal Louis. "Martin, it's Joseph. I just got word it was O'Rourke who was shot. He died tonight at Metro."

"Joseph, this is not good news. We may loose a few votes when the news breaks."

"Don't worry, Anton is on his way over to Metro to have the body moved to the Russoleni Funeral home. He will be buried quickly, and I will see it does not hit the press until after the election. We can say O'Rourke has been sent on a mission for the late Pope Leo. He was to deliver a letter to the pope's ailing brother. On the way back, there will be an unfortunate accident."

"Well done, Joseph. I will begin to circulate that story among the cardinals and the Swiss Guard. That should keep his absence from upsetting anyone. I think that you should be the one to inform Archbishop Valanti and do so quickly. He and the monsignor were very close."

"I will do that immediately." Pulaski hung up the phone. *This needs to be handled with care,* he thought.

"The archbishop is no one's fool." He stood up and began to pace back and forth in front of his desk. "I know Patrick had a letter and the key to give to the next pope. So he will have to be returning just after the election. I need to get a hold of that letter and the key. Patrick would have left the letter in his office, getting that will not be a problem. The last time I saw him, he had the key around his neck. The key may be a problem." He reached for the phone and dialed Anton's cell.

"Anton," he said. Not waiting for Anton to answer.

"Yes, your Eminence."

"When you get to the hospital, you need to collect O'Rourke's personal belongings. I need the key he was wearing around his neck."

"I will bring you everything." Pulaski hung up. He thought it would be better if he went to see Archbishop Valanti in person.

He quickly shuffled the papers he had been working on and put them in his center desk drawer. He tucked his cell into the pocket of his robe. Leaving his office, he encountered a hall crowded with visiting cardinals. He was stopped many times, greeting and shaking hands as he made his way toward the elevator. Every one seemed to want his attention. *This is going to take a while,* he thought, smiling, *but it is worth it.* He finally made it to the elevator, and he hit the down button and the doors opened. He pushed the button for the ground floor. As the elevator descended, he rehearsed in his mind what he was going to say to the archbishop.

The elevator stopped and the door opened. He stepped out and made his way to the archives. When he reached the door, the Swiss Guard snapped to attention. "Please inform the archbishop that I am here to see him."

"Sorry, your Eminence, the archbishop left ten minutes ago. He said he would not be back until the morning."

"Did he say where he was going?"

"No, your eminence."

"Was there anyone else with him?"

"No, the American Mat Mason was here earlier, but he left before the archbishop did."

"Thank you, Corporal."

That's odd.. I wonder what that old fox could be up to. It can't be good for me, he thought, going back to his office.

Running through the gauntlet of cardinals roaming the halls was a challenge. It took Pulaski nearly an hour to get back to his office. He made sure his outer office was locked. He did not want to be disturbed. He had funeral plans to take care of, not one but two.

His cell rang. Glancing at the screen, he saw it was Anton. "Yes."

"Eminence the hospital will not release the body until the autopsy reports are back. They will be silent on Monsignor O'Rourke's death."

"What about his personal belongings?"

"They were turned over to the Rome police. An Inspector Capleno has them."

"Isn't that a friend of Captain Sitzler?"

"Yes, I believe you are right."

"Is the Inspector still in the hospital?"

"I do not know"

"Well, find out!"

"Yes, eminence"

Well, this may not be too bad. If he has the key, he will have to give it to me, or the camerlengo. In either case, once elected, I will have the key, he thought as he waited for Anton to find out.

"Eminence, the Inspector has already gone."

"Fine, get back to the office. On second thought, check with the emergency room doctor to see if he saw a key around O'Rourke's neck or in his clothing. Call me back when you have something to report."

"Yes, eminence."

While he waited, he called the funeral home and spoke to Senor Russoleni.

"Alberto, how is your wife and children?"

"Fine, Cardinal Pulaski, thank you for asking. How may I be of service to you?"

"I need you to do me a favor."

"It will be my pleasure."

"There is a body at Metro. When it is ready for release, it needs to be picked up and prepared for burial very discreetly."

"I will handle it myself."

"Thank you, Alberto, you will be richly rewarded." Pulaski hung up, thinking, *Well, that is handled. Now to finish the pope's funeral and burial plans.*

He glanced at his clock. It was already after seven; no wonder he was tired. He had been working on this all afternoon. Sitting back, he closed his eyes only to be jarred awake by the ringing of his cell. "Eminence."

"Yes, Anton, what did you find out?"

"Someone had already inquired about seeing the key on O'Rourke. I spoke to the doctor and the nurse and they told me he did no have one on him."

"Who asked?"

"It was the inspector."

"Get back here to the office."

The cardinal's mind began to spin with many thoughts, most of which were not good. *I wonder what Mister Mason was doing with the archbishop? It has to do with the manuscript. I am sure of that. Mason was called here by Leo to finish what Sebastian had started. They must have some information. Sebastian must have left a clue in his room. Anton saw Monsignor O'Rourke with a bunch of the brothers the day before he disappeared. I will just have to get back into the archives through the secret tunnel Sebastian found out about from the manuscript.*

He hurried from his office, the corridors were quiet at this time of the night. Most of the cardinals were in their quarters or having a light supper in Rome. He made his way out and across the premier of the square. It was still filled with the faithful. He entered a small private garden near castle Grandolfo—the pope's home. At the end of the garden was a statue of the first Leo. Behind it, the wall was made of bricks with ivy growing on it. Pulaski pushed in the first three toes on the right foot of the statue and part of the wall behind it swung open. He quickly slid through the opening and pushed the wall panel back into place.

He took the flashlight he had brought and turned it on. The beam of light illuminated a narrow passage way. It was all stone with a low barrel ceiling. There were old, oil-soaked torches spaced along the wall. He did not need to light any of those. The passage sloped down for the first fifty feet or so then it leveled out. He was careful to stay in the center. The walls were damp with green slim dripping off them. The floor was slick from the constant dampness.

He had reached the midpoint where the tunnel began to slope upward. This would be the difficult part of the journey, trying to navigate the rise without falling. He had reached what appeared to be a solid wall, a dead end. He removed the two bricks at the top of the wall and standing on his tiptoes, looked into the archives through the two holes that were behind the bookcase.

The security lights were on, but the overhead lamps were off. He could see that the door to the archbishop's office was closed. Sticking his finger into one of the eyeholes, he felt the trip switch and pulled it down. A portion of the wall shifted and slid to the side. Just inside was another lever, which he pulled, and the bookcase against the wall sprung forward, giving him access to the archives.

Using his flashlight, he shone the beam slowly around the room. On a worktable there were several documents spread out. He walked over to examine them. They were drawings of Rome, where the cemetery is now and other drawings of the same area before the cemetery. Why would they be interested in the cemetery unless that's where Sebastian hid the manuscript? He could not tell what they had found, if anything, nothing was marked on any of the documents.

He went into Valanti's office. He searched the desk and cabinets. *Nothing*, he thought, *I will have to tell Carlos to ask Sebastian about the cemetery and have his men watch it*. Pulaski put everything back as he had found it and left through the passageway.

Chapter 40

Carlos felt jubilant as he walks down the steps of Metro Hospital toward his car. He had called the cardinal's secretary, Father Anton with the news of O'Rourke's death. Now he was heading back to the warehouse to deal with Sebastian. This monk had made him look like a fool. He had assured the don that he was dead. He was looking forward to giving him a good beating. Then if he didn't talk, he would use his favorite form of interrogation on him. He would chain him to one of the steel beams in the basement and run water over him. When he was good and wet, he would attach a battery charger clamp to various parts of his body. This always did the trick. He had seen grown he-men cry for mercy or death as he worked on them.

Carlos reached his car. As always, he perused the parking lot looking for anything or anyone that look suspicious. He had noticed a police car in its space near the door when he came in, and now it was gone. That was probably the inspector's vehicle. Seeing nothing suspicious, he opened his door, got in, and started his car. He slowly drove around the parking lot, making mental notes of the vehicles there, before he pulled out into the street. Normally, it would be a good forty-five minutes before he got to the warehouse. Maybe he could get there a little quicker, because traffic was light this time of the night. He looked at his watch; it was ten fifteen. He would not have a lot of time with Sebastian tonight, just a good beating to soften him up. The though of his fist smashing into Sebastian's face brought a smile to his face.

Carlos had a heart of pure evil. At the traffic light, he made a right turn onto the road, leading to the Forum. The Shrine to Italy's unknown was lit up but most of the tourists were gone. Glancing into his rearview mirror, he made a mental note of a dark sedan several cars behind him. He was making good time. He tuned in the Oldies station and sang along with Elvis. "I ain't nothing but a hound dog." *I am more like a pit bull,* he thought.

Up ahead was the Forum, he was going to turn right just up ahead. The black sedan was still behind him. Carlos made the turn and slowed down, looking in his rearview mirror. The dark sedan also made the turn, and it too slowed down. *I think I have company,* he thought. Carlos floored the Scion turning again right at the next street. The black sedan was keeping pace with him.

In the car behind him, the officer said, "I think we have been made. Call the inspector and see what he wants us to do."

Carlos knew he could not outrun the sedan, so he would have to outfox them. Up ahead was a parking deck. He had a block-long lead on his tail. He pulled in, got his ticket, and instead of going up to the next floor, he headed the wrong way down to the lower level. He pulled in between two large sedans and killed his lights. In just a moment, he heard the squeal of tires going up the ramp to the next floor.

When he thought they were far enough ahead, he slowly backed out and went back up the ramp. He could see the lights of a car spinning up to the next floor. Carlos pulled up to the cashier, paid his fee, and left the parking deck.

"Inspector, we have lost Carlos in the parking garage."

"You need to get out of there, and patrol the warehouse district and see if you can find him. That was the tail we had on Carlos, and they have lost him."

"How will we find Sebastian now?" asked Jason.

Carlos kept a close watch on the road behind him. No more dark sedans following him. He decided for safety sake to drive in a circle for a while until he was sure he had lost the police tail.

After a while, he felt safe and continued on to the warehouse. He parked the Scion in it usual place and entered the warehouse by the office door. Marino was still where Carlos had left him sitting in the cavernous room with the black sedan. "It's good to see you back. I was getting a little jumpy around that Father Anton. He gives me the creeps."

"Did Sebastian tell him anything?"

"No! He refused to talk to him at all. Looks like it's up to you to make him talk. You gonna start on him tonight or wait till tomorrow?"

"I thought I may just beat him tonight with that rope that we put the metal studs in. That should give him incentive to talk."

"Be careful, boss. Anton told me we could not kill him so be careful." Carlos swung his arm up, backhanding Marino, sending him tumbling across the room.

"Don't you ever tell me what to do? Do you get me?"

"Yes, boss," he said, getting back up on his feet, wiping blood from his mouth.

"Now get me the rope and be quick about it." Marino went over and opened a chest that was against the wall and took out a piece of rope that had metal studs embedded in it and walked back and handed it to Carlos. Carlos wound the end that was wrapped in duct tape around his hand, and he swung the rope in Marino direction and barely missed hitting him. "Get the key, and let's go visit our guest," Carlos said with a sneer.

Marino got the key and headed toward the basement door and opened it. He turned on the light in the stairwell. It was difficult going down the steep stairs. You felt like you were descending into a bottomless black pit. The stairs were always damp and slippery. When they reached the bottom, Marino flipped the wall switch that lit a single bulb hanging on a wire from the ceiling.

The ductwork and pipes were exposed down here, and the bulb cast shadows on the ceiling, giving it a foreboding appearance. They reached the last door, and Marino inserted the key and opened it, stepping aside to allow Carlos to enter first. "Good evening, Sebastian. Hope your accommodations are to your liking." Sebastian turned his head toward Carlos but did not speak. Carlos walked over to him and grabbed him by the hair with one hand, pulling his head backward while slapping him with the other. The blow broke the skin on Sebastian's lip. He could feel and taste the salty blood run into his mouth. "Didn't that whore of a mother teach you any manners?" Carlos sneered, bending down close to Sebastian's face.

Sebastian spat the blood into Carlos face, getting some into this mouth. Carlos backed up spitting and wiping his face with his sleeve. "You will regret that, monk," he said, letting the rope dangle in front of Sebastian. Sebastian raised his head and looked at Carlos.

"I am not afraid of you."

"I've heard that before. From much stronger men than you." Carlos brought the rope down hard across Sebastian's legs above his knees. He felt the metal studs bite into the top of his legs and despite his best effort, he let out a yell. "You still say you are not afraid. You screamed like a baby, and I have not even started yet."

Marino, get in here right now and bring that bottle of water and give the good monk a drink. Marino fetched the bottle and brought it over to Sebastian. He lifted up his head and opened his mouth, and Marino poured some of the water in. *That tastes so good,* he thought, swallowing the water.

"That's enough. Untie him from the chair and stand him up." Marino did as he was told and untied Sebastian. Getting him by the arm, he pulled him into a standing position. As soon as he stood, Sebastian whose legs were numb from sitting buckled on him, sending him crashing to the floor face first. His chest and face took the brunt of the fall. Now, his nose was also bleeding.

"What's wrong, tough guy? You can't even stand up," Carlos taunted. Carlos took his foot and forced Sebastian to roll over onto his back. "Marino, help the monk to his feet again." Marino walked around behind Sebastian. First getting him into a sitting position, then grabbing him under the arms lifted him to his feet. Having his arms tied behind his back, the force of being lifted caused all of the stitches that were in his chest wounds to be pulled out. Sebastian let out another scream.

"Oh, too bad, looks like the doctor did a sloppy job sewing you up." The pain coming from his chest was easing up a little, but once again the blood began to run down his chest in little rivulets.

"Get a wet towel and wipe off the blood." Marino did as he was told.

"Undo his belt and drop his pants, then unbutton his shirt, and take a knife and cut them off. Soon Sebastian was standing in only his boxers.

"That's much better, right, monk? I'm sure you were way too hot all dressed up in your suit." Sebastian stood, shivering in the cold dampness not saying a word.

"Marino, throw one of those chains over the black pipe overhead. Yes, that should do nicely. Now walk our guest over there under the chain. Very good, now tie his hands to the chain. Now you can cut off the plastic cuffs."

"OK, monk, this is the fun part, at least for me. Marino is going to pull on the chain until you hands are over your head. Now, we won't have to do this if you will tell me where the manuscript is located." Sebastian did not say a word.

"You realize that to get your arm up over your head both of your shoulder joints will have to pop out to allow that to happen or maybe both arms will break. Either way, the pain will be unbearable. Now make it easy on yourself and tell me what I want to know."

Sebastian stood with his head bowed, not saying a word. Carlos walked over to him once again, grabbing his head by his hair. He forced it up, so that he was looking into his face. "Last chance."

"No," said Sebastian through clenched teeth.

Carlos walked over and stood beside Marino. They both grabbed the chain. Looking at Marino, he said, "On three, we pull the chain together. One, two, three." Both men pulled hard on the chain. There was a grating sound and a loud squeal as the chain traveled over the large pipe.

Sebastian felt his arms being pulled up and behind him. The pressure on his joints and chest muscles became unbearable. He could feel his feet beginning to come up off the floor. All of his weight was centered on the joints where his arms joined his body. He heard a popping sound, and the pain was searing through his upper body. He heard himself screaming as the pain like hot irons was coursing through his upper torso. He felt tendons and muscles tearing, then a bolt of pain crashed inside his brain and then there was blessed blackness.

"Let the chain slacken slowly. It looks like our guest has decided to take a nap. While he is out, loosen his arms, and we will bring them around and tie them together in front. Bring the chair over here, and let's sit him in it." Marino got the chair, and he and Carlos lifted Sebastian into the chair.

"Tie his legs to the chair. Now let's retie his hand to the chain and pull it tight so that his arms are held up over his head. Take the rest of the water and pour it over his head. See if we can rouse him."

In a while, Sebastian began to stir. Carlos slapped his face. "Wake up, monk!" Sebastian opened an eye. Carlos was hovering just above him. He was sitting on the metal chair; the cold from the chair seeped into his body. His shoulders and arms ached; he felt pain in his chest, but all of this was bearable. He opened both eyes. "You ready to talk yet?"

Sebastian shook his head. Carlos stood up and brought the rope up over his head and brought it down hard across Sebastian's shoulders. The steel cut into his flesh, the pain caused his muscles to spasm. The pain was so great; he felt his bladder let go, and he felt the heat of his urine run down his legs, the odor and pain making him heave.

"Marino, looks like our guest just pissed himself. Get a bucket of water and wash him off." Marino went into the hall, found a bucket, filled it up with cold water, and poured it over Sebastian's head. The water stung the wounds as it washed over him. "Get that mop over there, and push the water toward the floor drain. This is just a sample of what's in store for you tomorrow. I will let you think about it for the next few hours. I know how to inflict pain. You will tell me what I want to know."

Carlos's cell began to ring, "Yes, I see. I will take care of that. No he has not said a word yet, but I have just begun. I will convey that to him." Carlos put his cell back into his pocket. "That was Cardinal Pulaski. He was just checking up on your health. Marino, finish cleaning up in here and bring in the battery charger. Then lock the door. You need to sleep here tonight."

"Yes, boss." Carlos headed back up the stairs. He had phone calls to make. He needed to post some guards around the cemetery before morning. With any luck, he just might catch a nun.

Chapter 41

The car carrying Patrick, Jason, the inspector, and his driver pulled through the gate and into the tunnel below the guard barracks. "How are you doing?" asked Jason.

"I'm fine. Just a little weak."

"We will soon be safely inside the guest quarters."

"Will you need any additional backup to guard the monsignor?" asked the inspector.

"No, I got it handled. The fewer people who are involved, the better."

"I agree with you, but if you change your mind, just let me know."

"Thanks, Lorenzo, I appreciate the offer." The car stopped. Jason and the inspector opened their doors and stepped out. Patrick was in the backseat, leaning against the other door. "I will come around and help you out," said Jason. Patrick nodded in acknowledgment. Jason opened the door and got Patrick by the arm and gently lifted him out. He was a little unsteady but managed to walk slowly toward the open door to the guest quarters hanging onto Jason.

Standing just inside the door was Archbishop Valanti. "Patrick, my son, let me take your hand." Patrick extended his hand to Valanti. He got on one side, and Jason on the other and helped Patrick across the room and into the bed, which had been readied for him. Patrick still had on the hospital gown. He let them lay him back onto the bed. He felt Jason picking up his legs and sliding him over to the center and pull up the covers and put another pillow under his head. "How are you feeling?" asked Valanti.

"All right, just a little tired."

"It is close to midnight. Get some rest. We will talk tomorrow."

"Jason, Inspector, let's move down to your office and let Patrick rest."

"Will it be all right for my car and driver to stay in the tunnel?"

"That should be fine. We won't be long. We just need to compare notes and plan what we need to do tomorrow," said Valanti.

Patrick closed his eyes as soon as they left. But sleep did not come easily.

Jason led the way to his office. When they were seated, he caught them up on what he and Mat had discovered and that Mat and his daughter were going to check out the entrances to the catacombs in the morning.

The inspector told Valanti about the phone call he received on the way over, telling him his men had lost Carlos. "In the morning, I will get every undercover officer busy, trying to locate Carlos. I am sure he will be moving in and out of the warehouse district. With any luck, he will be spotted. My men will have to be more careful next time."

"What can I do to help?" asked Jason. "Just keep the monsignor safe and out of sight."

"Will do, but I want to be involved when we locate Sebastian."

"I understand how you feel. I will keep you in the loop."

"Inspector, I will notify you if Mat and Sister Judith find the entrance. I have asked them to call me and to not venture in alone. I told them you and Jason need to go in with them."

"I will be looking forward to your call."

"Well, gentlemen, if that is all, I need to get back to my quarters. Tomorrow will be another long day. Good night, and may God watch over you." Valanti rose to go.

"I also need to stop by my office on my way home. I will call with any news," the inspector said.

"I will walk you out," said Jason, opening the door for them. The archbishop shook both of their hands and turned toward the main entrance to the guards' office complex.

Jason led the inspector back toward the tunnel. "Do you think we have a chance to find Sebastian before they kill him?"

"I don't know. If Carlos gets spotted again, we may have a chance, but the longer it takes, the odds go against us."

"This door will let you back into the tunnel. I am going to check on Patrick again before I call it a day." Jason and the inspector shook hands, and Jason closed and locked the outside door. Then he made his way back to Patrick's room.

Valanti felt like he was carrying the weight of the world on his shoulders. He loved his God, and he loved his church. "Please, God," he prayed, "give me strength to combat your foes, and the wisdom to do your will. Please touch your child Patrick with your healing hand and grant your protection to your servant Sebastian. Help, Jason and the inspector to do their jobs and find him." He was walking and praying as he made his way down the hall toward the main door to the Vatican office complex. Just as he was about to reach the door, it opened and standing there like a bad omen was Cardinal Pulaski holding a flashlight.

"Archbishop Valanti, how fortuitous! I had been down to the archives to see you earlier today. I have news about Monsignor O'Rourke that I thought you needed to know." Valanti's shoulders slumped. It looked like the air had gone out of him. He could hardly speak. Has someone seen them bringing Patrick in or had there been a leak at the hospital, informing them that he was still alive.

"News, you say" came the hoarse reply.

"Are you all right, Archbishop? You look a little pale."

"Yes, yes! I am fine. It's just a little late for me and seeing you coming in at this time of night, it just gave me a start."

"What are you doing out this time of night yourself?"

"Been cooped up all day in the archives, trying to get it in shape to present to the next pope."

"Yes, that will be happening soon, won't it?"

"Yes, cardinal. Now you said you have news for me about Patrick."

"I assume that you have noticed he has been gone since yesterday afternoon."

"I really haven't noticed, been so busy, you see."

"Well, he has gone to deliver a letter to Leo's poor brother who is ill and will not be able to attend the funeral. So Patrick will be out for a couple of days. I have arranged for Father Anton to sit in for him while he is away."

"That is most kind of you, Cardinal. I know Patrick would appreciate that."

"Well, anything we can do to help."

"Thanks for letting me know, I will pass that information along. By the way, Cardinal, did you fall on your walk? You have something all over the sleeves of your robe?"

"No, I must have brushed against the garden wall."

"Good night, Cardinal."

"Good night, Archbishop."

Well, that went better than I anticipated. Valanti seems to have bought the story. We still need to be careful, and this funeral and the conclave need to happen on schedule or there may be a lot of questions, thought Pulaski.

I hope I handled that OK. Won't Patrick and the others be surprised to learn that Patrick is on a trip to see Leo's brother? This is good news. I will call Jason and the inspector first thing in the morning. Valanti could feel Pulaski's eyes still on him as he opened the door and left the office complex.

Chapter 42

Mat's alarm clock went off at 6:30 a.m. This should give him enough time to shower, shave, and get dressed before he met his daughter. His thoughts went back to their home in Atlanta, Georgia, and to a time when Judith was a little girl, running around with one of her dolls bandaged up and playing nurse. They lived in an area of Atlanta called Druid Hills near Emory University where Mat was a professor of antiquities and his wife Taylor was a nurse in the hospital there. They had two children—Judith, who was Mat's cuddly bear, and a son, Matthew Junior, whom they called Chip. Judith always wanted to be a nurse like her mother. After graduating from the University of Georgia, she enrolled in nursing school at Emory.

They attended St. Anthony's Catholic Church, and Judith never missed a Mass. The church was a very important part of Judith's life. She had been befriended by several of the nuns of the Sisters of Mercy at St. Joseph's hospital where she got her first job after nursing school. Although Judith had dated a lot in college and after, she had just not found the right match for her. Hanging around the sisters, she realized that she had not found the right man because God had been calling her. She joined the Sisters of Mercy and became a nun. She had eventually ended up at the Vatican becoming Pope Leo's personal nurse.

At Judith's urging, the pope after Brother Sebastian was thought dead called her dad Mat to come and see if he could finish Sebastian's work. But when he arrived, Leo was dead. Archbishop Valanti and Monsignor O'Rourke asked him to stay and help them. Now, both Sebastian and the manuscript were missing. Their only clue was a note Sebastian was able to get to Patrick. With the clue from the note, Mat and Judith would be looking for the entrance to the catacombs that Sebastian had found.

Mat looked forward to spending the day with his daughter. The weather would be warm and no rain in sight. He pulled out his old khaki pants with all the pockets and a cotton shirt. His boots would be just right for a day of walking. He looked at the clock. Half an hour had already passed; he needed to get a move on. He went into the bathroom and shaved and started the hot water. He would shave in the shower; that would save time. Toweling off, he felt refreshed.

Oh my, he thought, *it's seven twenty-five*. He needed to speed up. Dressing in record time, he left his room promptly at seven thirty. He would just be a little late. He was meeting her in the lobby, and they would have breakfast somewhere close by. He picked up his backpack with the maps and his GPS, along with his cell and slung it over his shoulder and left his room.

She was standing near the front door when he arrived. "Good morning, cuddly bear."

"Oh Dad, good morning. I know a café around the corner. Let's go there." The street was very quiet. The tourists were not out yet so they had the whole sidewalk to themselves. Mat reached over and took her hand. She turned and smiled, and they walked together like that until they reached the café. It also was not busy. Rome obviously does not get up and out early in the morning. After they had ordered, Mat took out the map of the cemetery and told her about the note from Sebastian. Then he explained how they had marked this map, showing the entrances to the catacombs. Judith studied the map. "I have walked on the road that runs next to this wall and have never seen an opening to the catacombs." Pointing to the road, she said, "This is about a two-mile walk from here. Do you want to walk or catch a cab?"

"I was cooped up in the archives all day yesterday. Walking sounds good to me." Their breakfast came, and Mat folded up the map and put it back into his backpack. As they ate, they used the time to catch up on old friends and what was happening back home.

Then the conversation came back to what they must do. "Judith, you must keep what I am about to tell you in the strictest confidence. It is a matter of life and death."

"I will, Dad."

"First, the priest that was shot yesterday was Monsignor O'Rourke."

"Oh my god! How is he?"

"I don't know. The monk, Brother Sebastian, has been kidnapped by the mafia."

"How did you get the note?"

"Sebastian gave it to a nurse. That's all I know. The manuscript that Sebastian hid in the catacombs must be found before the mafia gets hold of it. It contains information that in the wrong hands could cause great harm. I am finished. How about you?"

"Me too. Let's get started, but before we go, let me see that map again." Judith studied the map once again, and Mat pointed to the places where there maybe an entrance. "OK, Dad, I have my bearing. Now let's get going." Judith led the way, walking the two miles going down narrow streets and wide avenues. "Look, Dad, that wall beginning at the next block is the wall to the cemetery. We will have to turn right, and we will be on the road you have marked." They reached the corner. There was a store that looked like it had been built into the wall. "That store is in one of the places that you have marked."

"We need to go in and ask the owner if he knows if there is an entrance there." They crossed the street and entered the store.

"Good morning."

"And good morning to you," Mat replied, walking up to the clerk. "My name is Mat Mason, and this is my daughter Sister Judith. You speak very good English."

"We get a lot of tourists in here."

"We are looking for an entrance to the catacombs. On an old map we have it, shows that there is one right here."

"There is not one here to my knowledge."

"Does the store have a basement? That is where it must be?"

"Why? Yes, it does"

"Would it be possible for us to have a look?"

"I don't know. I will have to call the owner."

"Please do so, and tell them that we are on a mission for the Papal archives." She went to the back. Mat and Judith looked around the shop.

"Mr. Mason, the owner said it would be all right for you to look. The door to the basement is back in the storeroom." She led the way and opened the door for them turning on the lights. "There is another light switch at the bottom of the stairs."

Mat and Judith descended the stairs; the basement was damp and had a musty smell. It was constructed out of large cut stones much like you would find in the ruins in the Forum. As the walked around examining the wall, they came to a break in the stones. You could still see an archway that had been bricked up years ago. "This must have been at one time an entrance, but these bricks have been here for hundreds of years. The map seems to be accurate. But we know this is not the entrance that Sebastian used. Let's go."

They came back up the stairs and thanked the clerk and left the shop. They continued their search. "Dad, where was the other entrance?"

"Looking at the map again, it looks to be about midway of the wall."

"This wall is at least three miles long."

"Look every so often they have built a niche into the wall and planted shrubbery."

"Dad, that would be a good way to hide an entrance." They stepped into each one, looking for an opening or some sign that someone had tried to get behind the shrubbery. But each time, there was only a wall.

"Dad, we have got to be getting near the midway point in the wall." They passed an intersection where a street dead ended in front of the cemetery. "Up ahead is another one of those planting." As they approached, they noticed that one of the bushes had several broken limbs near the wall. One caught Mat's eye. Attached to it was a piece of a plastic bag, the kind you get at the grocery store.

"We may have found something." Judith came up behind her dad.

"Look, there is a piece of plastic from what looks like a grocery bag under one of the front shrubs." Stooping down and getting on his hands and knees, he said, "Let's see if we can squeeze behind this bush." Mat pulled some of the limbs aside and made his way behind the bush. "Someone has been back here. The straw is brushed aside." Mat was able to stand up. He inched his way toward the center. He saw an opening in the bottom of the wall, large enough for a man to crawl into. He got the flashlight out of his pocket and shone it down into the hole. He could see a level area that opened into a tunnel.

"Judith, we have found it."

Little did they know but as they had been examining the wall, one of Carlo's men had been following them. The store where they stopped belonged to the don, and as soon as they mentioned the catacombs, the clerk had alerted Carlos. He, in turn, had called one of his men to stake out the store. He was at this moment calling Carlos, "Boss, I think they have found something. The man is behind the shrubbery. Now his daughter is crawling back there. What do you want me to do?"

"Call Ricardo and tell him to bring a car and meet you there. Bring me the man and woman."

"Yes, boss."

"Look, this has to be it. The straw, the way it has been moved shows someone else has been here." Mat shone the flashlight into the hole. "I am going in. Hold the light so I can see."

"But Dad, you told me the archbishop told you to just find the entrance and call him."

"I know he said, 'Don't go in,' but before I call, I need to make sure this is really the entrance, and I can't do that without going in. This could be just a hole the rain has washed out." Mat lowered himself into the narrow hole, feet first, sliding on his stomach. He could not feel the floor yet. He kept pushing, and when he was in up to his neck, he felt something solid and pushed himself all the way in. "Hand me the light," Judith got down on her hands and knees. She could see her dad standing stooped with his arms extended toward her.

"Here it is. Be careful." Mat took the light and in a stooped position, turned around shining the light into the darkness. Indeed, this was an entrance. He could tell someone had been here. There were footprints in the dust, leading back into the darkness. "This is it."

"Take the light, so I can pull myself back up." Judith took the light, and Mat pulled himself up and out. "Let's get back out to the road before too many people see us coming from behind these bushes." They made their way out. Once on the road, they began to walk back in the direction they had come.

Traffic was still light. Mat noticed a man in dark jeans and a black T-shirt, leaning against the wall about a half block away. He seemed to be watching them. Maybe he had seen them coming out from behind the bushes.

"Dad, stop a minute. You have dirt on your shirt and pants, and your shoes are covered in dust." Mat stopped and brushed himself off.

"That's better," remarked Judith.

"That man down there seems to be giving us the once over. Let's hurry and get past that guy," Mat said in a whisper. They picked up their pace, hurrying past him.

Mat's hair began to stand up on his neck as a big black sedan pulled over to the curb just ahead of them. The driver jumped out and came around the car and opened the front and rear doors. At the same time, Mat heard footsteps coming up fast behind them.

Before he could turn around, he felt a round cold object jammed into his neck. "Keep walking and get into the car, or I will shoot you and the girl." The driver stepped from the door and took Judith by the arm and pushed her into the backseat. Mat felt himself being shoved in beside her, and the door slammed. Judith was trying to find the door handle so she could get out only to find it had been removed. The only way to get out was for the door to be opened from the outside.

The driver and the man Mat had seen leaning against the wall got into the front seat. "Mr. Mason and Sister Judith, just sit back and don't give us any trouble. My boss, Carlos, asked me to pick you up. You will soon be joining Brother Sebastian as his guests."

Chapter 43

It had been a restless night for Patrick. Whatever way he turned, something hurt. He was grateful that morning had finally come. The clock on the nightstand had just hit 6:00 a.m. Pushing off the covers, he swung his legs off the bed and grabbing the nightstand, pushed himself up into a sitting position. He began to swing his right leg back and forth, trying to get the circulation going. Steadying himself, he tentatively stood up. Holding on to a chair and then to the wall, he made his way into the bathroom. After emptying his full bladder, he made it to the sink to wash his face and hands.

Looking into the mirror, he didn't look too bad, he thought. He needed to shave and wash his hair. He would not be able to shower for another day of two, depending on his wounds.

He was ready to get out of the hospital gown. His two puncture wounds where the bullet passed through has bled through the bandage and was on the gown. There was a razor and toothbrush in the cabinet behind the mirror, so Patrick shaved and brushed his teeth. This made him feel much more human. He returned to the bedroom and sat down in one of the chairs.

He heard men's voices, and the sound of footsteps as the guards moved out to their post. Soon there was a knock on the door.

"Come in." Jason came through the door, carrying a cassock and some of Patrick's other clothes. Following close behind him was a guard with what looked like a breakfast tray.

"Good morning, Patrick. I went to your room last night and brought you some clothes. I was not sure what you would want to wear, so I just grabbed several things."

"Thanks, I need a change," Patrick said, pointing to the blood stains on the gown.

Jason motioned for the guard to put the tray on a table. "Gustoff, go down to the clinic and have the doctor come up here and change the monsignor's bandages. Make sure no one outside of the guards hears you. While he is on his way, why don't you eat something? I am sure Archbishop Valanti will be here first thing this morning."

"Sounds like a plan. I am actually starving." Jason helped Patrick over to the table and poured both Patrick and himself coffee.

"Sleep well?"

"Not really. Just couldn't find a spot that wasn't sore." Patrick dug in, enjoying the food.

"Looks like your appetite was not hurt."

"Very funny." There was a knock on the door. Jason went over and opened it. The doctor was outside with his bag.

"Come in, Doctor."

The doctor went over to Patrick. "First, let me get your vital signs they are 120 over 70 with a pulse of 60 and no temperature every thing looks good so far. Can you stand and walk over to the bed?" Patrick steadied himself using the table and stood up. Seeing that he was a little unsteady, the doctor took Patrick's arm and helped him over to the bed.

"Let me take off the gown before you lie down." He untied the gown in the back and removed it. Seeing Patrick was nude, he asked.

"Would you like me to have Jason wait outside?"

"No, we go to the gym twice a week. He has seen me nude many times."

He helped Patrick onto the bed, and he lay back. The doctor changed all of the bandages on his arms and legs and the two on his sides. "Things seem to be healing nicely. Just be careful when bending or stooping. I will be back tomorrow morning to change the bandages again."

"Thanks, Doctor." Jason ushered the doctor out.

"You are just going to lie there naked or what?" Jason chided as he brought Patrick his clothes. He had to help him into his boxers and pants. After he was dressed, Jason helped him over to the chair and poured them both another cup of coffee.

"Got to go. I have to attend to my regular Vatican business. See you later." Jason left Patrick alone. After a while, he turned on the TV to the local Rome channel, hoping to catch the news. He was surprised to hear the commentator report this. "Unidentified priest who was shot and dumped near the Forum has died. We are still trying to get his identity. The Vatican offices nor the hospital will release any information until the family is notified. Now onto the weather."

"Well, that was interesting. Not to often one hears a report of his own death."

He was startled when the door opened. Archbishop Valanti stuck his head in. "Good morning, Patrick."

"Good morning. Please come in. Forgive me if I don't get up." Valanti came into the room and went over to Patrick and taking his outstretched hand.

"My, you almost look normal. I am relived to see you feeling well enough to be up and dressed." Valanti told Patrick about his encounter with Pulaski the night before.

"So they think I am dead but are putting out the story that I am on a mission to see Pope Leo's brother. And Anton is going to be in my office. You know why he is there? To search through my desk and files for the letter from Leo and the key. Well, both of the letters are tucked away in my Bible. I know Anton won't be cracking that book. I will ask Jason to go to my room again and pick up my Bible late tonight. I don't know if they have told you, but the key is missing. It must have come off when I jumped out of the car."

"Has anyone been back to where it happened and searched for the key?"

"I think the inspector sent some patrol cars to look. I haven't heard if they found it or not. The inspector should be coming by sometime this morning. He may have news."

"We must get that key back before the next pope is elected."

"I know, Valanti."

Jason came back from his rounds. "Good morning, Archbishop."

"Good morning, Jason. You need to get this news out to all of your men that Patrick is on a trip to visit the pope's brother."

"I thought he was dead."

"This is the story Pulaski told me last night. He does not want it to get out that Patrick is dead. He thinks it will cause too many questions from the rest of the cardinals."

"I see. They think Patrick is dead but don't want anyone else to know. That makes things interesting. That means, Patrick, you will be stuck here in this room."

"I know. By the way, have you heard from the inspector today?"

"No, not yet, but it is early."

"We need to know if thy have found the key."

"I'm sure he will call if that happens."

"Do you know if he has talked to the officers who first arrived at the accident?"

"Let me call and ask." Jason pulled out his cell and called the inspector. "Lorenzo, it's Jason. Did you have a chance to talk to the officers who first arrived? I see. Have you attempted to contact them? Thanks! Let me know."

"Seems like there were two American tourists who witnessed the shooting. The wife helped stop the bleeding and stayed with you until the ambulance came. The officers got their names and where they are staying in Rome. Lorenzo is sending a detective over this morning to interview them."

Catherine and Willard Phillips had just finished breakfast and were relaxing over another espresso. Wiping her mouth, she opened her purse to get out her lipstick when her finger touched the cold ornate metal of the key with its broken chain that she picked up yesterday. She had seen it on the street under the car near where the accident happened. She pulled it out and laid it on the table between her and Willard. The gold gave off a warm glow under the café lights. "This key is beautiful and heavy," she said, picking it up to admire. "There are many symbols up the shaft and around the top. This big one is the papal seal I remember seeing it carved over the door when we had our tour the other day. You know the way the officers acted when they looked at the priest identification. He must be someone important. I think we need to go over to the Vatican and find out whom to give it to."

"Catherine, that is a big place. How will we know where to start?"

"Let's ask at the reception desk. They may be able to help us." Catherine carefully placed the key safely inside of her purse, and they headed back toward the hotel. If they were going back to the Vatican, they would also need a cab. That too they could find at the hotel.

Lorenzo called over to this driver detective Remetta, "I want you to head over to the hotel Calone, and interview a Catherine and Willard Phillips. See if by chance they noticed that Monsignor O'Rourke had a gold key on a chain around his neck at the crime scene. Also interview the ambulance driver and his helper. It may be a good idea for you to search the ambulance also. Then go back over the crime scene and make sure the key is not in a sewer or under a vehicle. Then report back to me."

"Yes, inspector." Remetta decided to go to the hospital first and talk to the driver. It was the closest place to start. This proved fruitless. He knew personally both the guys and felt certain that they would not steal from a priest or anyone. The search of the ambulance also turned up nothing. Returning to his car, he headed out across Rome to the hotel.

Being an officer of the law and in an official car, he pulled up to the front door and parked. He flashed his badge, and the doorman immediately opened the door for him. Remetta crossed the lobby to reception. "May I help you, sir?"

Once again, Remetta flashed his ID badge. "I am looking for two American tourists—a Mr. Willard Phillips and his wife Catherine."

"They are guests here?"

"You have just missed them."

"Do you know where they are going?"

"Sorry, Detective, I was not the one who helped them. Let me call Renaldo." He motioned to the other clerk on duty, and he came over.

"The detective wants to ask about the Americans, you know, the Phillips."

"Yes, nice people. I hope they are not in any trouble."

"No, they witnessed an accident yesterday. I just need to get some additional information."

"They were just here asking if I knew who they should see at the Vatican. Mrs. Phillips found a gold key. They are in a cab as we speak."

"Who did you tell her to see?"

"Probably someone in the office of the curia or possibly one of the Swiss Guards could help her."

"Thank you."

Remetta hurried back to his car. On the way, he called the inspector. "Inspector, I am at the hotel. The Phillips have the key and are on their way over to the Vatican to return it. They will be asking for a member of the curia or the Swiss Guards."

"Come pick me up as quickly as you can." The inspector hung up and called Jason.

"Jason just found out that the American tourists, the Phillips, have the key, and they are on their way over to the Vatican with it. They may approach one of the guards or ask to see a member of the curia. I will be over shortly."

"Thanks, Lorenzo. The key is on its way. I need to notify my staff to be on the lookout for an American couple named Phillips. Archbishop, you need to do the same with the Vatican personal. Whoever they contact should bring them immediately to the Swiss Guard office. We need to make sure they do no get to the curia office." Jason left Patrick's room on the run. Valanti went over to the phone and called the main switchboard.

"Vatican central"

"This is Archbishop Valanti. Get a message out to all staff that interacts with our visitors. An American couple named Phillips will be contacting someone about returning a key. They need to be brought quickly and quietly to the Swiss Guard office. Use the utmost respect in doing this."

"I will get the message out immediately."

Valanti turned toward Patrick. "Soon we may have the key back."

"That will be an answer to prayer."

The cab ride was uneventful. The Phillips reached Vatican square, and they were let out near the obelisk. It took them a while to make there way through the crowds that were in the square. They wanted to go up the front steps of St. Peters and across to the Vatican museum, but it was roped off to make lines for the people trying to get into the church and pay their respect to Pope Leo who was lying in state there. Some had been in line since yesterday and had camped out all night. The lines wrapped around the square several times and into the street.

"Willard, lets walk around to the other side. I saw some guards on duty behind a fence where they are working on the building."

"Yes, dear." Facing St. Peters, they made their way to the left side street, running along the square. There was a construction fence, and they could see a guardhouse toward the rear. Caroline began waving at the guard. Seeing her, he waved back. She began to motion for him to come over. Thinking she was just a tourist wanting to make his picture, he ignored her. "Willard, you must do something."

"What do you want me to do?" Willard began to also wave his arms at the guard. Thinking they would not give up, he finally walked up to them.

"Do you speak English?"

"Yes, madam." Catherine pulled the key out of her purse. "We found this yesterday at the scene of the accident involving the priest who was shot. We want to return it. The clerk at the hotel said to give it to one of the guards or ask to see someone in the office of the curia." The guard looked at the key and instantly recognized the papal seal on the top of the key.

"Follow the fence around to the other side. See that building just beyond the end of the fence? That is the office building for the Vatican. You will find the curia office on the fourth floor. They will be able to help you."

"Thank you." Willard and Catherine began to make their way to the other side toward the office building. The guard went back to his guardhouse. He heard the phone ringing as he returned. "Post five. How may I help you?"

"This is Captain Sitzler"

"Yes, Captain."

"Be on the look out for an American couple named Phillips, trying to return something they found."

"They were just here." He looked out of his window and saw them rounding the corner of the fence and walking up toward the building. "I sent them over to the fourth floor of the office complex to the office of the curia. I can see them just now walking toward the door."

"Oh shit," Jason said as he slammed up the phone. He busted through his door and ran down the hall to the main door of his offices in a full-out run. Reaching the hall, he made a left toward the executive offices. Just as he rounded the corner of the main hallway, he was just in time to see a couple step into the elevator and the door close. His heart racing, he ran to the stairway, taking two steps at a time. He finally made it to the fourth floor. He saw the Phillips going down the hall toward the door to the curia offices. Jason took a deep breath and called out. "Mr. Phillips!"

Willard took his hand off the door handle and turned toward Jason who was bent over trying to catch his breath. They did not know what to do. Jason looked up to see Willard reach out again for the door handle. "Mr. and Mrs. Phillips, please wait a moment," he said, walking slowly toward them. "I am Captain Jason Sitzler of the Swiss Guards. We have been expecting you. I believe you have a key to return. Please come with me." Willard took his hand off the door, and he and Catherine followed Jason down the hallway.

They had not gone five steps with the door to the curia office opened and Father Anton called after them. "Captain Sitzler, what's all the commotion about?"

"Sorry to disturb you, Father Anton. It was just a mix up in destinations." Anton stepped back inside and closed the door.

"Mr. and Mrs. Phillips, the Rome police called to tell us your were on the way here. I tried to alert all of my guard to be on the lookout for you. When I called the guardhouse, he must have been out talking with you. I will escort you to my office where I will call Archbishop Valanti, who is the keeper of the papal archives, and you can give him the key."

They all got into the elevator and took it down to the ground floor. The Phillips followed Jason back to his office. "Please have a seat. Can I offer you something to drink?"

"Yes, some water would be good."

"Corporal! Please bring in two bottles of water for our guests" While they were waiting for the water, he called Valanti. "Archbishop, would you please come to my office? I have some guests you will want to meet."

Then turning to the Phillips. "He will be here in a moment. How did you come by the key?"

They related the whole story to Jason. "The priest you helped was a dear friend of mine. I am so great full for your help."

"We were so saddened to learn that he died." The corporal opened the door for the archbishop and brought the water in to the office. He set the water down on a table. Archbishop Valanti walked over to them offering his hand as they stood to greet him. He held their hands and blessed them. Jason told Valanti how Mrs. Phillip had helped Patrick.

"I too am most grateful to you for your kindness." Catherine reached into her purse and brought out the key and handed it to Valanti. "Words cannot express our gratitude and appreciation to you. This key belonged to our beloved Pope Leo, and it must be passed on to the next pope. The priest you helped wore it around his neck for safekeeping. Is there anything that we can do for you while you are in Rome?"

"We were hoping to see the Sistine Chapel, but we understand it is sealed off for the conclave."

"Yes, it is. But if you are ever in Rome again, it would be my honor to give you a personal tour. In the meantime, I will send over to the hotel a book showing the chapel as well as other parts of the Vatican to you. May God richly bless you," Valanti said as he shook their hands again and left the office.

A moment later, Inspector Capleno arrived.

"Inspector, may I introduce to you Mr. and Mrs. Phillips. This is inspector Capleno of the Rome police. I was just about to offer the Phillips a ride back to the hotel."

"Captain, I need a few minutes of your time. I have an official car and driver outside. Allow me the honor of giving Mr. and Mrs. Phillips a ride back to their hotel."

"Thank you, Inspector. I will have my corporal escort Mr. and Mrs. Phillips out to the inspector's car. If there is anything I can do for you while you are visiting here, please let me know. Here is my card with my personal number on it."

"Thank you, Captain."

As the corporal escorted them out, the inspector said to Jason, "Let's go back to Patrick's room I am sure getting the key back will brighten his spirits."

Chapter 44

The light from the hall brought Sebastian's head around toward the door. Even though it was a single bulb, it was blinding, coming out of total darkness. He blinked his eyes, trying to make out who was standing in the doorway. It did not take long once Carlos opened his mouth.

"Good morning, Sebastian. I hope the accommodations were to your liking." Sebastian could hear the sarcasm dripping from his mouth. He did not answer. He couldn't even if he wanted to. His mouth was so dry that no sound would come out. "What's wrong? Cat got your tongue? Marino, bring some water over here and give our guest a drink."

Marino came over to Sebastian, and he opened his mouth. Nothing had ever tasted so good on his parched throat and tongue.

"That's enough," yelled Carlos. "We don't want to spoil our guest, do we?" Carlos walked over to Sebastian, cupping his hand under his jaw. He forced Sebastian to look up at him. "Ready to tell me what I want to know?" Sebastian just looked at him. "Marino, roll the battery charger over here to me. See this little box? I can generate enough juice to cook you. But I will do it slowly so that you will feel every jolt passing through your body. If you tell me what I want, and we find the manuscript, I will make it easy on you. How about a bullet right between your eyes? That way, you will meet your maker instantly." Sebastian could see the evil force in Carlos's eyes. He sat there and said nothing. "Maybe a little jolt to get things started will loosen up your tongue. Marino, go over there to the wall, and plug in the charger, then bring in the water hose. We will give out guest a little shower." Marino came in with the hose and began to run water over Sebastian. The cold water stung the cuts Carlos had opened on his chest and the new ones he has inflicted across his back and legs with the barbed rope. "That's fast enough."

Carlos reached down and connected one of the cables of the charger to the metal chair. Turning up the power lever to about one quarter, he held the other cable in his hand. He placed a metal rod on the end he held. Putting on rubber gloves, he stood over Sebastian. "Where did you hide the manuscript?" Sebastian just looked at him. "Last chance. Where is the manuscript? OK, monk, you had your chance." He took the rod and touched it to Sebastian's bare chest. There was a cracking sound that turned into a sizzle of flesh. Sebastian arched back in the chair as the electrical charge passed through his body. Every one of his muscles contracted at once in an agonizing spasm of pain. He felt a scream forming in his throat but nothing came out. Carlos pulled back the rod.

The skin on his chest was blistering up and the smell of charred flesh filled his nose, causing him to gag. The bile from his stomach rose up his throat and came out of this mouth and nose. He heaved again, spewing it out and all over Carlos. "You son of a bitch," Carlos yelled at him. "You have ruined my clothes. Marino, rinse him off while I change clothes. And while I am gone, untie him from the chair and tie him up to the chain and tighten it so that he will be standing. When I get back, I will help you, and we will pull the chain so that he is hanging up by his arms." Carlos left.

Marino untied Sebastian's legs and helped him stand. He walked him over to where the chain was hanging from the ceiling and did as Carlos instructed. He then took the hose and rinsed Sebastian off. This time, the cold water felt good on his burned chest. "Brother Sebastian, please tell Carlos what he wants to know," pleaded Marino. "He is a very cruel man. He will take great pleasure in inflicting pain on you. Please, God, forgive me, I don't want to do this, but he will kill me and my family if I don't do as he says."

"I understand, Marino, but I can't let him find that manuscript. You don't understand the evil that can be loosened on the world. God will give me the strength I need. I forgive you, and God will forgive you." Marino went over and picked up the bottle of water and gave Sebastian another drink. "Thank you!"

They both heard the heavy footsteps coming toward them as Carlos came down the stairs. He came through the door dressed in clean clothes. "Come here, and help me pull up the monk." Marino came over, and together they pulled up the chain until Sebastian was hanging several inches off the floor. "Marino, hang the hose up over the beam and let it down until it is just over the monk's head. That's good. Now go and turn on the water and let it run slowly over him and into the drain in the floor that should make a good ground. Now attach the cable to the chain just above his head. He looks too comfortable. Take your knife and cut of his boxers, I want him nude. How do you feel now, monk? Nothing is more degrading than to be stripped of your clothing. You will tell me what I want to know. I have never failed to get everything out of my special guests. Now what you got before was mild. Turn up the dial to half power, Marino. Talk, monk! Where did you hide the manuscript?"

Sebastian just looked at Carlos and shook his head. "Well, let's start at the bottom and work our way up. Most don't let me make it past their balls before they tell me what I want to hear, and by then, they are crying like a baby." Carlos took the electrical rod and touched it to the ball of Sebastian's foot. It felt like a bolt of lighting coursing through his body. His arms and legs jerked like he was a puppet on a string. This time the scream that formed in his throat came out and echoed through the basement. As Carlos removed the rod, his muscles relaxed, and he just hung limp. Pain shot through his entire body as he hung there. His brain ached, and he tasted the salty blood and felt it dripping from his mouth where his teeth had bitten a whole in his tongue.

"How did you like that, monk?" This went on for what seemed like an eternity to Sebastian as Carlos slowly moved the rod up his body. He had burns from the bottom of his feet to his calves thankfully, the last jolt had been so painful that he had blacked out. Even the water running over him could not bring him to.

"Marino, might as well turn the water off. It looks like he will be out for a while."

"Yes, boss." Carlos turned off the charger and lay the rod down. He took off his rubber gloves and laid them on top of the charger. The smell of burnt flesh mixed with urine permeated the basement. Sebastian hanging there looked more dead than alive. Carlos looked at his watch. It was close to noon.

Carlos's cell began to ring. It was one of his men that he sent to watch the American and his daughter the nun.

"Yes!"

"Boss, we have the American Mat Mason and his daughter. They may have found where the monk had been hiding. We are in the car and heading that way."

"When you get here, bring them directly into the warehouse. I will meet you there. Marino, I am going upstairs to wait on our newest guests. Loosen the chain so the monk can lie on the floor. It may help to awaken him." Marino did what he was told. He laid Sebastian on his back on the concrete floor. Feeling sorry for him, he covered him up with a towel as best he could.

Carlos climbed the stairs into the main part of the warehouse. He opened the door to the driver's side of the sedan and sat down to wait. "This monk was a lot tougher than he thought he would be. Most men would have cracked before now. But it would not be long now. He had never had anyone withstand having the rod touch their balls. Once cooked, they would immediately begin to swell, and if the man was unlucky, it would burst at this point, and he would tell you anything to stop the pain. Most of the toughest men would beg to die, and being the man he was, once he got everything he wanted. He would either put a bullet between their eyes or jam the rod against the chest at full power and watch the blood spew from their nose and mouth as the blood in the heart boiled.

The garage door began to open, which brought Carlos out of his revelry. He watched as another black sedan pulled in beside the one he was sitting in. Carlos got out of the car and closed the door. Nicholas got out of the driver's side and walked around to where Carlos stood.

"Open the door, and let our guests out." Nicholas opened the backdoor, reached in, and got Mat by the arm and pulled him out.

"Stand over there beside the back of that car." Then he reached in and pulled out Sister Judith. "Get over there and stand beside your father."

Carlos greeted them. "It is not often that we have such distinguished guests," said Carlos, walking over toward them and standing in front of Mat and Judith. "We have a monk downstairs that I know you have been looking for. Turn around and face the car and place your hands on the roof. Nicholas, tie their hands behind their backs and take them downstairs."

Nicholas led Mat and Judith toward the basement door. Carlos motioned Plato to get out of the car. "You on vacation or something? Get downstairs and help Marino and Nicholas. I have some calls to make. Caprice!" Carlos called the don.

"Carlos, you got any news for me yet?"

"I have not been able to get the monk to talk, but Nicholas and Pablo have just brought in the American and the nun. They found where the monk has been hiding."

"Did they find the manuscript?"

"No, but I think Sebastian will talk if he thinks I will do to the nun what I have done to him."

"The cardinal is getting anxious. Get me some results."

"Yes, don. I will not fail you."

"You better not or you will find yourself on the end of that battery charger. Caprice?"

"Yes, boss."

Chapter 45

Father Anton had just settled into his office and was going through the messages that had come in for the cardinal. He was also making a list of those cardinals who were lined up to vote for Pulaski as the new pope. Cardinal Louis had done a good job of politicking in secret. Of course, he had an ulterior motive. He had been promised that he would become the head of the curia, the next most important position in the Vatican under the pope. Pulaski also had incentive for Father Anton. After Pulaski became pope, Anton would be elevated to the title of archbishop and would replace Valanti as curator of the papal archives. Tallying up the votes, it looked likely that Pulaski had just enough to be elected.

The door opened and Cardinal Pulaski breezed in, his red sash flying behind him like a kite tail. "Anton, I have a job for you," he said on the way into his office. Anton got up to follow him in. Pulaski stopped by the credenza to pour himself a cup of coffee from the carafe. Anton made sure it was there every morning. Settling himself into his overstuffed chair behind the massive desk, Anton came and stood before him and offered him the messages and the tally sheet. Pulaski waved it away. "Just put it on the corner of my desk and sit down. You know that I don't like people standing above me." Anton was over six feet tall and usually towered over the five foot six Pulaski. Anton sat in one of the chairs facing the desk. The chairs had been specially ordered to have unusually short legs, making those sitting there look up at the cardinal. Sitting there caused Anton's knees to be nearly up to his chin—a very uncomfortable position. "I want you to go into the office of Monsignor O'Rourke and take his calls and messages. We need to find out what he and that old fox Valanti found out from Sebastian. Also search his desk and files discretely and see if you can find the letter Leo left for the next pope or any other correspondence he may have left. See if you can find the papal key Leo was wearing when he died. O'Rourke may have hidden it. We know Valanti doesn't have it, or they would not be looking for it. Check the voice mail also. Now go and report back to me anything you find." Anton got up and left.

Pulaski reached over and started going through his messages and his schedule that Anton had left. He was scheduled to meet with several cardinals to try to obtain their votes with some type of bribe. Things had not changed in a thousand years. People who wanted to be pope still had to buy and bribe votes. He picked up the tally sheet and smiled. *I won't have to do too much work,* he thought. He began making his calls.

Anton approached Patrick's office and was stopped by the Swiss Guard stationed there.

"May I help you, Father? Monsignor O'Rourke is not in at the moment."

"I have been sent here by Cardinal Pulaski to man the office and answer any questions the visiting cardinals may have."

"I was told not to admit anyone."

"Call whomever you must, but I am going in."

The guard immediately called his Capitan's cell phone. "I have a Father Anton wanting access to Monsignor's O'Rourke's office."

"Let him pass."

"You may go in." Anton brushed past the guard and entered the waiting room. He passed through it into Patrick's office. He locked the door behind him. The light on the answering machine was flashing. There were twenty-five messages, nothing of importance. Methodically, he searched Patrick's desk and then his files in the credenza behind the desk and came up with nothing. He saw some papers in the trash and came across a phone number he thought he recognized and a name he knew—Brother John. That's how Sebastian contacted O'Rourke. He knew it. He put the paper into his pocket. *I will deal with you later, my fine Brother John, for lying to me,* he thought.

Pulaski's stomach began to growl. He looked over at the clock—ten until twelve. He decided to take a break. He called his friend Cardinal Louis to accompany him to lunch. They had plans to make and that needed to be done away from the Vatican. They met outside the executive offices where Pulaski had his car and driver waiting. The driver opened the door and helped the cardinals into the backseat. This was one of the safest places in Rome to talk. Pulaski and Louis settled in as the car pulled away from the curb and into the Rome lunchtime traffic.

"Take us to that little café Giovanni's just outside of Rome," the cardinal instructed his driver. On the way to the restaurant, they plotted their take over of the Vatican and relished the power and wealth they would have. They entered the restaurant and took their usual corner booth in the back. The waiter came over with their favorite drinks. Just as they were about to toast themselves, Pulaski's cell began to ring. He took it out and looked at the caller ID.

"It's the don. I need to take this."

Hello, Vincenza, hope you have good news. Ah, so you have been released from St. Joseph's. You call and interrupt my lunch with this trivia. Well, now that is what I want to hear. Call me immediately when you know something. Ah, dear Martin, we can celebrate. Carlos men have picked up Mat Mason and Sister Judith and have taken them to the warehouse where they are holding Brother Sebastian. Carlos thinks he will tell us where in the catacombs the manuscript is located in if Carlos threatens to harm the nun. She and her father have provided us with the entrance Sebastian used. Our friend, Don Amato, is on his way over to see to things personally. It won't be long now. We will have everything needed." Pulaski and Martin raised their glasses and drank to success.

Back at the Vatican, Jason, Valanti, and the inspector were still in Patrick's room. The inspector's driver had dropped off the Phillips at their hotel and was on his way back to the Vatican. "Well, the Phillips are safely back at their hotel. It's one o'clock. Anyone hungry yet?"

"If you are buying, Lorenzo, we all are," answered Jason for all of them. "You know I thought we would have heard from Mat by now. They only had two possible entrances to check out."

"They may have just stopped for lunch," commented Valanti. "That may be so, but knowing Sister Judith not hearing from her surprises me."

"Jason, don't worry if we have had no word by the time we return. I will send out a couple of patrol cars to check on them."

"Jason, you and Lorenzo, go ahead. I will have something sent in for Patrick and me."

There was a knock on the door, and the corporal stuck his head in. "Sir, the inspector's driver has returned, and he is outside."

"Thank you, Corporal. Patrick, do you feel like getting out for a while? We could have the car brought around into the tunnel and get you out before you can be seen."

"Thanks, Jason, but it is too dangerous for Sebastian if I am seen. Valanti and I will just eat in, but thanks."

"OK, we should be back by no later than two thirty." Lorenzo and Jason left the guard quarters and went out by the main entrance to

Lorenzo's car. Lorenzo climbed into the front seat by the driver, and Jason got into the back. As they pulled away from the curb, the radio in the car came on paging. "Delta one, come in. Delta one, do your read me?"

Lorenzo motioned to the driver that he would get it. "Delta one here."

"Delta one, I have a report from one of the patrol cars cruising the industrial and warehouse area that one of Don Amato's cars has been spotted entering a garage in that district. They also reported sighting another dark sedan already parked inside." The Scion Carlos was driving earlier is parked in the lot adjacent to the office.

"Roger that. Have the patrol keep watch, and stay out of sight and call for backup. Do not approach. Repeat, do not approach. Just keep me apprised if something changes."

"Yes, Captain."

"Do you think that may be where they are keeping Sebastian?"

"That is a good possibility, Jason, but for now, we need to just watch and wait. Let's eat at Victories. It will be quick."

"Sounds good to me." Detective Remetta turned at the next intersection onto Via del Babuind and headed for Victories on Via Del Carrozze across from the Spanish Steppe's.

Chapter 46

Mat and Judith would never have made it down the steep slick steps with their arms tied behind them if Nicholas and Palo had not held them tightly. The smell of feces, old urine, and burnt flesh attacked their noses as they reached the bottom of the stairs.

The hall was wide enough to allow their captors to walk beside them while holding onto their upper arms. The further down the hall, they went toward the opened door the stronger the odor became. It was so bad, Judith involuntary reached bending over, and Nicholas kept her from falling. Mat began to breathe only through his mouth, trying to stifle the smell. Judith did the same.

At the door, Nicholas let go of Judith's arm and pushed her through the door. Palo did the same to Mat. In addition to the other smells, there was an underlying odor of rot and mold. It took a few minutes for their eyes to adjust to the darkness coming in from the hallway. At first, they only saw a piece of equipment in the center of the floor and a metal chair. Then they saw a chain hanging from the ceiling with a water hose suspended above it. Looking down, Judith noticed something on the floor. She strained, trying to make it out. She could define the outline of what must be a body. She drew back in horror.

"Don't be shy," Marino said, pushing her toward the figure lying on the floor had enough that she fell. Hitting the wet floor, she slid toward it on her stomach coming to rest against it.

Nicholas walked over and lifted her to her knees. Mat screamed at them to leave her alone. Marino walked over to him and punched him hard in the midsection, causing him to double over onto his knees. Palo walked behind him and taking his foot kicked him in the back, causing him to slide over also toward where Judith was. Marino kicked Mat in the side several times, then taking his foot rolled him over onto this back. Grabbing him by the shirt, he pulled him into a sitting position.

"Get onto your knees," he yelled while repeatedly kicking him in the legs. He then spun him around so that he and Judith were facing the same direction. Judith had turned her head and was watching Marino and Palo beating her dad. She now turned back toward the body that was lying in front of her. She could tell it was a man who had been severely beaten and tortured. His face was turned away so she didn't know who it was.

She could see his chest rise and fall so she knew that he was still alive. Marino walked over and turned Sebastian's head toward her. Judith gasped when she saw who it was. "Recognize your favorite monk now?"

"Yes! What have you done to him?"

"Tried to make him talk, but he turned out to be a stubborn bastard. Said he won't talk. He would rather die."

"Marino, have you been entertaining our guest?" said Carlos, strolling through the door. "Pick up Mr. Mason and tie him to the chair. Now untie our good sister's arms from behind her back and tie her to that chain over here. Pull it tight enough that she is hanging there just able to touch the floor, and by the way, strip her down to her bra and panties."

It took all three men to do as Carlos said. Judith fought them with all that she had. Mat strained against his bonds until his arms and legs were bloody from pulling against the plastic ties.

"Marino, go and get another chair, Then you and Nicholas pick up the monk and tie him to it. Place him right in front of the nun." When they picked up Sebastian, the towel fell off, and he was tied to the chair totally nude in front of Judith. "I hope the sight of a naked male does not offend you too much. I've heard you nuns get it on with the monks and the priest all the time. Looks like this monk could do some damage with that dick. Ever had any of that?"

"Don't talk to my daughter like that, you filthy pig."

Carlos walked over to Mat and backhanded him so hard, it knocked out one of his teeth. "Don't speak to me again like that if you want your daughter to live." This time, he punched Mat in his face breaking his nose. Blood ran down from his nose, dripping off his chin.

"Marino, get a bucket of water and throw it on the monk. We need to wake him up." Marino went out and got the water and did as Carlos had told him. Sebastian still did not wake up. "Marino, go upstairs and look in the cabinet by the desk where we keep some medical supplies and bring me some ammonia." Carlos got a hand full of Sebastian's hair and pulled his head up. He lightly slapped him across the face a few times. He still got no response.

Marino came back down holding a bottle of ammonia. Carlos took the bottle and uncapped it. He held the bottle under Sebastian's nose. Sebastian's head jerked back from the bottle and slowly opened his eyes. He did not know where he was. He tried to move but couldn't at first. He thought he was paralyzed.

Everything looked blurry. As he looked up in front of him, he thought he saw Jesus on the cross. "Forgive me, Lord, for I have sinned," he mumbled. Once again, Carlos grabbed him by the hair and held his face up toward Judith. As he stared up at her, his eyes cleared, and he recognized her hanging there before him. "Sister Judith."

"Welcome back, monk." His mind began to clear, and he remembered where he was. The sound of Carlos voice had jolted him back into reality. His mind was having a hard time conceiving what he was looking at. A nun stripped to her underwear. "You will surely pay for this outrage, Carlos. I damn you to hell for all eternity."

"Damn all you want, monk. Cardinal Pulaski has already given me absolution. Now tell me where the manuscript is hidden. We already know the location where you entered the catacombs, thanks to your nun friend here and her father."

"Tell him nothing, Sebastian. I have no fear of him or death," screamed Judith.

"We'll see about that. Marino, turn on the water hose, and you and Nicholas pull up the chain until our good sister here is hanging off the floor." The water began to run over Judith beginning with her head. As it ran down and soaked her bra and panties, they seemed to disappear leaving her hanging there nude. Both Mat and Sebastian bowed their heads and closed their eyes, not wanting to see her like this.

"What's wrong, Sebastian? Don't you like what you see? That looks like prime stuff to me. How's about you, guys? I wouldn't mind tapping that. How about you Palo?" asked Nicholas.

"Yeah, I'd pop that a few times," he replied.

Carlos put his hand under Sebastian's chin and forced his face up toward Judith. "Open your eyes, monk, or she will pay the price." Sebastian slowly opened his eyes and locked his eyes onto hers. "Bring the charge in a little closer, and let's give the girl a little thrill." Marino rolled it over, and Carlos put on his rubber gloves. He turned the poser dial up low. "Tell me, monk, now!" Judith shook her head so Sebastian remained silent.

Carlos let go of Sebastian and moved toward Judith. He reached out with the rod and touched her on the toe. There was a zap, then a sizzling sound as the arc of electricity jumped from the rod to her toe. The smell of fresh burned flesh, and Judith's scream filled the room all at once.

Mat yelled, "No!" at the top of his lungs, as did Sebastian.

"I'm sure you remember from earlier today how that feels, don't you, monk? I will keep moving up her body and increasing the voltage until you are ready to talk. Her pain is on your head."

"No, please, stop. If you will let her down and cover her up, I will lead you to the manuscript."

"I thought you would. Just tell where it is, and we will go and get it."

"I have hidden it in a place that you would never find. I will have to take you to it."

"Palo, take her down and help her into her blouse and pants and then tie her to that chair next to her father. Marino, go upstairs and get something for the monk to wear and some shoes." Nicholas and Palo untied Judith from the chain and helped her dress and then tied her next to her father. Marino came back with the clothes for Sebastian.

"Boss, the don is upstairs and wants to see you."

"OK, bring the monk up when you are finished."

Nicholas, stay here and guard our guest. Palo, I want you to come upstairs with me."

Marino and Nicholas dried off Sebastian and dressed him in sweats and sandals, then retied his hands this time in front of him. They placed a leather belt around his waist and tied his bound hands to the belt.

Marino took Sebastian by the arm and began to lead him toward the door. After one step, his knees buckled, and he went down. He would have landed on his face if Marino had not had a hold on him.

"Get up!" Sebastian tried but just couldn't. "I can't," he said with his trough-parched lips.

"Nicholas, look in that ice chest and get me one of those sports drinks." He brought it over to Marino who uncapped it and held it to Sebastian's lips. He drank greedily, taking in too much too fast. As soon as Marino removed the bottle from his lips, it all came right back up. Sebastian heaved again, but this time nothing came up. "Too much to fast he whispered." Marino took a towel and wiped his face.

This time, Sebastian took just a little. The waited a few minutes and then he took a little more.

"What's the hold up down there?"

"I was giving the monk some sports drink, so he will be able to stand. We are coming now. Drink the rest if you can. It may be a long time before you get another chance." Sebastian downed the rest that was in the bottle.

"Nicholas, give me a hand."

With the help of both of them, Sebastian was able to stand. Marino held his arm with one hand and got hold of the belt with the other. Holding him up this way, they moved slowly to the door and toward the steps.

"Hey, boss, send Palo down. He will never be able to climb these steps without a lot of help." Palo came down the steps. He took the other arm and the belt and between them, they made it up the steps.

"Brother Sebastian, I'm sure the cardinal will be pleased that you have decided to help us. Put him in the backseat of that car. Who is going with you, Carlos?"

"Just Marino and me. The fewer people, involved the better. I thought I would leave Nicholas up here and send Palo down to the basement to guard the nun and her father."

"Good, good. Call me as soon as you get the manuscript."

"Yes, don."

"Carlos, I will open the garage door for you, then after I call the cardinal, I will be going home. You can call me there."

Marino got in the back with Sebastian, and Carlos got in the driver's seat. The don opened the door and Carlos backed out, turned the car around, and headed toward the cemetery.

Chapter 47

Cell phones began to ring at various restaurants around and about Rome. First one to ring was that of Inspector Lorenzo Capleno. He was in mid-bite when his rang. "Inspector Capleno speaking."

"Inspector, this is Gillespie. I am with the units watching the warehouse. The don arrived about thirty minutes ago. When he pulled his car into the warehouse, there were two cars already parked inside. From the partial plate we had, one of the cars parked inside is the one used to abduct Sebastian and the monsignor. The door just opened and one of the cars just left with Carlos driving, and there were two other men in the backseat, and I couldn't make out who they were."

"Another car is leaving now. It is driven by the don."

"You stay put. Have one of the cars there follow Carlos and have another follow the don. Tell your men to call as soon as the reach their destination."

"Will do!"

He turned to Jason. "Seems like Carlos and the don are on the move. Call the archbishop and see if he has news about Mat and Sister Bridget."

Jason made the call and bought the archbishop and Patrick up to date on what was happening. "Have you heard from Mat or Sister Judith?"

"No, and we are beginning to worry."

"OK, I will get back to you."

"They have heard nothing."

"I will make a few calls and see if one of our informants can tell if they are still out on the street."

Cardinal Pulaski and Cardinal Louis were on their second bottle of wine, enjoying a plate of antipasto awaiting their meal. Pulaski's cell rang. Glancing down at the number, he recognized it as belonging to Don Amato. "Yes, what is it. I am having lunch," he said into the cell.

"Sorry, your eminence. But I thought you would want to know Carlos and Marino are in the car with Brother Sebastian on their way to pick up the manuscript."

"Did you say manuscript?"

"Yes, your grace. We should have it soon."

"Now that is the kind of news I want to hear. Call me the minute you have it in your hand at the warehouse."

"Yes, your eminence."

"That was the don. I should have the manuscript and the monk along with Mason and the troublesome nun very soon now. Things are beginning to come together. Let us toast to power."

"To power," they said, touching their glasses together and drank deeply.

Meals were being served at both cafés. One table ate in worried silence, the other in jubilant celebration.

Another lunch was taking place in Patrick's room at the Swiss Guard headquarters at the Vatican. "Patrick, I am worried about Mat and Sister Bridget. They had only two places to check out."

"I am sure they will be OK. They may have just stopped for a long lunch and time to catch up on family and friends. I have been thinking that it is time for us to involve someone else."

"What do you mean? We already have the help of the Rome police."

"I think someone else here at the Vatican needs to know what we have found out about Cardinal Pulaski."

"You may be right. From what I hear, he is the most favored to be elected as our next pope."

"You know, we can't allow that to happen. What do you know about Cardinal Alveraz, the camerlengo?"

"He is a good man, well respected among the other cardinals. He has not served long here in Rome, so he is not involved in the intrigues that abound in this city. Why do you ask?"

"I think since he is acting head of the church until the election. He should know what is going on."

"I feel that he can be trusted but much of what is going on only a pope should know."

"I agree, but Valanti, much of that may soon come out, and those that can be trusted will be good allies in keeping the secret. If we had known what we know now, Pulaski would not have been able to gain so much power."

"This is true, but it was not our decision. This knowledge has been held by the reigning pope for thousands of years."

"I understand, but we need important allies if a confrontation with Pulaski happens."

"I agree, but we must keep it to a small trusted group."

"I agree."

"Call him and see if he will meet with you in Jason's office. Then bring him back to my room, and we will fill him in on that is happening. We cannot let Pulaski be elected pope."

"You are right, Patrick." Valanti walked over to the nightstand and picked up the phone and placed the call.

"This is Archbishop Valanti. I wish to speak to the camerlengo."

"One moment please" came the reply.

"Yes, Archbishop, how may I help you?"

"This is of utmost importance. I need to meet with you in secret. I have information you need to hear. Will you meet me in the office of Captain Spitzer as soon as it is possible."

"I am in the middle of finalizing the plans for the conclave. Can't you tell me this over the phone?"

"This has to do with the Pope's death and the priest being shot. This matter is very delicate."

"I see. I will meet you in one hour."

"Thank you, Cardinal Alveraz."

"One hour, Patrick. Let's finish lunch and then it should be time to go and meet him.

"Inspector, is that your cell again?"

"I did not hear it ring, Jason," he said as he stood and removed it from his from pants pocket. "Inspector Capleno speaking, that does not sound good. When did this happen? I see. Call in a special unit to meet us at the warehouse. Waiter! Check please" He said as he motioned the waiter over to the table.

"What's going on?"

"Mat and his daughter were seen being forced into a car at the cemetery by one of my informants." The waiter came over and laid the lunch tab on the table. Jason picked it up and threw down twenty euros. He and the inspector hurried to the door. "How far is it to the warehouse?"

"About thirty minutes. We could make it in less time using the sirens but that would alert anyone inside, and we do not want to do that."

"I have a special ops squad on the way. We should get there about the same time they do." Both jumped into the inspector's car. "Head toward the warehouse district, and the warehouse we are staking out. Looks like you will be having a late lunch today," he told his driver Detective Remetta.

"Got a radio message that the don is at home."

"Call and tell the patrol officers to stay out of sight, and let us know if he leaves."

Remetta made the call. "Delta one, do your read me?"

"This is Delta one."

"We are trailing Carlos. They have just parked across from the cemetery. Carlos is getting out. The two in the backseat are also exiting the vehicle. One of the suspects I can identify. It is Carlos's man, Marino. The other suspect appears to be in shackles. Hands tied in front of him and attached to a leather belt around his waist."

"Can you now identify him?"

"No, sir."

"Hang back and watch. Let me know if they leave."

"Will do Delta one."

"Something is going on over there. That has to be Sebastian. Something has made him give them the location of where he hid the manuscript."

"Lorenzo, he would not have done that unless they do have Mat and Sister Judith."

"I agree. We need to free them and set a trap for Carlos when he returns."

"What makes you think that they will go back there?"

"Just a hunch."

"Delta one, come in."

"This is Delta one, go ahead."

"Looks like Carlos has cut the cuffs off the man's hands. He and Marino have him by the arms and are crossing the street toward the long wall that runs along the cemetery."

"Just watch and wait. Let me know when they return."

"Out."

"How much further to the warehouse, Remetta?"

"We should be there in fifteen minutes, depending on the traffic."

Patrick and Valanti finished their lunch. "I will bring the camerlengo back here before I tell him anything."

"I think that is a good idea. The shock of seeing me will make him more responsive." Valanti left Patrick and made his way back to Jason's office to wait. Valanti did not have to wait to long. The corporal ushered in Cardinal Alveraz, the camerlengo into Jason's office. Valanti looked at the clock. It was one thirty.

"You are early, your grace."

"I was hoping you would be early yourself, Archbishop. I have had more than a few questions put to me especially since the priest was shot and killed. Although, I have not been serving here long, in Rome, rumors travel fast as I have learned. The many ways one plays for power are learned quickly if one is to survive. I have known Leo for many years, and I spoke with him often. I knew something was bothering him but to my knowledge was that he was in good health. My sympathies are with you my friend for I know you were very fond of him."

"Thank you, your grace. Leo and I go back a long way."

"Do you know when Monsignor O'Rourke will return from his trip?"

"That is one of the many things we need to discuss. But first, I have something you need to see. Please come with me." Valanti led the cardinal out of Jason's office and back to Patrick's room.

"Where are we going?"

"Just to this room right here." The guard stepped aside, and Valanti opened the door for the cardinal. Upon entering, he saw Patrick sitting in a chair by the fireplace. He just stopped and just stared. Yes, it was Monsignor O'Rourke, but he looked somehow different so pale and was struggling to stand to greet the cardinal.

"Please come in, your grace. It is good to see you."

"What's going on here?"

"Please sit down, and we will explain." The cardinal sat down, and Patrick and Valanti did also. Patrick started, "Your grace, remember the priest who was shot two days ago and was reported dead? That priest was me."

"Then how are you here? I was told that you were on a trip for Pope Leo."

"That was a lie your grace to cover up my murder."

Over the next hour, Valanti and Patrick laid out all that had happened beginning with the pope's death up to calling the cardinal.

"I must say that is an unbelievable story. What proof do you have?" Patrick pulled up his shirt and showed the cardinal his wounds. Then he opened his Bible, Jason had gotten for him from his room and showed the cardinal the letters from Leo. Archbishop Valanti pulled his letter out and also showed it to the cardinal. For the next few minutes the Cardinal studies the letters and contemplated all that he had been told.

Valanti's cell rang. "Sorry, your grace, I must get this call. It is from Inspector Capleno."

"Yes, Inspector. We will pray for your success. Mat Mason and Sister Judith are being held in the don's warehouse. The inspector has a special ops unit there now and will attempt to free them. Carlos has who the inspector thinks is Sebastian at the cemetery entrance to the catacombs. He needs to rescue Mat and Judith before they return with Sebastian and the manuscript. Cardinal Alveraz, if Cardinal Pulaski goes to the warehouse, it would be good for you to witness what happens."

"I want to be there also," said Patrick.

"Yes, Archbishop, you are right. I need to see for myself how the rest of this unfolds. I am going back to Captain Sitzler's office to make a few calls. Come there, and get me if we need to leave. I will call, and have a car and driver standing by. Monsignor, I understand why you want to be there. But you can hardly stand. I feel it would be too dangerous."

"I will not hinder anyone, your grace, but please let me try."

"I will let the archbishop make that decision." The cardinal rose to go. With great effort, Patrick stood and bent down and kissed his ring. Valanti ushered the cardinal out. Patrick forced himself to walk over to the bathroom, then back to where he had been sitting. He did this several times as Valanti watched.

"Save your strength, Patrick. You know I would not deny you accompanying us to the warehouse or where ever this plays out."

"Thank you, Valanti," he said, collapsing into a chair.

Chapter 48

Sitting tied to the metal chair, Judith shivered in the cold dampness. Water from her wet hair dripped down her forehead and ran in rivulets down her back, keeping the blouse wet. The cold from the metal seemed to be absorbed by her blouse and transferred to her damp skin. She rocked the chair with her shivering, giving the silence an eerie sound. The burn on her foot where Carlos touched it with the rod ached and had blistered up and was oozing blood. She looked over at her dad; the blood from his broken nose had run down his face and was crusted on his lips and chin and what had dripped onto his shirt had already turned to a rusty brown color. His face had turned blue on the cheek, and his eye was black where Carlos had punched and slapped him. The tooth that had been knocked out lay beside his chair, shining in the darkness, reflecting the light from the lone bulb in the hallway. His head was hanging down onto his chest, and his eyes were closed.

"Dad, Dad," she whispered.

Mat slowly raised his head. "I am so sorry, Judith. I felt so helpless. I will never forgive myself for what happened to you."

"It's not your fault what these evil men did."

"Yes, it is. I should never have called you in the first place to accompany me."

"You didn't know what would happen."

"I knew that they had Sebastian and that the mafia and the cardinal were involved. I should have realized just how dangerous it was."

"Dad, it's all right. I love you, and we will get out of this."

"The only way out for us, Judith, is death."

"Don't say that."

"But it is the truth. We know too much. I can only buy us a little time, working on the manuscript. Once they get what they want, it is over. I can only pray it will be quick for both of us. I just can't stand the thought of them hurting you."

"Hey, both of you shut up! Anymore talking, and I will duct tape your mouths shut."

"Could we have some water?"

"So what do you think? This is a five-star hotel with room service?"

"No, sir. If you don't want to give me any that's all right, but please give some to my daughter."

"All right." Palo went out to the hall.

"Judith, when he is not looking, try to rub your ties against the metal chair. Hopefully, the friction will weaken the plastic ties."

"I told you, no talking." Palo uncapped the bottle and held it to Judith's lips. The cold water made her feel better. Palo walked over to Mat and also gave him a drink. The cold water hurt his lip and where his tooth was gone, but at least, it washed out the taste of blood in his mouth.

"Thank you," he told Palo. Palo walked back into the hall and yelled up the stairs, "Have you heard anything yet, Nicholas?"

"No, nothing."

Across the street, things were beginning to heat up. Jason and the inspector arrived just after the special ops rescue team had. The inspector walked over with Jason to the team lead. It was Sergeant Tunelly. "Nice to have you onboard, Sergeant." He introduced the sergeant to Jason. "Like you to meet Captain Jason Sitzler. He is the commander of the Swiss Guard over at the Vatican."

"Good to meet you, sir."

"We need to get into that warehouse very quickly and overpower whoever is inside and secure the building. It must look normal to Carlos when he or the don returns. We need to secure the cooperation of any of the don's men he left inside. Any ideas?"

"We have called for plans of the warehouse to be sent over. Let's walk over to the van which is our command post." As they entered, the officer at the screen said, "Plans have just arrived. I have sent them to the printer."

Sergeant Tunelly walked over and pulled them off. He laid them on the table, and all three gathered around. "From what we see hear, we can enter from the office area. That lock can be easily picked. I will send a two-man team to do that and disable the alarm system. We have the latest in stun-gun technology. We can put a man down quietly at fifty yards, and they will not make a sound."

"How long will they remain paralyzed?"

"About ten minutes tops."

"Call you men together, and let's get this done."

A two-man team circled the block and came in on the blind side of the building. They were in the office in less than three minutes. The office was dark so they crept forward toward what they knew from the plans was the warehouse door. Finding the door locked once again, they used their picks and unlocked it. Cracking the door just enough to slip a slim cord, which had a camera in the front, the man spotted Nicholas sitting at a desk facing the door. He had his iPhone out and appeared to be texting or playing a game on it. In any event, they would be seen the moment the door was opened. He signaled the man behind him to back up and return to the front door. He withdrew the cable and followed him out. Once out of ear range, he pressed the send button on his headset, "Sergeant, we have spotted one subject sitting directly in front of the door. We need some kind of distraction to get his attention toward the big garage doors."

"Copy that. Get back in position and give us forty-five seconds." They crept back into position at the door. He inserted the cable back through the door again. Nicholas was still sitting at the desk where they had last seen him.

They were both crouched on ready. Suddenly, Nicholas jumped up from the chair, turning it over, looked toward the garage doors. The lead man popped opened the door and fired at Nicholas's back. He toppled over and hit the floor. Hitting his mike switch, he said, "Target down."

The inspector, Jason, Sergeant Tunelly, and the rest of the team quickly crossed the street and entered the building through the office. Tunelly's lead man had Nicholas sitting on the chair with tape over his mouth. He was still out. Tunelly using hand signals deployed his men throughout the warehouse to secure it. There was a door standing open at the back of the warehouse with steps leading down to a basement. They could see a light on down there, but they did not go down.

Two of the team held Nicholas down onto the chair by the arms while another stood behind him, grasping him by the shoulders. Nicholas head began to move, and his eyes slowly opened. Feeling the pressure being exerted on his body and having his mouth taped shut, his eyes filled with fear. All he could see were men dressed in black combat gear holding rifles. One of them bent down and whispered into his ear. "Is anyone else in the building with you? Don't try to speak, just nod your head in response." Nicholas did not respond. Tunelly motioned to one of his men holding onto Nicholas arm. Nicholas felt his arm being raised, and the man took hold of his middle finger. A question was whispered into his ear again, "I there anyone else here with you. Tell me the truth or he will break your finger." Nicholas still did not respond. He felt the man change the hold on his finger and felt an increase in pressure. He quickly began to nod his head up and down. "That's good. Is there anyone up here?" He shook his head, no. "OK, are they downstairs?" He shook his head up and down. "Is there more than one?" He shakes his head, no. "I am going to remove the tape from your mouth, and I want you to call him to come up here. If you try anything, the officer behind you will snap your neck. Do you understand?" He nodded his head, yes. Sergeant Tunelly slowly peeled off the tape. Nicholas took a deep breath. He felt the officer place one hand on his forehead and the other on his jaw. "Now, call your friend."

"Palo, I need you to come up here. Palo, do you hear me?"

"Be up in a sec, Nicholas."

The two officers standing on either side of the door heard footsteps climbing the stairs. They could tell by the sound that it was only one person, and he was getting closer. Palo popped through the door and was on the floor and in cuffs, before he knew what had hit him. They brought Palo over to where Nicholas was being held. The inspector and Jason stepped out of the shadows. "Check out the basement" Two of the officers descended the steps with weapons drawn. "Where are Carlos and Marino?"

Neither man said a word. "Secure Palo to that chair and bring him over here."

"Now I will ask you again, where are Carlos and Marino? And who else is with them?" Still silence.

"Sergeant, draw you pistol and put a silencer on it. If I do not get an answer this time, begin by shooting Palo in the knee."

Turning to Palo and Nicholas, he asked, "Now where are they?"

Still silence. "Shoot Palo." The sergeant took the safety off and aimed it at Palo's knee.

"No, no, please," Palo screamed. "Carlos will kill us."

"You are dead anyway. All I have to do is put word out on the street that you talked to me, and you are dead either way. The only difference is you will be walking on crutches and living in a lot of pain. It's your choice."

"Pull the trigger, Sergeant."

"No, please. Carlos has taken the monk and has gone to the catacombs."

"Shut up, you fool," said Nicholas, scowling at Palo.

"Sergeant," called one of the policemen from the basement.

"Yes!"

"We have found two hostages down here."

"Bring them up." Inspector Capleno turned back to Palo. "Are they coming back here?"

"Yes."

Mat and Judith came through the door. "Oh Jason, Inspector Capleno, I am so glad to see both of you" as she ran toward them giving each a big hug.

"Are you all right?" Jason asked.

"I am now."

Turning to Mat, he said, "You look like you have been a dog fight."

"I was but as you can tell, it was one sided."

"Do either of you need medical help?"

"As you can see, I need a dentist," Mat said, grinning at Jason, showing he had a missing tooth.

"We can have that taken care of soon. We have just learned that Carlos will be coming back here. You may have to go back to the basement and be tied up again. We need to lay a trap for all that are involved." He looked at Nicholas and Palo. "You two will cooperate with us, or you will go down with the don and his friends. I will have you put in a safe place where you will be able to live out your lives in peace, or you can die now. What will it be?"

Palo answered first, "I'm in.

"How about you, Nicholas?"

"What about my wife and my two sons?"

"You will be able to take them with you."

"OK, I'm in too."

"All right, here's the plan. Jason, call Patrick and the archbishop."

"Patrick is alive?"

"Yes, Sister. I will explain later.

Chapter 49

"Marino, are you sure this is where they picked up Mason and the nun?"

"Yes, boss."

"Hey, monk, is this the right place?"

"Yes, Carlos."

"I am going to circle the block one time to see if we are being tailed, then we will park across the street." Carlos circled the block. He did not notice the car following him had stopped and was reporting in. He drove the car back around the block and parked two cars away from his tail. Marino opened the backdoor and got out as Carlos exited the driver's seat. Marino grabbed Sebastian and pulled him out by his arm. When Carlos came around, he cut the plastic cuffs off Sebastian, and with each of them holding onto one of Sebastian's arms and the belt. They propelled him across the street. "Where do we go from here, monk, and don't try anything heroic? I am only one phone call away from your friends. I'm sure you don't want to return to the warehouse to find them burnt to a crisp, do you?" Sebastian shook his head, no.

"OK, which way?"

"We need to walk about half way down this block toward that planted area in front of the niche built into the wall." Sebastian was still very weak from the torture and having no food but only the sports drink. He was half pushed and half dragged down the street. He was breathing hard when they arrived. "We need to get behind those bushes. There is an opening back there to the catacombs."

"There better be," Carlos growled. Marino went first, trying to bend the bushes back, so Sebastian and Carlos could squeeze by without having to crawl on their hands and knees.

"I don't see any opening."

"It's just over here. We will have to crawl in."

"Marino, you go first. Here, take this flashlight." Marino got down on his hand and knees.

"You have to lower yourself, feet first," cautioned Sebastian. Marino turned around, sticking his feet and legs into the hole. Pushing with his hands and arms, he slid in. "I'm in, boss. It's big once you get in."

"OK, Sebastian, you go next. Here comes the monk. Watch out." Sebastian backed his way in followed by Carlos. Once inside, they moved carefully into the darkness. The tunnel was wide enough that they could walk abreast of each other. Marino and Carlos held tightly onto Sebastian by the belt. Soon they were at the point where Sebastian slept. "So this is your little hideout. You got another flashlight?" Sebastian reached under his blanket and got out the one he left. With three lights, it was easier to see. They made their way down the passage until they reached where it split. Sebastian stopped like he didn't remember. "Which way?"

"I am confused. Let me think a moment." Carlos and Marino loosened their hold on Sebastian for a moment. Feeling the pressure let up, he took his flashlight, using it like a club, knocked the light out of both his captors' hands. In the confusion, like a football player, he faked right, then turned his light off and ran left. He could hear Carlos cussing, and the sound of them trying to find their flashlights in the dark and then the lights being picked up.

He stopped and stood dead still and held his breath. He could hear footsteps running first in a circle, then down the right-hand passage. He quickly lit his light and made his way down the passage to the room where the manuscript was hidden. He removed the brick and reached in, getting the handle of his briefcase. Removing it, he set it on the floor and opened it up. Inside was the manuscript. He gently untied the velum cover. He turned the pages until he found the place that told the location of the two other keys. He gently removed these pages and placed them back into the briefcase. Sebastian then put the briefcase with the remaining part of the manuscript into the crypt and put the bricks back. He took dirt off the floor and threw it onto the wall until any trace of where the bricks were removed was gone. He stooped down, picked up the remaining pages, neatly rewrapped them in the original velum cover, and stepped back into the passageway.

He was about half way down, returning to the split in the passage way when he saw lights coming toward him. "Don't move, monk," screamed

Carlos. "Thought you would outsmart us, did you?" Carlos raised the butt of his pistol and brought it down hard across Sebastian's face. The result was a deep cut from his ear to his chin. The force of the blow brought Sebastian to his knees. Carlos hit him again this time just over his right eye. Sebastian dropped the manuscript. "You, sorry piece of shit. You better not try anything else. If you did not have some value to the cardinal, I would kill you right here and now."

Carlos bent down and picked up the manuscript. "Get him to his feet. We need to get moving." Marino bent down and took a hold of Sebastian's arm and helped him to his feet. Marino used the tail of Sebastian's sweatshirt to wipe off the blood streaming down his face, and he leaned Sebastian against the wall to steady him. "Carlos, I need something else for his face to stop the blood."

"He has some blankets where he slept. Let's get him up there." Together they got Sebastian up and headed in that direction. Marino spread out a blanket on the floor and helped Sebastian sit down. He found another blanket and a bottle of water. He gave Sebastian a drink and used the rest of it to wash his face off. Rummaging through his things, Marino found a couple of the gauze bandages Sebastian had bought and some of the tape. He put the bandages across the cut and taped it into place. Sebastian's eye above the cut began to swell shut.

"That's enough. We need to get out of here. We don't have time to coddle him. Get him up and let's go." Sebastian tried as hard as he could, but even with Marino's help, he just could not stand.

Carlos leaned over him. "Get up, monk!"

Sebastian tried again. "I just can't." Carlos tucked the manuscript into his belt. Getting Sebastian's other arm, he and Marino got him up. With more drag than walk, they managed to get him back to the entrance of the catacombs. Getting him through the opening was another question.

"Marino, you go out first, and I will push from here while you lift him." They first had to lean Sebastian against the wall. Marino made his way out. Carlos walked Sebastian over and raised his arms up and into the opening. "I can't reach him," Marino yelled.

"You are going to have to lift him up some." Carlos got behind Sebastian and tried to lift him from the waist. Sebastian did not move. Carlos laced his fingers together, making a double fist. He hit Sebastian with them in the middle of his back, making Sebastian to take a deep breath, causing him to raise his arms some. "OK, Carlos, I have his hands." Carlos bent down and put his head between Sebastian's legs, straining he pushed upward. He could feel the weight lifting as Marino pulled. Finally, they had him through to the outside. Marino dragged

Sebastian clear of the opening so Carlos could get through. Marino and Carlos sat while Sebastian lay there not moving.

"Here, Marino, take the keys and bring the car over here, and park as close as possible." Marino crawled out from the bushes and crossed the street toward the car. He was covered in dirt from getting in and out of the opening.

"Look, Thomas," one of the officers called to his partner. "Here comes one of the don's men. Looks like he has been crawling in the dirt. Get down!" They watched as Marino got into the car and made a U-turn, parking across the street. He got out and helped Carlos get another man into the backseat. As they pulled away, Thomas made a call, and in the other car, Carlos did also.

Officer Thomas called the inspector to alert him that once again Carlos was on the move. Carlos call was to the don to let him know they had the manuscript and were on their way back to the warehouse. The don in turn made a call to Cardinal Pulaski to let him know what was happening.

Earlier in the day, Jason had called Patrick's room to let them in on the plan the inspector had to catch the don and hopefully the cardinal. Now that things had been set in motion, there was no turning back.

At the warehouse, the inspector was busy getting his people in place. Soon Judith and Mat would have to go back downstairs and be tied once again to the chairs like Carlos had left them. Accompanying Palo to the basement would be two of the sergeant's squad hidden from sight. The inspector was fairly sure Palo would cooperate. Nicholas was another worry. The inspector had sent for his wife and two sons. Once they were there, he would have a good hold on Nicholas. They had about thirty minutes before Carlos arrived. If they needed more time, he had a team ready to throw roadblocks at every road, leading to the warehouse. That should give them another fifteen minutes or so, any longer would cause Carlos to become suspicious. For this to work, all of his players needed to be in place before Carlos arrived. It would not matter if the others like the don or the cardinal were late. He just hoped they would show up.

Chapter 50

After the call came in from Jason, the archbishop went to Jason's office to alert the camerlengo of the inspector's plan and the part they would have in it. He and the camerlengo would go to the warehouse and be in a hidden location where they could witness what went on. The inspector and Jason would be near by for their protection. The inspector had several officers from his team hidden within the warehouse, and the place was surrounded with swat teams stationed along the perimeter. The camerlengo had a car ready, and they were leaving Jason's office when Patrick came in leaning on the guard that was stationed outside of his door. "Patrick, what are you doing here?"

"You said that I could go with you."

"I know what I said, but I still think that you are too weak. This may get dangerous."

"Please, I must go. You never know what will happen, and I may be of some use."

"You can stay here and pray for us."

"Valanti, you of all people know that Leo was like a father to me. Please."

"What do you think, Cardinal?"

"For some reason, I cannot explain, I think he should be there. With our help, he should be all right."

"Thank you, your grace," Patrick said, leaning heavily on the guard's arm.

Cardinal Pulaski ended the cell call from the don. "Martin, we have some important business to take care of. I need to get something from my office and pick up Anton." He called Patrick's office and got the answering machine. So he dialed Anton's cell.

"Where are you?"

"Just returning from lunch, your eminence."

"Meet me in my office. I should be there in half an hour. I have some business to take care of, and I need you to go with me."

"Yes, eminence."

"Martin, sorry to cut our lunch short," said Pulaski, motioning over the waiter. "Tab please."

"I will be right back with it." When the waiter returned, Pulaski lay his credit card down.

"Let me take care of this," said Martin.

"No, no, my friend. It is my pleasure." The waiter took the card.

"What is this pressing business?"

"I told you the don's man Carlos is on his way back with Sebastian from the catacombs, and he has something I need."

"And that is?"

"The manuscript he said, signing the tab." He stood, following his lead, Martin also stood, and they made their way out of the restaurant.

The cardinal's car was standing at the curb. Seeing his boss exit the restaurant, the driver quickly got out and went around and opened the rear door for them. "Take us back to the Vatican," Pulaski told his driver as he settled himself back in the seat. The lunch-hour traffic was still heavy, making the trip back to the Vatican longer than expected. It took an hour to get through the Rome traffic, which normally would have been half that time before the car pulled up at the curb in front of the Vatican offices.

"Meet me back here in twenty minutes, he told Martin as he exited the car." The main floor halls were filled with the visiting cardinals. Pulaski smiled and shook hands as he made his was toward the elevator. He tried to avoid any prolonged conversations without appearing rude. He pushed the up button. Many of his supporters came by for a quick word. He was relieved when the door opened, and the nuns inside stepped back to allow him to get in. He spoke to several of them as the car rose to the fourth floor.

On this floor, only the usual staff was around, so he moved quickly to the door. Entering the curia offices, he saw Anton sitting at his desk, looking at the schedules. "Anton, put those away. I forgot to tell the driver to leave the car out front. See that this is done immediately and tell him you will be driving, and he can have the rest of the day off."

"Yes, eminence."

Pulaski went into his office and locked the door. Then he walked over to his desk and sat down. He unlocked his lower desk draw and removed the small chest that he had found in the archives. Inside was the piece of the manuscript and the two halves of the keys he had found hidden. He carefully put the key halves in his pocket and tucked the old piece of papyrus into his sash, being careful not to tear it. He had memorized the words printed there, but had never used the key without the papyrus being present. He had a feeling that all the power was held within the key itself, but why take any chances. The only thing left to get was the small bag that contained the white powder made from the bones of dead saints. Now armed with what he had come for safely tucked away, he walked back to the door and unlocked it. He had told Martin to be back in twenty minutes. By the time he ran the gauntlet of cardinals on the main floor that should work about right.

"Anton!"

"Yes, eminence"

"Did you call the driver? And is the car outside?"

"Yes, eminence."

"Good. We need to leave now. You go on ahead, and stand by the car."

"Where are we going?"

"To the warehouse to meet the don and finish our business with Brother Sebastian. We are meeting Cardinal Louis in about fifteen minutes from now."

"Is it prudent to take Cardinal Louis along? There may be some, how should I say it, unpleasantness that he does not need to witness."

"Anton, Martin is just about as deep in this as I am. It may serve me well for him to have a little blood on his hands as well. Now go! We don't have a lot of time."

"Yes, eminence."

They both left the office. Anton taking the stairs so that he could be there ahead of the cardinal while the cardinal took the elevator. Pulaski exiting on the main floor waved and smiled and shook a few hands as he made his way out of the building. His car was parked at the curb with Anton just opening the rear door for Cardinal Louis. Pulaski quickly made his way over and got in. Anton closed the door and walked around and got into the driver's seat. "I see you are not using your usual driver, Joseph."

"We need to keep our little journey a secret. The fewer people who know, the better." They settled back for the ride across town.

At the warehouse, Jason's cell began to ring. "Captain Sitzler, this is Gustoff. I thought you would want to know that I saw Cardinal Louis and Pulaski coming in from lunch about twenty minutes ago, and now they are leaving again. The thing that made me call you is that Anton is driving them."

"Which way did they go?"

"Looks like they are going in the direction of the Forum."

"Thanks, Gustoff. Lorenzo, we may be having more company than we were expecting. I have a hunch that Father Anton, Cardinal Pulaski, and Cardinal Louis are coming this way. I am going to call Archbishop Valanti and alert him. I know that they want to be here and witness this. Is there any way we can get them here ahead of the others?"

"I can have all of the streets that lead to the warehouse temporarily blocked. That will cause a traffic jam and hold every one up.

Jason called Valanti's phone number, "Archbishop, looks like things are coming to a head over here."

"We have a car standing by and can leave immediately."

"Lorenzo, do you have any patrol cars near the Vatican to escort them?"

"Let me check."

"Archbishop, we may be able to get you a police escort. Hurry to the car, and I will call you back."

"Patrick, you sure you are up to going?"

"Yes."

"Cardinal, we need to leave immediately." Patrick got to his feet. Valanti came over and offered his arm to Patrick, and they left heading toward the car.

Valanti's cell began to ring. "Archbishop, we will have you an escort out front in five minutes. Whose car are you coming in?"

"The camerlengo's vehicle."

"Looks like this will be quite a gathering. Have the driver bring you to the office entrance of the warehouse." Jason gave him the name and street number. "I will meet you out front." Valanti hung up his cell.

With the Camerlengo on one side and the archbishop on the other, they got Patrick out of the building and into the car. Valanti gave the driver the address. The patrol car pulled alongside, and Valanti gave the address to the officers and with sirens blaring, they pulled out into traffic and headed toward the warehouse. People moved aside as they sped down the road. They were able to keep up a good pace, cutting the travel time nearly in half.

Pulaski turned from his conversation with Cardinal Louis. "Anton, what seems to be the matter? We keep stopping and starting."

"The police are rerouting traffic which has caused a massive jam."

"Don't you know another way to get there?"

"Yes, your eminence. I should be able to turn at the next avenue and get us around this mess."

The don found himself in the same traffic tie-up once he reached the Forum. The police had all of the streets leading toward his warehouse blocked off, and they were detouring traffic in what he thought was a circle. He did not see a wreck or heard of a road rally taking place down in this area. Maybe something was happening at the Tomb of the Unknown Soldiers just down from the Forum. He turned on his police scanner and still did not learn anything. He wanted to be there when Carlos returned with the monk. He needed to make sure they had what the cardinal wanted before he arrived. He did not want to disappoint him again. One encounter with whatever it was the cardinal sent to him was enough.

The trip through Rome for Patrick, the archbishop, and the camerlengo was fast. They had weaved in and out of traffic, rounding corners on what felt like two wheels. The camerlengo's driver proved to be as good as the police car he was following. In his weakened condition, being thrown back and forth between Valanti and the cardinal, felt almost like being at sea during a storm. Patrick felt sick and dizzy. He was doing his best to not vomit. He kept swallowing. Being thrown from side to side, he caught his wound on the cardinal's elbow. He stifled a moan, and he felt something warm trickle down his side. He was relieved when they pulled into the parking lot of the warehouse. Jason opened the door of the office and came out to greet them. The cardinal exited followed by Patrick and Valanti. "Patrick, are you up to this?"

"I would not miss this for anything."

"All of you need to get inside quickly." Jason leaned in and told the driver to follow the police car and wait with them out of sight.

Inside the office, Lorenzo was waiting for them. "I will release the roadblocks, so we will have about thirty minutes to get ready. We don't know exactly how this will play out. The don's men that are here are working with us." A woman and two small children came in escorted by two policemen. "You must be Nicholas's wife and children?"

"Yes, sir."

"Take them to see Nicholas then get them to a safe location." After they were gone, Lorenzo continued. "Mat and Sister Bridget will be downstairs where I have two men stationed. I hope they will be brought up to the main warehouse by the don, if not we may have to go down there for the confrontation. Until that time, you three will be hidden inside some large crates we have prepared for you at the back of the warehouse. We have two chairs in there and will bring in another. You should be able to see what is going on. I will give you an earpiece so that you can hear the conversations. We have directional mikes and cameras all throughout the building and will be recording everything. I will leave it your discretion if and when you will want to reveal yourselves. Are there any questions?"

"I need to find a toilet and some water before we go into our hiding place," said Patrick.

"I think that would be wise for all of you. We don't know how long this is going to take." Jason led the way through the office to the toilets. When Patrick got into the toilet, he unbuttoned his cassock and pulled up his shirt. Sure enough, blood was seeping out of his wound on his left side. He wet paper towels and pressed them against his side. Pulling off several more, he folded them and placed them against the wound. Redressing, he relieved himself and returned to the hall so that Valanti could get in.

"How are you holding up?" asked Jason.

"I will get trough this. Having you here means a lot my friend." Jason led then all back to the main office with Patrick leaning on his arm.

"Jason, go ahead and get them in place. I had another chair brought in, and there is water in there. I will caution you to be as quiet as possible when the don's men return. Sound carries quiet well in there. Don't talk or move the chairs. We don't want our cover blown before it is time, and we have all the evidence we need. It is time for you to get into place so follow Jason out."

Jason took Patrick by the arm and led them into the warehouse. At the sight of Patrick who he thought was dead followed by the archbishop and the cardinal made Nicholas's knees feel weak, and he began to sweat. "What's wrong, Nicholas? Never seen someone come back from the dead?" He did not respond. He just kept watching the parade as it passed him and faded into the recesses of the warehouse.

"OK, gentlemen, these will be you quarters for the next several hours." The cardinal went in first followed by Valanti and finally Patrick. They could see the warehouse through the slits that had been cutout of the sides of the crate. They could also hear Nicholas as he paced back and forth near the front. "I see what the inspector meant about sound carrying," said Valanti.

"Put on your ear pieces. You can walk around a little back here. We will alert you in time to get back in here and sit down. I must get back, so I can get into place also." They nodded to Jason in reply and watched as he walked back up toward the front. All three stood and moved around while they still could.

The inspector was waiting for Jason in the office. "While you were getting the cardinal, archbishop, and Patrick in place, I called and had the roads unblocked. My patrol cars have been on watch for the don, Carlos, and the cardinal's vehicles. They have been spotted and are headed here as we speak. I just checked with my men, and they are ready down in the basement. I have sent word to all up here to get into place and remain silent. You and I need to go into our little control center we set up in the closet used for cleaning supplies. We will be able to see and hear everything that happens. They both cleared the office and went into the supply closet. All was in readiness.

Chapter 51

"Anton, I thought you knew a way around this traffic mess."

"I have tried several different streets that go to the warehouse and each has been blocked off, your eminence. It looks like it may be finally breaking up some what."

"Let's hope so. As I was saying, Martin, you may get to see my power today. So don't be alarmed when things seem to appear out of thin air. I am always amazed to witness it myself. I have only used it a few times—twice on Leo and once on the don. I must say that there were two very different outcomes. I have never seen it in action myself, so this will be a first for me also. Just remember, I will be in control at all times so you will have nothing to fear."

"Just from what you have told me, it gives me goose bumps. Maybe I should stay in the car."

"Nonsense, I told you, I will always be in complete control. Plus, you need to be there and witness the power I have, and from what I understand, this is just a small part. The manuscript holds many secrets, some have been hidden for centuries"

Traffic was also breaking up for the don. This circle he had been on was over. He should be at the warehouse in five minutes. He had the shortest drive. He must be there before the cardinal got there. He wanted to make sure that when he presented him with Brother Sebastian and the manuscript, that all was in order. He had been promised that he and his whole family would be free from having to spend any time in purgatory and that all of his future sins no matter how grievous would be forgiven. He had found over the years that the cardinal could be very generous with money if he was pleased. And the don had made a lot of money over the years getting rid of the cardinal's sins now turn about was fair. The prostitute that was killed was one of the cardinal's sins that was getting out of hand and needed to go away. It worked out well to use her to smear the monk's name. *What is it they say? Killing two birds or something like that,* he thought. The don smiled in satisfaction. He would even forgive the cardinal for putting him through a taste of hell. He was a changed man. No more sin for him; he had pre-forgiveness.

"What the shit is going on here?" mumbled Carlos. "We've been sitting in this traffic for what seems like hours."

"I know what you mean, boss. We've been going in circles."

"I want to get back before the don and cardinal arrive. I need to make sure that everything is as it should be. I don't want to end up on the end of that chain being fried."

"Me either, boss." The street up ahead was being unblocked. Traffic began to creep along at a quicker pace. Carlos looked into the rear view mirror at Sebastian the bandage across his face was soaked in blood, but it was no longer running down his chin. The sweatshirt, however, was covered in blood around the collar and down the front. "Hey, monk, you still with us?" called Carlos. Sebastian opened his eyes and just looked at him in the mirror. "We should have you back to the warehouse in about five minutes."

As fate would have it, all three cars arrived at the warehouse at the same time. "Mother f—," moaned Carlos, seeing the other two cars behind him as he pulled into the parking lot and stopping in front of one of the garage doors. He looked over to see the don, staring at him and in the rear view mirror was Father Anton with whom he felt sure was Cardinal Pulaski in the backseat.

He quickly called Nicholas cell. "Yes, boss" came the reply.

"Open both doors and prepare to get three cars inside."

"It will take a minute. I need to move the ones already in here."

"Open the doors first."

"Yes, boss." Carlos and the don watched as the doors begin to rise. Inside after pushing the button to open them, Nicholas hurried over to the first sedan and began to pull it to the back. Carlos pulled in behind him, far enough to allow Anton to get in behind him. Nicholas ran to the other car and also moved it to the back. The don pulled in behind that one next to the cardinal. Carlos was the first one to exit followed by Marino. Carlos hurried over to the don's car and opened his door. The don stepped out. He and Carlos stood beside his car and watched as Anton got out and came around to open the rear for the cardinal. Anton held his hand out and Pulaski took it, and Anton helped him out.

The cardinal stood adjusting his robes. Much to the don's and Carlos's surprise, Anton extended his hand again and helped out another cardinal. It was Cardinal Louis. He also had to adjust his robe and sash.

The don walked over to the cardinals. "Your graces, it is an honor to have you here."

"I trust I am not going to be disappointed again, Don Amato, especially in front of my dear friend Cardinal Louis."

"No, your grace."

Turning to Carlos, the don asked, "Where is the manuscript and Brother Sebastian?"

"Still in the car," replied Carlos.

"Well, get them out and bring them to me so that I can present them to the cardinal."

Carlos went to the back of the warehouse where Marino stood by the backdoor of the sedan. Carlos reached into the front seat and retrieved the manuscript. Then he went to help Marino get Sebastian out of the backseat. The loss of blood from the many wounds sustained made him very weak. It took both Carlos and Marino to carry him to where the cardinals and the don stood. To be able to help carry him, Carlos had to lay the manuscript on top of the vehicle.

Back in the control room, Jason and the inspector were watching and listening to what was going on via the many cameras and video feeds. "Did not expect that," said Jason, pointing to screen five whose camera was aimed at the cardinal's car.

"Me either," replied Lorenzo. "I wonder just how deep this conspiracy goes within the college of cardinals?"

"I don't know."

"Are we recording all of this?"

"Yes, both in here, and in the van we have across the street."

"Does the operator in the van also have eyes and ears?"

"Yes."

"How many are in the van?"

"Just one."

"Can he be trusted?"

"Yes, Sergeant Tunelly is manning the van."

"Patrick, the archbishop, and the camerlengo can all hear, but do you think their line of sight was blocked when they moved the vehicles further into the warehouse?"

"It will be a limited view but good enough."

Watching Carlos place the manuscript on the top of the car, Jason asked, "Do we have anyone close enough to grab that without being seen?"

"Maybe."

As Carlos, Sebastian, and Marino approached, the cardinal said, "Don, I told you I need him alive." Looking at Sebastian, it was hard to tell. His feet were not moving, his eyes were closed, and his head hung limp. He had apparently fainted when they stood him up.

"Anton, get that chair over there and bring it to me."

"Yes, your excellency." He brought the chair over, and they sat Sebastian down. Marino had to hold onto him to keep him from sliding down and hitting the floor. They could tell he was breathing from the rise and fall of his chest.

"Are you sure this is Sebastian?"

"Yes, your grace."

"Let me see his face." Carlos came over and grabbed a hand full of Sebastian's hair and pulled his head up and tilted it back so the cardinal could see it. "Wake him up. I want to make sure I am not getting damaged goods. He could be an idiot after your torture."

"Marino, get me a bottle of water and a clean piece of cloth."

"Where are the other two, you know whom I am talking about—Mason and the nun?"

"They are still in the basement."

"Well, get them. I need to see what shape they are in."

"Nicholas, go downstairs and tell Palo to bring up the two prisoners." Nicholas left. Marino came back in and wet the towel and began to wipe Sebastian's face. The cold water helped to revive him. As he opened his eyes, he was looking at a sea of red. Both cardinals were standing right in front of him. Marino brought the bottle to his lips, and he took a small sip.

"Bravo one, see if is possible for you can slide out of your position and retrieve the package that Carlos lay on the top of the car."

"Roger that." Jason and Lorenzo watched as they tried to revive Sebastian. The longer it took, the better; it was a great distraction for them. They did not want them to see the action going on in the back. One moment the package was on top of the car, the next, it was gone. "Delta one, mission accomplished" came the voice of Bravo one.

"Now that is going to cause quiet a commotion when Carlos goes back to pickup the manuscript and finds it gone. Only he, Sebastian, and Marino know for sure that it was there."

Sebastian had taken several sips of water and was able to sit in the chair unaided. Noise from the back of the warehouse caused all of them to turn their attention in that direction. Palo came out of the door first followed by Sister Bridget whose hands had been tied in front of her. Then came Mat also with his hands tied and being helped along by

Nicholas. They made there way around the parked cars and toward the front where the rest of them awaited. Just a couple of steps behind them, still on the steps, were the two special ops policemen hanging back until they had a chance to move into position in front of the first car.

"Sister Judith, you should be more careful being out on the streets of Rome dressed like that. Your habit would have kept you safe."

"I doubt that, Cardinal."

"Watch your mouth, nun, or you may live to regret it. Mister Mason, you too would have been safer had you not meddled where you don't belong. Don Amato, our American guest, looks like he has not had a good visit with you."

"I do my best, your grace."

"Well, it looks like I have most of what I came for. Where is the manuscript?"

"I will get it for you," volunteered Carlos.

"Don, have your men get a few more chairs, and let's move over to the desk."

"Marino, come over here and set up the chairs around the desk." Mat and Sebastian were taken and seated on one side close together. The two cardinals took their place on the other side. They left Sister Judith where she was. Everyone else gathered around the ends. "Clear off this stuff. We need to be able to lay out the manuscript so Sebastian and Mister Mason can read it for us." Marino and Palo cleared away everything that was there and laid it on the hood of the don's car.

"Well, Don, I am waiting"

"Carlos, what's the hold up?"

"I can't find it. I laid it on the top of the car when I went to help Marino get the monk out of the car and brought him up front."

"What do you mean, it's not there?"

"Don Amato, I hope for your sake and the sake of your family that Carlos finds it in a hurry. Am I making myself clear?"

"Marino, did you and Carlos have the manuscript?"

"Yes, boss. I swear on my mother's grave, it was back there."

"Well, it may have been knocked under the car. Go back there and help him find it and be quick about it." The don could feel sweat begin to bead up on his forehead, and some began to trickle down his chest. His mind flashed back to his office, and the thing that attacked him that the cardinal controlled, and one encounter was enough.

"How long should we hold back? We have enough on the don and the cardinal to put them away for a long time."

"I know but I won't to be able to pin the murder of the prostitute on them. Let's just wait a minute or two longer, but let's be ready. This is Delta one, be ready to move out on my signal."

"Boss, it's gone. I swear to you, it was there."

"Things just don't disappear or walk off on their own. What kind of a ruse are you trying to pull on me, Don Amato? I thought I had taught you a lesson. Well, it seems to take some people longer to learn than others."

"Cardinal, I swear to you, Carlos told me he had the manuscript." Don Amato reached into his jacket and pulled out a Beretta.

"Carlos, where is the manuscript?" He pointed the gun at Carlos.

"Please, boss, I have always been loyal to you and did what you told me to do. I had the manuscript just like I told you."

"Carlos, you told me you had taken care of killing the monk along with the prostitute for the cardinal, and I still see the monk."

"But, boss, I threw him and her into the bay at the same time. I had the manuscript when I got out of the car."

Back in the control room listening to what was happening in the warehouse the inspector said. "Thank you, Carlos. It's time to move out. We don't want our star witness killed." He hit the button for his mike switch. "Move out." He and Jason left the closet and made their way through the office and exited at about the same time his men broke out of their hiding places.

"Drop the Beretta, Don Amato," yelled the inspector as he and Jason burst through the office door at their backs.

Black-clad police officers seem to come out of nowhere, holding assault rifles trained on them. The don dropped the Beretta, and it was quickly retrieved by one of the team. Cardinal Pulaski rose and turned toward the inspector and Jason.

"Captain Sitzler, I am so relived to see you. We have been held captive by the don and his men. Anton, please go and open the door to the car for us. Come along, Martin, we need to move along, so the inspector and his men can do their jobs." Cardinal Louis rose, and the three of them headed toward the cardinal's car.

"One moment please, your excellency, you need not be in such a hurry. We have everything on tape since you arrived. Bravo one, bring me the package." All eyes turned as one of the inspector's men came from behind a car, carrying the manuscript and handed it to the inspector.

"See, boss, I was telling the truth."

"Don Amato, you almost killed one of your most loyal employees."

"I'll take that, Inspector. It belongs to the papal archives," said Cardinal Pulaski, boldly walking toward him with his hand extended.

They had their attention on the confrontation first between the don and Carlos, then the surprise of being surrounded, and finally, having the missing manuscript produced that they did not notice the three people moving slowly and quietly from the back of the warehouse until Archbishop Valanti spoke.

"No, Cardinal, as curator of the archives, only myself and the pope are privy to its contents."

"And you are not pope yet, Cardinal," said the camerlengo.

Both Cardinals Pulaski and Martin nearly had a heart attack as they turned to see the archbishop, Patrick, and the camerlengo standing just beyond the officers.

"I thought you were in control," said Cardinal Louis through clenched teeth.

"I am." Taking the two parts of the key out of his pocket, he put them together. He took a bag from his pocket containing the bones of the saints and stooping down draws a circle before him and a pentagram in the center, laying the key on the pentagram. Pulling the Papyrus out of this pocket he called out the names written around it then ancient Hebrew he intoned the words, "Come and serve me." The air in the warehouse seemed to become thick like a dense fog and began swirled around in front of the cardinal like a mini tornado. Things became blurry; it was like looking at the world underwater. There appeared an eerie opaque light, and in the midst of the room, in front of the cardinal, a door began to take shape.

It was a large bronze door with many ancient writings on it. The cardinal picked up the key from the circle and walked up to the door and inserted the key under the serpent handle and turned it. The door began to slowly open. From the inside came a light like a flickering flame. Everyone but the cardinal was frozen in place. They could not comprehend what they were seeing. Fear gripped all of them. The light from the door was suddenly blocked by what appeared to be a black cloud of smoke. The cardinal held up the key and said in Hebrew, "Come and serve me," and the black figure came toward him and seemed to kneel. The cardinal pulled out the old piece of Papyrus that he had tucked in his sash and read the Hebrew words written on it. "Rid me of these evil creatures." The figure moved and the cardinal turned toward Cardinal Louis who was frozen in fear. "I told you I had it under control."

The figure moved in the direction of the don and Carlos who was just in front of the Inspector and Jason. The inspector fired and the bullet just passed through the figure and hit the car just behind it, just missing one of his men. Arms seem to appear out of the blackness, and they grabbed Carlos by the throat and seemed to sink into his skin. Carlos tried to fight, but he could not move. He opened his mouth to scream and the blackness descended down his throat and nose filling him. Carlos was thrown to the ground, his body going into spasms. The blackness that was not inside Carlos began to go back toward the open door dragging Carlos body long with it. When it reached the door, it poured out of Carlos's mouth and nose, surrounding him, pulling him to his feet. Now Carlos's screams could be heard, resounding throughout the warehouse as the blackness enveloped him and pushed him through the doorway.

They were all filled with pure terror; the sound of Carlos's screams made the hair stand up on the back of the don's neck.

Everyone stood in stunned silence, even the cardinal had not moved. Patrick was the first to move. He staggered toward Jason but stopped and knelt down beside Sebastian's chair, putting his arms around him. The archbishop and the Camerlengo came up behind him. Once again, the figure emerged from the door.

All eyes turned toward it. "Not them, pointing at the don, Marino, and Nicholas, who had been standing by Carlos, but all of these," the cardinal screamed at the blackness, pointing to the special ops team, the inspector, and Jason.

The black figure came slowly into the room and went in the direction of Jason and the inspector, but it stopped and turned toward Marino. The don, Nicholas, and Palo broke and ran toward the office door. They did it so quickly that they caught Jason and the inspector off guard, and they were knocked to the floor. Seeing what he thought maybe his only chance, Father Anton fled followed by Cardinal Louis. "Let them go," hollered the inspector. "They won't get far."

They all watched in horror as the blackness enveloped Marino and dragged him screaming through the doorway. Patrick, Judith, Valanti, Sebastian, and the Camerlengo dropped to their knees and began to pray. Seeing this Jason and the inspector and all of his men dropped their weapons and dropped to their knees.

Now, only the cardinal was left standing. He had the key in one hand and the piece of the manuscript in the other.

For the third time, the blackness filled the doorway and drifted back toward the cardinal. Once again, he commanded, "Rid me of this evil." The blackness rose and circled each of those who were left. Then it returned to the cardinal.

"Evil can only enter where it is invited and had been before. There is only one left whose heart harbors evil," the voice boomed eerily through the warehouse, and all those who heard it shivered at the sound. Many of the officers prostrated themselves on the floor. The cardinal was so shocked hearing the voice that he dropped the key and the piece of manuscript. Sebastian watched in fascinated silence as the manuscript fell to the floor. The sound of the key hitting the floor in the silence sounded like the peal of a church bell tolling doom.

Before the cardinal could gather his wits and bend down and pick up the key, he was encapsulated in blackness. He could not breathe. The blood in his veins ran cold; he was paralyzed in fear. He opened his mouth and gasped for breath, but all he pulled in was the blackness. It filled every part of his body. He tried to move, to run, to escape, but he had no control of his body. He was like a puppet someone or something was in charge of. His mind was filled with thoughts of all the evil he had done. He could only see blackness all around him. He felt himself being moved, and suddenly, there, in the darkness, was a bright light, and a sudden rush of unbearable heat enveloping him. He was standing on the other side of the door. He could still see the others kneeling in prayer. He looked down; all of his regal priestly robes had been burned off and were gone, and he was standing nude. He tried to call for help, but they could not hear him.

With the exception of the sound of prayers, all was silent. The warehouse was lit brightly by the light coming from the inside the door. Then there was darkness again as the room filled with the black figure. The figure drifted over toward the key. Black arms came from the darkness and picked it up. Holding the key, the figure slowly circled the room as if looking for someone or something. It stopped before each of the persons kneeling and then moved on. It came and stopped where Sebastian, Patrick and Valanti were kneeling, arms around each other. The voice boomed, shaking the windows of the warehouse and breaking light bulbs. Those still kneeling hit the floor and covered their faces. Only three were upright. Sebastian was in the chair, and Patrick and Valanti were kneeling on either side of him. The voice said, "You are most worthy" as it dropped the key before one of them.

The End

Chapter 52

AFTERWORD

The one holding the key twisted it, and it came apart. The blackness returned to the door, and the door closed. He got up slowly and made his way to the door, inserted the key into the lock and turned it. Once again, the air seemed to get thick and vision became distorted as the door slowly vanished.

Jason picked up the piece of the manuscript off the floor and brought it over and laid it on the desk beside the rest of the manuscript.

The inspector and his men got up off the floor and helped Patrick, the archbishop, the Camerlengo, Sebastian, Mat Mason, and Sister Judith out of the warehouse. Sergeant Tunelly had called an ambulance, and they loaded Sebastian and Mat into it. Judith went also to be there with her dad. Jason brought the manuscript out of the warehouse and gave it to the archbishop to be returned to the archives. The Camerlengo's driver bought his car around and he, Patrick, and the archbishop went back to the Vatican.

The don and Cardinal Louis were apprehended, leaving the warehouse as were Nicholas and Palo. True to his word, Nicholas and his family and Palo were relocated to safe location. Father Anton is still at bay. No one has been able to figure out how he got by the police that were surrounding the building. Tape was put up, and the don's warehouse is no longer in business and neither is the don.

Two days later, a tile in the ceiling began to move. A figure dressed in black let himself down from his hiding place in the attic. He moved quietly into the men's toilet. In one of the lockers, he found some gray sweats, and he quickly changed out of his clerical garb and stashed it in the trashcan. With the building closed, it would be weeks, months, or maybe never before it was found. The guards posted at the warehouse had become lax. He watched, crouched at the window, and when the opportunity came, he slipped out and faded into the night.

News quickly spread around the Vatican that Cardinal Pulaski had resigned his post and left the Vatican along with Cardinal Louis. With the front runner gone, the college of cardinals was in turmoil. The stories circulating about Sebastian, Patrick, and the archbishop made them heroes.

The pope's funeral went without any problems. Patrick, Sebastian, Archbishop Valanti, Mat Mason and Sister Judith had front row seats just behind the college of cardinals. Leo would have been proud of them.

A lot had happened in these last few days. Now the conclave to elect Leo's successor had begun. The cardinals were sealed in the Sistine Chapel. The square was filled with the faithful watching the smoke stack for the white smoke signaling the election of the new pope. It had been a busy day, and Patrick had retired to his old room to read and rest. He would soon be moving to a new location and a new assignment, and someone else would be serving as the next pope's secretary. Most of his things were packed, and he was ready to go where the new pope sent him. Valanti was getting the papal archives in readiness for the new pope and the person to fill his position. The key was back in its place in the book and the secret compartment in the bookcase. The manuscript was on his desk. He would put it back into its hiding place later. Tonight, he would lock it in his safe. Sebastian had gotten out of the hospital, and, after the funeral, had accepted Jason's offer to stay for a few days in the guest quarters Patrick had used. He was still the only one that knew that only a part of the manuscript was in Valanti's office. Once the new pope was elected, and he was up to it, he would get the rest and return it to its proper owner.

Around midnight, after the fist round of voting took place, to everyone's surprise, a white smoke came pouring from the chimney pipe. A roar came from the crowd. The cardinals looked at each other and smiled; it was God's will. Viva Papa. Viva Papa could be heard coming from the courtyard.

It would take a while for the crowd to greet the new pope, because he was not in the room. The vote had been unanimous. The cardinal who read out the name on the ballots turned to cardinal Alveraz. "As the camerlengo, it is your duty to go and ask the newly elected pope if he will serve. Then bring him back to us so that we can pledge ourselves to him.

Alveraz left the Sistine Chapel and made his way to the man's room to the one who was deemed most worthy. As he knocked on the door, his heart raced. It had been centuries since other that a cardinal, a prince of the church, had been elected Pope. When the door opened, he knelt. "Holy Father, will you serve, and what name will you have?"

"Yes, and I will take the name David."

It was said about David that he was a man after God's own heart. "Then they asked for a king. God gave them Saul son of Kish a man from the tribe of Benjamin, for forty years. Then he removed him, and raised up David as their king; of him he testified. 'I have found David, son of Jesse, *a man after my own heart; he will carry out my every wish*'" (Acts 13:21-22).

Several months had passed since the new pope had taken office, and many changes had been made. Late one night, long after everyone was fast asleep, a hooded figure wearing a monk's robes crept out of the palace. Staying close to the shadows to avoid being seen, he quickly made his way out of the Vatican grounds and headed into Rome.

Legacy of the Keys
Book Two

KEY OF ILLUMINATION

Chapter 1

All was quiet in the papal palace. The offices had been long closed; the only people up were those members of the Swiss Guard who had pulled night duty. All the lights in the apartments had been turned off. Someone standing in the courtyard below would have noticed one lone light shining through the window of the papal apartment. The shadow of a lone figure crossed in front of the light casting a long shadow upon the window. It was nearing three o'clock, and soon the guard stationed outside the Pope's door would be taking his usual break. The pope pulled on the old rough robe that had belonged to him when he was Brother Sebastian. The rest of the manuscript was still safe in the catacombs in an old tomb where he had hidden it several weeks ago. A lot had happened during that time. Upon his election, Brother Sebastian had taken the name of David. The new pope had made several changes. Archbishop Valanti had been elevated to Cardinal and was now head of the Curia. Monsignor O'Roark had been made an Archbishop and taken over the post of curator of the papal library and archives.

To save the church embarrassment from a public trial of one of its Cardinals, the new pope had worked out a deal with the Rome police department with the help of Inspector Capleno, a friend of Captain Sitzler, for the church to send away Cardinal Louis for his part in helping Cardinal Pulaski with his plans to steal the key and the manuscript and use its power to have himself elected pope. He wondered how Cardinal Louis liked his new assignment on the Russian side of the cold and desolate Chinese border in that little monastery deep in the Caspian Mountains where there was little interaction with the outside world. No Internet, no cell service and only the electricity produced by an old generator. It would give the former Cardinal Lewis, now a lowly brother time, to pray and fast for his sins. Several in the College of Cardinals who were still loyal to Cardinal Pulaski asked where he had been reassigned. His quick departure and disappearance still had to be dealt with. He would leave this up to his new Cardinal Valanti to come up with a plausible story. No one would believe the truth of what happened. You would have had to witness it to believe it, and still he was having trouble believing it was a reality. The tapes made at the warehouse during the battle with Pulaski by the Rome police had been given over to the Vatican, and Pope David had them sealed in the archives under the guard of Archbishop O'Roark, never to be viewed during his lifetime.

The pope was jostled out of his thoughts by the sound just outside his door as the guard left his post. There would be maybe a ten-minute time frame that he could make his way out of his apartment and down to the door that led to the stairs leading out of the building. Pope David pressed his ear against the door trying to detect the sound of the receding footsteps echoing off the tile floor. He thought he heard a door opening at the other end of the hallway leading to the rest of the building. He placed his hand on the door handle and began to turn it slowly, the lock released and he gently cracked the door open just enough to be able to see that the hall was empty. Easing the door open, he stepped out into the hallway, his slippers hardly making any noise as he quickly ran to the doorway leading to the steps that led outside. Just as he closed the door, he paused to listen before descending the stairs. He heard the footsteps of the new guard coming down the hall toward his post. Being very careful not to make any noise, he crept down the stairs. When he reached the outside level, he paused and pressed his ear against the door. Hearing no sound, he gently opened it and looked down the passageway. The only lights on were the exit signs over the doors and a security light in the middle of the hallway. Seeing no one around, he exited the stairs and walked toward the outside door. The doors would be locked at this time of night, but only from the outside. He could get out, but getting back in would be a problem. Reaching inside of his robe, he pulled out a wad of paper with tape wrapped around it. He would place this in the doorjamb keeping the door from locking. He began to pray, "Dear Father, please don't let anyone use this door until I return."

He pushed the center bar on the door and it opened easily. The hinges squeaked loudly, and looking around to see if anyone heard, he placed the paper in the doorjamb, exited and gently closed the door. David pulled on the door, trying it and it opened. His paper jam was working.

Staying as close to the wall as possible to keep in the shadows, he made his way down the outside steps and into the Plaza that was in front of Saint Peter's. This was going to be the tricky part. The Plaza was always lit so he would have to keep to the far outside edges in the shadows. There was a fence along the left side of the Plaza where work was being done on the front of the office complex. If he stayed close to the fence and could avoid being seen by the guard on duty, he would be all right. Edging along the fence, he turned to peer inside. He could just make out the guardhouse nestled close to the office complex. He could just make out the light illuminating the interior. A shadow crossed the window so he was sure the guard was inside, but he could not be sure he was not looking out. Bending low, he crept along the fence. As he rounded the corner near the street, he was blinded by the lights of a quickly approaching vehicle. Turning, he could see the long shadow he cast beyond the fence. Suddenly, security lights lit the interior of the fence, and he could hear the sound of footsteps running in his direction. He lifted his robes and sprinted toward the street and the shelter of cars parked on the other side. Reaching the other side, he knelt behind a car. He could also hear the sounds of running boots and guard dogs barking. There was an alley about a half a block from where he was; if he could reach it he would be safe, but he must move quickly.

Unnoticed by the new pope was a shadowy figure hidden in a doorway watching. He had kept a constant vigil of the palace and St. Peter's since he had climbed out of the ceiling of Don Amato's warehouse, still dressed in the clothes he had stolen, a janitor's uniform. Father Anton burned with hatred for the new pope and those who had destroyed his patron's plans. It should be Pulaski who was in power, and he would be at his right hand. He watched as the hooded figure crawled behind the cars and then sprinted to the alley and disappeared. He dared not move to follow the figure because the guards and the dogs were now at the edge of the fence and were unlocking the gate. It would not be long before they were across the street and would discover his hiding place. He would like to follow the hooded monk, but he was too far from the alley. He had no choice but to turn in the other direction and run, and run he did. Anton was a man alone, but he was a man wanting revenge. He knew that there were other keys out there, and he was determined to keep watching until his chance came. He also knew that he needed help. Pulaski was gone and Cardinal Louis would be of no help where he was. His only hope would be to hook up with some of the don's men who had not been caught yet. He knew that the Cardinal had secreted away money over the years, and he knew how to access it. Money would not be a problem. A new identity was the first thing he needed to purchase. Looking over his shoulder, Anton could see that the guards had not gone down the alley but were in hot pursuit of him.

Unaware of the eyes watching, David ran down the alley. At the end was a narrow residential street. In the distance he could hear the barking of dogs and the excited talk of the guards. The alley was like a megaphone amplifying the sound. It sounded like the guards bypassed the alley and had continued down the street. He felt safe for the moment. He stopped at the next corner to get his bearings. He was about two miles from the entrance to the catacombs where he had hidden. That seemed like a lifetime ago. He was still in pretty good shape and had several weeks to heal. Being Pope was a strenuous job, but it did not require a lot of activity. He thought he could make the three miles in about and hour. Once there, it would not take long to retrieve the manuscript and then another hour to return. If his calculations were correct, he should be able to be back into the main building around five thirty. It would be difficult to get back into his apartment at that time, but he would deal with that when he returned. The next change of the guard would be a six AM. He began to trot down the narrow street. He knew that he would not be able to keep up this pace because of the injuries he had sustained at the hands of the don and his men. The longer he could trot, the more time he would have to get back earlier.

The new pope was not the only one still up. Down in the papal archives, the light was on in the office of the new curator, Archbishop Patrick O'Roark. With him that night was his new friend, Mat Mason. They had been pouring over the manuscript for the past several weeks since the election of the new pope. They were beyond the point in the manuscript where the then Brother Sebastian had translated giving the location to the first key. Patrick had carefully replaced the key in its prior resting place, part of the key in an old book, and the other part in a compartment in the bookcase against the back wall. They had been able to ascertain that the next key had something to do with great knowledge, and it was not located here in Rome. He used the term "next key" because near the end of the page they were working on, another key was mentioned. It was referred to as the *Key of Destiny*. The mention of that key was the reason he and Mat were still working that night. They had only a few more pages to go and they wanted to get to the end. "What do you make of what we have found out so far?" asked Patrick. "I am surprised to learn of two more keys. I wonder if there are any more listed in the rest of the manuscript. I have a feeling the part we have here does not tell the location of either one of these keys. Do you know where the rest of the manuscript is to be found?"

"In the note from brother Sebastian it said that the rest of the manuscript was still in the catacombs with directions to the sight."

"Do you still have the note? We need to go tomorrow and retrieve it?"

"Jason gave the note to Cardinal Valanti when he returned from the hospital after having found that we had been taken hostage by the don's men. That night in the warehouse Cardinal Valanti still had the note. I will call him in the morning and see if he will give it to us."

"Without the rest of the manuscript, we are at a dead end," commented Mat as he leaned over the last pages spread out on Patrick's desk.

A hooded figure hurried through the night headed back to the catacombs, which had been a safe heaven for the then brother Sebastian. Thinking of the darkness and the rats scurrying about made his skin crawl. When he closed his eyes, he could still hear the sound of their claws scratching the rock as they made their way to the pool of water near where he laid. He neared the street where the wall of the cemetery began; it would not be far now. He saw the light of a car coming down the street. It looked like a dark sedan. The sight brought back memories of Carlos and the time spent in the basement of the warehouse. He quickly ducked behind the bushes that were planted at intervals along the wall. He caught himself holding his breath as he watched the car pass. He let his breath out in a sigh of relief as he watched it pass. It was just a cab heading back to a line in front of a hotel in the heart of Rome.

He moved out of the shadow of the bushes and once again continued his journey toward the entrance to the catacombs. He was only a block away and his heart began to race as he picked up his pace. The bushes had not grown back where Carlos had cut them back so that they could get by them easier. Pope David slipped behind them and made his way to the narrow entrance. Getting down on his hands and knees, he lowered himself down to his stomach, and then backed into the crevice. Pushing himself inward, he felt his feet touch solid ground. He pulled the rest of his body through the entrance. Stooping, he turned around and took a few steps into the darkness and stood up. Reaching inside of his robe, David pulled out a flashlight he had brought with him and began to walk deeper into the cave.

CPSIA information can be obtained
at www.ICGtesting.com
Printed in the USA
LVHW041653260619
622438LV00003B/31/P

La Conner Regional Library